Chasing Paris

Jen Carter

To my family

Prologue

Eva stood at the end of a long, sloping driveway lined by linden and oak trees. She looked toward the house sprawling across the hilltop in front of her and thought about the silence filling that house. She thought about the loneliness emanating from it. Warm air whipped Eva's hair against her face, and she thought about her sister's last days taking place in that silent, lonely house.

She clutched six envelopes, each containing her sister Lizzie's final wishes and regrets.

The notes are ready, Eva had said minutes before, standing beside her sister's bed and noticing that Lizzie's frail body was nearly swallowed by the pillows surrounding her. *The one to Billy,* Eva continued, *the one to your friends in Paris, the one to your granddaughters, and of course the three separate ones to your children. I've done my best to mimic your handwriting, and they are all sealed away in envelopes, ready to be mailed.*

Lizzie had nodded, closing her eyes and straining to swallow. Her hair lay scattered across the pillows like silver strands of moonlight, a beautiful and unfair contrast to her gaunt, lined face.

Don't mail the one to the granddaughters, she had said. *I've changed my mind. I don't want to end my life by beginning a family quarrel. Now is not the time. Please go send the others.*

Eva had nodded and left her sister's room. Now, outside the house, standing at the bottom of the hill and next to the mailbox, she mulled over her sister's words.

And she thought about their seventy-five years as sisters. The laughter of their childhood. The freedom of their teenage years. The recklessness of their twenties. Lizzie's mistakes. Eva's faith. Fiercely protective, all they ever had was each other—from the beginning until now, when Lizzie's cancer was about to declare itself victor.

Eva looked at the six envelopes. One by one she placed them in the mailbox. Holding the last one in both hands, she studied the names on the front and thought about Lizzie's words one more time. *Don't mail the one to the granddaughters. I don't want to end my life by beginning a family quarrel. Now is not the time.*

Eva pictured the girls. Inseparable sisters. Fiercely protective sisters. Sisters whose love for each other rivaled that of Eva and Lizzie's.

Still picturing the girls, she put the final envelope in the mailbox.

"Actually, now is the time," she said under her breath.

For a moment, she gazed toward the cloudless sky, feeling the warmth of late spring on her face and listening the breeze push past her. Then she brushed wind-blown wisps of hair behind her ears and began climbing the hill back to Lizzie's cold, silent house.

It was time to say goodbye.

One

Los Gatos

"Get up."

The words flew from April Winthrow's mouth as she swung open her sister's bedroom door. Standing in the doorway with folded arms, she continued without pause. "We've got a problem, and Dad's coming over right now to explain."

Amy was used to her sister's wake up calls. Normally, however, they came on weekdays when Amy was going to be late for work. This was Sunday. She lifted her head and squinted at her alarm through the curly blonde hair criss-crossing her face.

"It's not even ten o'clock," she groaned. "Why are you waking me up on a Sunday before ten o'clock?" Her head dropped back to the pillow.

"It doesn't matter what time it is," April said, tightening her arms across her chest. "You need to get up. Now."

Amy peered toward the doorway with unfocused eyes just in time to see her sister's fuzzy outline whip around and stalk down the hall. She yawned.

"April, I don't want Dad to come over," she called. "I want to sleep."

"Doesn't matter," April called back from the kitchen.

Amy groaned again, rubbing her eyes. She rolled out of bed and found her way down the hall to the shower. Ten minutes later—with the help of a blast of hot water—she joined her sister in the kitchen, finally feeling like herself.

"Coffee," she muttered, breezing past the kitchen table where April sat and heading straight for the coffee pot on the far counter. She poured a cup and said over her shoulder, "Thanks for making this."

April didn't respond.

Amy sipped from her mug and walked toward the table. Sitting down, she said, "What do you have there?" She nodded at a piece of paper on the table.

April slid the paper toward her sister until it touched Amy's coffee mug.

"This," she said, "came in the mail." She took a sip of her own coffee. "This morning I remembered that we didn't grab the mail yesterday, so I went out to get it. And this is what I found."

Amy picked up the piece of paper. She scanned the longhand, trying to place the writing. The words did not compute the first time, but upon her second reading, she began to understand April's less-than-cheery mood.

To my granddaughters—
My greatest sadness is in not knowing you. This I cannot change, but I do hope that you can forgive my absence. I have loved you from afar, and I have cherished the pictures and stories about you that Eva has shared with me. Please accept the gifts coming to you as a piece of my heart.
Elizabeth Hathaway

Amy's eyes met April's. They had lived side-by-side most of their lives—throughout childhood, most of college, and even now after college—and despite their different personalities, they had the ability to read each other's thoughts. Amy knew April was as confused as she was, but she couldn't stop herself from asking the obvious question.

"What is this?"

April shrugged.

Amy read the note again, slowly, focusing on one word at a time. The new reading strategy didn't help.

"This is why Dad's coming over—to explain this? When is he getting here?"

"He's already here," their father said, letting himself into the little house his daughters rented. Spenser Winthrow smiled at Amy and April as he turned the corner to the kitchen, but the smile looked painfully uncomfortable. "Good morning," he said.

He sat down across from them at the kitchen table. His often-sunburned skin was redder than normal, and dark circles rimmed his blue eyes. He was a big man, solid and strong, who most often carried his bulk with the energy of a man half his age. As a professor of Classics, he claimed it was the combination of old philosophers and bright young minds that kept him on his toes. This morning, though, he looked tired.

"Who the hell is Elizabeth Hathaway?" April asked. She leaned back in her chair and crossed her arms in the same manner she had when waking up Amy.

"May I see what came in the mail from her?" Spenser asked.

Amy handed him the note. He studied it, taking his time to read and reread it.

Amy and April exchanged glances. April raised an eyebrow at her younger sister and then said, "Dad, it doesn't matter how many times you read it—the words aren't going to change."

"Okay," Spenser said, placing the note on the kitchen table. He sighed, leaning back in his chair. "Okay, here we go."

Amy crossed her arms to match her sister's.

Spenser cleared his throat. "Elizabeth Hathaway," he paused, eyes still on the note, "is your mom's mother. Her biological mother. She is," he paused again, "Eva's sister."

He lifted his eyes toward his daughters and waited for a reaction, but none came. Amy and April stared at their dad, each sure he would say more. When they realized his explanation was over—that it really was a basic as it sounded—April broke the silence.

"What?"

Spenser's shoulders slumped. "I guess there is no way to sugar coat this." He leaned forward, clasping his hands and resting them on the table. He kept his eyes down. "Your mom had it tough when she was a little girl, and she doesn't like to think about her childhood. Her father died, and then her mother abandoned her and her sisters. Elizabeth's sister—Eva—stepped in and adopted them. Eva became your mom's mother. She became your grandmother. Your nana. But biologically speaking, Nana is really Mom's aunt."

Amy and April's eyes grew. They continued to stare at their father, but they could feel each other's surprise—a strength in their shared confusion—which grew with every passing second.

Spenser continued, "No one even knew where Elizabeth was until about the time that you girls were born. We imagine—" He stopped himself and shook his head. "It doesn't matter what we imagine was going on while she was gone. When she did return, she wanted to make amends with your mother, but too much damage had been done. There was no relationship to recover."

Spenser picked up the note again. Amy and April watched their father as he fiddled with its corner.

"So Nana's not really our grandma?" April asked.

Spenser shook his head. "Not technically."

"Mom really didn't want a relationship with her mother when she came back?" Amy asked.

Spenser shook his head again. "Would you?"

Amy looked at her sister. "I don't know. I might want to find out if there was a reason she left in the first place."

Spencer laid the note on the table and leaned back in his chair. "I suppose your mom had put enough pieces of the puzzle together as she was growing up. Enough to know that she didn't want to have a relationship with Elizabeth—or, Lizzie, as Eva always calls her." He pointed to his daughters. "And I suggest that you don't bring this up to your mom. I can promise you the conversation won't go well. If you have any questions about the items Lizzie left to you, go through me. I'll be working with Nana to sort out her sister's things."

"Speaking of that," April said, "do you know what was left to us?"

Spenser nodded. "I spoke with Nana yesterday when we found out Lizzie had passed away. She gave me a run-down of the will. Lizzie put money into special accounts for each of you. It has to be used for education. She will pay for you to go back to school for a graduate degree, wherever you want, whatever degree you want, no matter the cost."

Amy's eyebrows rose.

"Ugh," April muttered. "That's wasted on me." She looked toward her sister. "You can get two degrees and take the money set aside for me."

Amy's eyebrows rose higher. "Really?"

"Sure." April turned back to Spenser. "Anything else?"

Spenser pursed his lips. "Yes, but April, if you didn't like the money, you're not going to like the rest." He looked from his oldest daughter toward his youngest. "Amy, it's right up your alley though. She also left you a library full of books to share. Over a thousand books. But it's complicated—so you won't get them right away. Of all those books, about fifty were left to someone else. We have to go through and find those particular titles and deliver them to their new owner."

"Can we help?" Amy asked.

Spenser shook his head. "No."

"Okay, wait," Amy said. She cocked her head to one side and narrowed her eyes. "You found out yesterday that this Elizabeth-Lizzie person died, and you didn't call us about it?"

Spenser shifted his weight. "Well, if she hadn't sent you that note in the mail, I don't think you'd know even now. Mom got something in the mail from Lizzie yesterday, too. When we saw it, we thought she might have sent you something. But then we didn't hear from you, so we figured we were in the clear. We probably would have told you the gifts from Lizzie were from a long-estranged relative and left it at that."

The sisters looked at each other. April stood and walked to the counter where they kept their coffee pot. She poured herself another cup. Then she reached for another mug and filled it.

"I'm done here," she said, walking back to the kitchen table and placing the second mug before her father. "Books, school, and an old lady who died. That's all I needed to know." She paused and pointed first at her father and then at Amy. "But, Dad, I think you might be here awhile answering her questions." She nudged the coffee cup toward Spenser. "Drink up."

And April was right—Amy had a lot of questions. Spenser wasn't surprised by his daughters' reactions. While they had similar appearances with their blonde hair and green eyes, the similarities stopped there. April was headstrong and abhorred change; she would convince herself that nothing was different and remain happy that way. Lizzie would have no impact on her life. Amy was curious and often let her imagination sweep her away; she would mull over the situation and play out a thousand scenarios in her head.

If Mom never forgave Lizzie, did Eva ever forgive her? Amy asked. *Did Lizzie leave Mom anything? Do we know why she wants us to further our education? What was special about the fifty books that Lizzie didn't leave to us? Did Lizzie live nearby?*

Spenser couldn't answer many of her questions, but Amy continued for twenty minutes, rewording and rethinking the questions, hoping to trigger a couple satisfying answers from her father.

When the questions slowed and Amy began staring out the kitchen window in thought, Spenser rose from the table. "I better get back to Mom and Nana," he said.

Amy turned from the window and looked toward her dad. "When is the funeral?"

He shook his head. "No funeral. That was stated in the will. She'll be cremated, and we'll do as she asked with her ashes."

"What's happening with the ashes?"

Spenser halfway smiled and patted his daughter's shoulder. "I don't know yet."

"Are we going to have dinner tonight at Nana's like we normally do on Sundays?"

Spenser shook his head. "I don't think so, honey. I think everyone needs some time to process Lizzie's death."

Amy nodded and said goodbye as her dad headed for the front door. Her eyes fixated on the kitchen table where Elizabeth Hathaway's note lay. She picked it up and read it once more before folding it and sliding it into her pocket.

Two

All day, Amy tried to put Elizabeth Hathaway out of her mind, but the words of Lizzie's note rolled around her head, pulling her from everything happening around her. By dinnertime, April was tired of Amy's random, rhetorical questions about the mysterious Lizzie Hathaway.

"Enough already," April said, handing her sister a set of car keys. "Go drive around or get a cup of coffee—get out of here, and get that woman out of your head. Go—before I strangle you."

Amy knew April was right. She needed some fresh air to clear her mind. But instead of going for a drive, she put the car keys down, packed her messenger bag, and went for a walk.

By the time Amy arrived at the park, dusk was falling. The streetlights cast orange circles in random sidewalk squares up and down the street, giving the impression that night was closing in. People moved all around her as she sat down on a bench, and for a moment she watched them coming and going. Then she reached into her bag, rummaging around for her notebook. She pulled out a novel and looked at the cover for a moment. She smiled at her favorite book and then put it on the bench next to her so that she could continue looking for her spiral notebook. Upon finding it, she flipped to the page she had used to store Lizzie's note.

> *To my granddaughters—*
> *My greatest sadness is in not knowing you. This I cannot change, but I do hope that you can forgive my absence. I have loved you from afar, and I have cherished the pictures and stories about you that Eva has shared with me. Please accept the gifts coming to you as a piece of my heart.*
> *Elizabeth Hathaway.*

She read it twice, each time hoping to find something in it that she hadn't found the last two hundred times she read it. When nothing jumped out at her, she folded the note again and touched the tip of her pen to the notebook.

A single letter inked the page. *J.* Amy followed it with a dash, not bothering to write out the whole word. Looking at the paper, she paused, collecting her thoughts. Then the pen began moving across the next line—like it always did—seemingly without any encouragement.

> *April doesn't understand why I like to come out here sometimes, especially during spring and summertime. She thinks it gets too crowded, and she thinks that we exhausted and exploited this place by the time we graduated from high school. But I don't know. It just feels like home to me, and so I can't help but continue to come here, especially when I need to sort out my thoughts.*

> *Miles doesn't think it's a good idea to come out here either—not when I come by myself and stay until after dark. He worries about everything. All the time. But I don't care. Where else can I go to get away from the silences in my life? I like to pretend that I'm sitting on an old porch swing with a dear friend who can name all the stars above—or at least point out Venus at dusk and Jupiter at dawn.*

Darker and darker shades of blue wove themselves into the violet sky as she wrote, and the orange streetlights brightened. Faces continued to pass by; bits of people's conversations floated around her. She kept writing, noticing none of it.

> *I've been thinking about this Lizzie thing all day. What if it had been reversed? What if we grew up with Lizzie as a grandmother and never knew Nana? That would have been such a loss, and I wouldn't have even known it. I wonder if missing out on Lizzie has been a loss—a loss I haven't realized. I wish I could talk to Mom about this. Maybe I can talk to Nana. I just don't understand, and I feel like I should understand.*

Amy dropped her pen against the paper and stared across the street. She remained there, still, staring, letting minutes slip away. Not even the man walking in her direction broke her trance. He stopped a few paces away, waiting for her to look toward him.

When his presence didn't interrupt her train of thought, he sat down next to her.

Amy nearly jumped. "Miles! You surprised me!" She clutched the notebook to her chest. Slowly she lowered it back to her lap, careful to place her hand over the top of the page.

"I'm sorry." Amy's boyfriend smiled at her. "I didn't mean to. April said that you were probably here, so I thought I'd join you. What do you have there?"

"Oh nothing. Just thinking on paper." She closed the cover and shifted her body to face him. A grin formed on her lips, and her eyes grew. "Guess what—I have a plan to figure out who exactly this Lizzie was—"

"Amy, what are you doing?" Miles' face darkened. "This morning you told me your mom didn't want you involved—"

"I know, but just listen—"

"No, you can't—"

"I'm—"

"No, you can't." He shook his head. "You've got to stay out of it."

Amy studied Miles' furrowed eyebrows and felt a familiar frustration choking back her words.

He continued, "Your mom doesn't want you or anyone else making waves. Let it go. Just forget—"

"Why? I'm not—"

"You *are*. You're just going to make it worse."

She pushed a curl behind her ear, feeling heat rising to her cheeks. "I'm not, Miles. I'm *not* going to make it worse."

"But you are, and—"

"I haven't even done anything yet. I haven't hurt anything. I just want to know who this Lizzie person is. Who she was. I want to know more about where I came from. There's this whole family history we didn't know existed. What's wrong with wanting to explore it?"

He pursed his lips. "Why can't you be content with what you know right now?"

Amy's face went blank. She blinked. Her stomach tightened. She blinked again. "I am content with what I know right now. Everything is fine. But what's wrong with wanting to know more?"

"You should do what your mom asks." He looked around the park as though sensing something new in the air. "And what are you doing out here right now? It's cold and dark."

Amy sighed. Slowly, quietly, she slid her notebook back into her messenger bag and said, "Miles, I'm not a little girl. Don't talk to me like I'm one."

"Yeah, but you still—"

"Okay, stop it. Let's go." She stood up and slung her bag over her shoulder. A chill ran down her arms. "Let's go." She started walking away, forgetting the novel she had laid on the bench when looking for her notebook. She didn't wait for Miles to stand up, and she didn't look back to see if he followed.

But, of course, he did—without noticing the book on the bench either.

Three

Los Angeles

Will Chase stood on the balcony of his Westwood apartment, grinning, looking down at the group of girls on the sidewalk. He leaned against the rusted railing and wondered if they would ever take *no* for an answer.

"Why won't you come out with us?" Sarah, the ringleader, asked. Clad in a black dress and red heels, she planted a hand on her jutted hip and shook waves of brown hair off her shoulders. The two girls flanking her adopted similar poses.

Will continued grinning. "I wish I could, my friends. But finals are around the corner, and I'm way behind with studying. It's time to buckle down."

"You went out with us last night," Sarah countered.

"Exactly. And that's why I'm behind now."

Out of the corner of his eye, Will saw his roommate step onto the balcony next to him.

Chris leaned against the railing, his additional weight bending it outward an inch. "Ladies," he said, releasing the railing with one hand to pat Will's shoulder, "I'm sure you'd like nothing more than having the legendary Will Chase accompany you down to the bars of Westwood Village tonight, but alas, he is booked for the evening. That being said," he let go of the railing with his other hand and held a finger up, "his replacements are headed downstairs right now. I promise they will take good care of you."

As if on cue, Will and Chris' other two roommates walked out of the building and appeared next to the girls.

Will looked down at the group standing on the sidewalk for a moment, then at Chris, and then back at the group below. He hadn't expected this.

Ralph, the short, bald roommate looked up to the balcony and called, "Don't worry, buddy. We'll drink a beer in your honor."

"And we'll text you if you're missing anything interesting," Brian, the tall, blonde roommate added.

With that, Will's roommates waved at him and then

gestured toward the end of the street as if asking the girls to accompany them down toward the village center.

"How easily I'm replaced," Will muttered, watching the bar-hoppers walk down the street. He couldn't keep a sheepish smile from creeping across his face. He shook his head. "The girls didn't give it a second thought."

Sarah turned around, wobbling slightly in her heels, and called, "The old Will would have come with us no matter what. Not even finals would have stopped him." She turned back around, wobbled again, and threaded her arm through Brian's as they continued toward Westwood Village.

"She's already had too much to drink," Chris said. "Can't even stand straight." He patted Will's shoulder again. "You're welcome, by the way." He walked back into the apartment.

Will thought about Sarah's words. *The old Will would have come with us no matter what.* She was probably right. And the old Will would have bought beers for everyone. Or ended up in a fight. Or shown up at the wrong apartment at the end of the night. Or done a combination of those things.

The new Will wanted to get back on track for graduation in a year. When his parents told him they would only pay for four years of school, he knew it wasn't an empty threat. Paying for fifth year on his own—due in large part to his immaturity rather than impacted classes—wasn't an option he wanted to explore.

He looked at the sky. A sprinkling of stars peaked through the Los Angeles smog. *Not long now*, he thought. *One more week of class, and one week of finals. School will be over, I can relax, and I can go back home where smog doesn't hold the night sky hostage.*

"Will, get in here," Chris called. "When I said you were booked, I meant it. I need your help."

Will walked into the apartment and left the sliding glass door open behind him. He watched his roommate set a backpack on the kitchen table and crack open a beer. One swig later, the beer landed on the table next to the backpack.

"I have an English paper," Chris said. He unzipped his backpack and peered inside. "It's due in nine hours."

Will looked at the clock. It was eleven. "You have a paper due at eight in the morning?"

"Sure do." Chris tossed a book to Will. "Time for you to work your magic."

Will walked to the hand-me-down futon they used as a couch, looking at the book.

"I assume you haven't started it." Before Chris could answer, Will sat down and continued, "You know, when I agreed to help you with English papers, I didn't expect you to spring them on me at the last minute."

Chris tossed Will a beer and took another swig of his own. "And when I agreed to help you with any class involving numbers, I thought you'd at least know how to add and subtract." He walked toward the couch and placed a piece of paper on the coffee table. "Here's the essay prompt."

"Go get my hat," Will said. As Chris followed his orders and disappeared toward the back bedroom, Will held up the tattered book with the words USED—UCLA BOOKSTORE splayed across its spine. "This book is for Professor Hollings' class, isn't it?"

"Yep," Chris answered from the bedroom.

"Great professor."

"I know. You recommended him."

"We used this book when I had him. It was a different class, but the same time period."

"I know. You told me at the beginning of the quarter." Chris emerged from the bedroom and threw a San Francisco Giants baseball cap at Will. "There's your hat."

"Thanks." Will slapped it over his head backward, covering his dark hair. "I can't write a paper without it." He picked up the paper prompt.

"I know. You say that every time you help me with a paper." Chris picked up a basketball left under a side table and tried spinning it on his finger. "Okay, so what should I write?"

Will finished scanning the prompt and leaned back on the couch. "Where are your notes from class?"

Chris cringed. The basketball fell to the ground and he kicked it back under the table. "I don't really take notes. I figured I could borrow Janine's notes since we were taking the class together." He walked toward Will and sat down on the coffee table. "But then—"

"She broke up with you," Will finished.

"Right." Before Will could comment, Chris continued quickly, "Don't think I was entirely irresponsible though. I did ask her for the notes after we broke up. But she said no."

Will rolled his eyes. "Chris, this assignment asks you to write about a really hard Shakespeare poem. And nothing on the internet will give you what Hollings is looking for. Go into my bottom desk draw and get the notebook labeled English 151."

Chris walked back toward the bedroom.

Will flipped to the index of the Renaissance poetry book to locate Shakespeare's Sonnet 129. "Hey," he called to his roommate. "While you're back there, grab your laptop. Then you can start typing up the cover page."

After finding the poem in the index, Will flipped to page 312 and saw Sonnet 129 staring at him. Next to those printed words were handwritten words—obviously written by the book's previous owner. As he read the notes, Will's eyebrows rose. He read the handwritten words again. And then again.

"Hey," he called toward the bedroom, "did you know that love is supposed to be like a midsummer night's dream?"

"What are you talking about?" Chris emerged from the hallway. "I can't find that notebook. How about the notebook for English 164—will that do?"

"No, dumbass. English 164 covers a completely different time period. Go find the right notebook." Will turned his attention back to the handwritten words next to Sonnet 129.

Why isn't love always like a midsummer night's dream?

Strange. He flipped the page and saw more of the same handwriting in the margins. And on the page after that, he saw even more. Page after page he saw notes next to poems—notes that didn't look anything like the notes he had ever taken on Professor Hollings' lectures.

He whispers and he sighs
And softly, so softly come his goodbyes
that I know tomorrow
is only a moment away

His eyes jumped to the handwritten words on opposite side of the page.

> *Sleeping silently,*
> *He lies.*

Will's eyebrows furrowed. "This is really odd." He fanned through the pages and stopped at the next random page with blue ink in the margin.

> *I still remember—I fell in love with you on a Wednesday.*

Chris walked back into the living room with his laptop and a notebook.

"I found the right one," he said. "How's the paper coming? Do you have my thesis statement done yet?" He sat down on the couch and slid the notebook across the coffee table toward his roommate.

"Have you noticed the margin notes in this book?" Will asked. "The notes made by the previous owner?"

"I haven't actually opened the book." Before Will could react, Chris added, "Professor Hollings' lectures are so interesting. There doesn't seem to be a need for the book." He opened his laptop and started typing, avoiding eye contact with his roommate.

Will said, "The person who owned this book before you used the margins sort of like a journal. She wrote things like, 'I still remember—I fell in love with you on a Wednesday' and 'Why isn't love always like a midsummer night's dream?'" He flipped the page. "'Slipping through the fingers of concern, he lets me go.'" He looked up at Chris. "Strange, huh?"

Chris looked over from his laptop and shrugged. "Yeah, strange. Do you think any of those notes will help me write my paper?"

Will flipped back to page 312 and looked at the sonnet Chris was supposed to analyze. Next to the poem, the blue handwriting in the margin stared at him. He shook his head. "Whoever wrote in here was right—Sonnet 129 is nothing like a midsummer night's dream, but that's not going to get you very far." Will turned on the lamp next to the couch for the additional light needed during intense concentration. He repositioned his hat and reached for the notebook on the table. He tossed it to Chris. "Okay, here we go. Find my notes on this poem. We'll start there."

"And what are you going to do while I look up *your* notes in *your* notebook?"

"I'm going to look through here." Will held up the textbook. "And find some inspiration."

Chris sighed. "This is going to be a long night. How did I end up with the only roommate in the world who would get distracted by comments written in the margins of a used textbook?"

"You're what's distracting me. Just be quiet so I can think." Will stood up and walked toward the balcony. "Good papers need inspiration. I'll be back in five minutes with an idea for you." Once on the balcony, he closed the screen door behind him and sat in his favorite fraying patio chair. He flipped the page and read the note in the margin.

How am I supposed to talk if I have nothing to say?
Do you want to see how empty I really am?

Four

Los Gatos

Amy leaned against the counter in Eva's kitchen, watching her mother wash vegetables at the sink. "Can I help, Mom?" she asked.

"Oh no, honey, that's okay," Debbie said over her shoulder. "I'm almost done here, and Nana's lasagna is almost done, too."

Amy smiled. She loved that her family had dinner together every Sunday. She had been sad to miss last Sunday's dinner but understood why her mother and Nana probably needed some time to themselves after the news of Lizzie's passing. She was relieved that this Sunday's dinner resumed as normal.

"You know your mom and her salad," Eva said, crossing from the counter to the oven. "It's an—"

"Art form," Amy and Debbie finished together.

Amy watched her mom and Eva move about the kitchen. She had never given much thought to family resemblance, but since learning of Lizzie, she found herself examining what she had never examined before. Debbie's skin was fair, her hair was light and curly, and her face was round. Eva was much darker and more angular. Though her hair was gray, it had once been nearly black, complimenting her green eyes and olive skin. It also had always been long and straight, almost an extension of her angular facial features. Debbie looked nothing like Eva—and come to think of it, she didn't look like Grandpa either.

A roar erupted from down the hall, carrying into the kitchen and catching the three women off-guard. The rest of the family and Miles were watching a baseball game in the family room. From the sound of their cheers, Amy surmised that the Giants had scored.

"My goodness," Debbie said, slicing through a tomato. "You'd think they were watching the World Series out there."

Eva opened the oven and peered at the lasagna. "They think every game is the World Series." She closed the oven and looked at Amy. "Is Miles as passionate about the Giants as the rest of them?"

Amy rested her forearms on the counter and leaned on them. "I don't know. He'll watch a game, but I don't think he cares quite as much. When given the choice between watching a game or helping in the kitchen, he'll always choose the game."

"Then he's a good sport for putting up with those three," Debbie said.

Amy nodded and shrugged.

"Honey, I know what you can do to help," Eva said. "Upstairs, on my dresser, there's a jewelry box. Right inside is a small, black box with earrings in it. Grandpa gave them to me for our anniversary last week. Will you run up and grab them? I want to show you and your mother."

Amy followed Eva's directions, stopping only for a moment in the family room to get the game's score. Her sister, dad, and grandpa sat on the edge of the couch, hunched forward with eyes glued to the television. Miles sat on the recliner, feet up, paging through a magazine. He waved at Amy as she paused in the doorway.

"Score?" she asked.

"We're up one," April answered without taking her eyes off the television.

Amy continued upstairs, heading for her grandparent's room. From their doorway, she could see the jewelry box sitting on the dresser. She crossed the room and opened its lid. Grabbing the small black box, she noticed a folded piece of paper under it. Specifically, she noticed a word on the folded piece of paper. *Lizzie.*

She picked it up and unfolded it. The longhand was vaguely familiar—narrow and slanted—a bastardized calligraphy. Amy's eyes scanned the first line. A moment passed before she realized what she had found.

> *The following is the last will and testament of Elizabeth Hathaway. I wish that my sister, Eva Knodt carry out my wishes.*

Amy gasped, her heart suddenly thundering in her ears. She read word after word, but none of them seemed to have meaning. *Lizzie's will. Lizzie's will. Lizzie's will.* Her hands trembled. *This is Lizzie's will.*

"Amy, did you find them?" Eva called up the stairs.

The sound of Nana's voice tore Amy from her trance. "Yes," she called over her shoulder, refolding the paper and replacing it in the jewelry box. "Yes, I found them. I'll be right down." She snatched the earrings from the jewelry box and headed downstairs.

"They're beautiful, Nana," Amy said, crossing the kitchen and presenting the earrings to her mother. She hadn't looked at them, but even with her heart still thundering, she knew what to say.

"Oh, they are beautiful," Debbie said. "Did he pick them out all by himself?" She wiped her hands on a dishtowel before taking the box from her daughter.

"He certainly did. I was shocked when I opened them. I joked that he must have a girlfriend who helped pick them out. He's never had an eye for jewelry."

Amy's mind raced as her mother handed the earrings back. She wasn't listening to the voices around her—she could only think about what she had found upstairs.

"Nana, do you want to put them on now?" Amy asked. "Or would you like me to take them back to your room?"

"Oh heavens, they're too nice to wear," Eva laughed, sitting down at the table. "Would you mind taking them back?"

"Not at all."

Amy turned and raced toward the stairs, unaware that Miles waved as she passed the family room.

After returning the earrings to the jewelry box, she snatched the will and power-walked down the hall to the spare room where Eva and Aidan kept their computer.

Again her heart thundered in her ears as her eyes focused on the words staring at her.

> *I, Elizabeth Hathaway, being of sound mind, willfully and voluntarily...*

She skimmed line after line, seeing names she recognized and names she didn't—but with her nerves strangling her mind, she could process none of it.

She approached the printer sitting next to the computer. Scanning the buttons on the machine, she muttered, "Copy, copy, copy, doesn't this thing copy?" A moment later she abandoned the idea of copying the will and feverishly patted the pockets of her jeans. "Ugh," she spat under her breath. "Why didn't I grab my cell phone downstairs?" Silently, she added, *Taking a picture would have been much easier.* She didn't dare go back downstairs to get it and chance getting stuck in a conversation with someone. Instead, she grabbed the legal pad at the desk's edge. Quickly, she took notes with a shaky hand. Not only was Lizzie's writing strangely angular, but it also was very small, and it covered both sides of the page. *Faster, faster*, she told herself, cursing her unsteadiness. She would never get the contents down in its entirety—not even with the shorthand she used in college.

Minutes ticked by. She hoped no one missed her downstairs.

The backside primarily listed books. She skimmed the list. *Huck Finn, The Inferno, Canterbury Tales*. The list seemed endless. She recognized most of them and promised herself that she would remember them.

"Amy! Dinner!" April yelled up the stairs.

"Coming!" she yelled back. She ripped her page of notes from the legal pad, folded it, and pushed it into her pocket. "I'll be right there!"

***

The following day after work, Amy let herself into her quiet house and wandered to the kitchen, glancing in the family room along the way to see if her sister was around.

"April?" she called, dropping her purse on the kitchen table. "Hello?" There was no answer. She walked to the counter where the day's mail lay. Two or three of the envelopes were bills; two or three were credit card applications. Next to the mail sat a yellow Post-it note. Amy picked it up and read April's handwriting. *Miles called at five. He'll be here at seven. Order a pizza.* Amy looked across the kitchen at the microwave clock and then threw the Post-it and credit card applications into the garbage.

"You're home?"

Amy looked up and saw her sister walking into the kitchen from the back of the house, yawning.

"Yeah, I'm home," she answered, opening a bill. "Were you taking a nap?"

April nodded. She walked further into the kitchen and lifted herself onto the edge of the counter near Amy. "Did you have a good day?"

Amy shrugged. "I guess." She put the bill on the counter and looked at April. "Except I think I lost a book I've been reading on and off. I couldn't find it at lunch. And I can't remember the last time I read it, so I don't know where I might have left it. I thought it could have been at the coffee shop, but when I called them, they said they didn't have it." She picked up the bill again and looked at how much they owed the cable company.

"That's what you get for wasting money every morning at a coffee shop. If you made coffee here, you'd save money and still have your book. Hey, did you get my little note about your boyfriend calling?"

"I did."

"Super." April looked at the clock and yawned again. "What's-his-name is going to be here soon. Have you ordered a pizza yet?"

"Not yet." Amy dropped the bill back to the counter and crossed the kitchen to fill a teapot at the sink.

"I'll order one. Extra-large pepperoni? I'll have them deliver it at seven." She slid off the counter and headed toward the family room for the phone.

"You're the best."

"Hmm," April responded, her voice trailing away as she disappeared through the hallway.

Amy set the teapot on the stove and watched the flames dance around its base. Work had worn her out—Mondays always left her with rounded shoulders and a searing lower back. All she wanted since noon was a cup of raspberry green tea and two Advil. When the water boiled, she made her tea and sat down at the kitchen table. From her purse she pulled the paper she had been thinking about all day.

Last will & test.
Me & sis—$ for edu. Any edu—trips, school, books, etc.
Mom & siblings—divide rest of $$
Nana—house and furniture. 1800 River Way—Saratoga
Billy Strath—books listed on back and the accompanying letters
Me & sis—rest of books
Marie and Jean Lambert —house in Paris
Ashes—to Paris. Lamberts will know what to do

"What are you doing?" April said, reemerging from the family room.

Amy pulled her eyes from the paper and smiled at her sister. "Come here—I'll show you."

April walked toward the table and sat down. "Uh-oh, you have that sneaky look on your face."

Amy considered her sister's observation. "Well, maybe. But look at this anyway." She slid the paper across the table to April.

"It looks like your chicken-scratch." She slid it back to Amy. "Just tell me what it is."

Amy's smile widened, and she leaned over the table as though about to share a secret. "This," she said, "is better than the plan I originally thought up." She tapped the paper. "Yesterday when we were at Nana's, I found Lizzie's will. So I copied down the key points, and now I'm just trying to figure out what it all means. It's a good place to start, huh?"

April shook her head. "You're insane. Figure out what it means? It means just what it says." April snatched the paper from Amy and read, "me and sis—money for education. Mom and siblings—divide the rest of money. Nana—"

"I know what it says," Amy snatched the paper back. "I want to figure out what it means. What *happened*. I want to know why we didn't know her." Amy pointed toward the top of the page. "Look, here is the address of the house that now belongs to Nana. I can go there and see it." She pointed further down the page. "And here's the name of two people getting a house in Paris. Who are Marie and Jean Lambert? I don't know, but I can do some research and figure it out. They've got to be pretty important because her ashes are supposed to be sent to them as well." She pointed above Marie and Jean Lambert's names. "And who's this? Billy Strath? He's the guy who gets a handful of books from her library, *and* he gets letters—that must be important. He must be important. I can find him too. Someone's got to be willing to talk, right?"

April shook her head. "Do what you want, but I'm pretty sure Mom will flip out if she finds you snooping around behind her back."

"She won't find out."

"Why don't you just talk to Nana? She's probably not as uptight as Mom about this. Sisters put up with each other's craziness all the time."

Amy raised an eyebrow at April before looking toward the kitchen window. "Yeah, I know. But I think it's too soon to talk to Nana. She clearly had a relationship with Lizzie—she even told Lizzie stories about us and showed her pictures of us. Lizzie's note to you and me said that specifically. She's got to be grieving. Right? And at the same time, she's so close to Mom. She might tell me to let it go—for Mom's sake—just like everyone else."

Before April could respond, the front door creaked open. Amy grabbed her paper and folded it knowing that Miles had just arrived.

"Yeah, you better hide that," April said. "He's such a kiss-ass that he'll tell Mom if he finds out what you're doing."

Amy scowled at her sister as they heard footsteps coming down the entryway. She knew April was right.

Five

Los Angeles

Spring quarter was at its finest in the days of late May and early June. The lull between midterms and finals permitted students to relax a little longer on the campus' green hills between classes, and it gave them the energy to stay out a little longer at fraternity parties and bars after dark. In spring, UCLA's atmosphere came straight out of a picture book. Elementary schools took fieldtrips to the campus to play among the watercolor trees, staircases, and fountains. Backpack-clad students roamed along the main campus path, lovingly called Bruin Walk, often stopping on brick steps or grassy knolls to chat with friends. People picnicked in the Sculpture Gardens, listened to live music in coffeehouses, and played sports on the intramural field. Beautiful nineteen, twenty, and twenty-one year olds walked around with tanned toes and sun-lightened hair, smiling at each other in their beach-inspired clothes. They talked about last weekend, this weekend, the sneak-preview movie showing in the school's adjoining Westwood Village, and the get-together that night at Sam's or Dave's or Phil's apartment. Those were the days when life was at its best.

And it was noon on one of these spring days—one of the last before finals. Lunchtime. Will sat with Chris and their other two roommates on a hill bordering Bruin Walk. They reclined on their elbows, the row of four young men looking nearly identical in their sunglasses, white T-shirts, and black or khaki shorts. They watched students walking to and from campus, eating Korean Barbeque across the way, and ignoring the solicitors who lined the walk.

Chris took a bite of his Taco Bell burrito and then looked down the row of his roommates. "Hey Will," he said. "I just got my paper back from Professor Hollings' class. Guess how I did."

Will finished chewing a bit of his own burrito. "I don't know—how'd you do?"

"I got a C. Thanks for all your help." He smirked.

Brian and Ralph looked at Will.

"You, the English major, helped Chris with a paper, and all he got was a C?" Brian asked.

Will shrugged. "He was writing on one of Shakespeare's hardest sonnets, and he didn't exactly give me much time to help him."

"I don't think that was the problem, buddy," Chris said. He crumpled up his burrito wrapper. "The problem was that you were too distracted by the comments written in the textbook, and I was left to decipher your awful writing from the English 151 notebook—which wasn't very helpful in piecing together a paper."

Ralph and Brian looked as though they were watching a ping-pong game, turning back and forth between Will and Chris. Their eyes now settled on Will.

"What comments in the book?" Brian asked.

"Why didn't you tell him what to write?" Ralph asked.

Will shook his head and looked at Ralph. "I did tell him what to write. My suggestions were shot down. *All* of my suggestions were shot down." He turned toward Brian. "And the comments—well, Chris, do you have that book with you?"

"Yeah." Chris reached for the backpack at his feet and rummaged around for the requested reading material. When he found the collection of Renaissance poetry, he tossed it over Ralph's lap to Will.

"Look at this," Will said, opening to a random page. He smacked the page with the back of his hand before reading, "'Are my dreams just ink stains on a page?' Who writes that in a book?" He flipped to another page. "'Your eyes are such a troubling blue—and yet I'm drowning in my own silence.'" He looked toward his roommates. "I mean, this stuff has nothing to do with Renaissance poetry."

Chris exchanged a glance with Ralph and Brian. "See what I mean?" he asked. "Distracted."

"That was the night Sarah wanted you to go down to the bars, right?" Ralph asked. "You should have just gone out with us. It doesn't sound like you got anything done anyway."

"Besides going around in circles with this idiot for three hours?" Will nodded at Chris. "No, I didn't get anything done. He didn't like any of my ideas."

"The ideas couldn't have been that good," Brian said. "He

got a C."

Will shoved the last of his burrito in his mouth and crushed the wrapper into a ball. "You guys are idiots." He stood up and tossed the wrapper into a nearby garbage can. "And if I want to pass my classes this quarter, I've got to stop hanging out with you fools and trying to help you write papers." He grabbed his backpack. "I'm going to study. See you all at home." He pointed at each of his roommates one by one. "Who's making dinner tonight?"

Ralph raised his hand. "My turn."

"Ah, that means a hearty meal of Spaghettios. Very good." He held up Chris' book and continued, "I'm borrowing this." He shoved it into his backpack.

As he began the uphill walk toward the north end of campus, Chris called after him, "Why? Are you going to use it to *not* help someone else write a paper?"

Before Will could turn around and respond, Ralph yelled, "Hey, the girls want to go out again tonight. You in? Or will you be busy coming up with bad thesis statements?"

Will decided against turning around. Instead, he waved over his shoulder and kept walking. He hooked his thumbs around his backpack straps and looked at his feet while climbing the hill toward Royce Quad. *No wonder it's hard to stop being a jackass,* he thought to himself. *I'm surrounded by them.*

Will reached the water fountain at the edge of the quad and scanned the scene. Students milled about, walking across the quad and into the surrounding buildings. Royce Hall and Powell Library, two of the school's most beautiful buildings—inspired by the architecture of Italian churches—buzzed with the energy of a looming finals week. Along the face of Royce stood a row of arches that students often used as shaded benches for studying, and today was no different. In fact, a student with an open book leaned against every arch, leaving no room for Will. A smattering of students sat on the steps leading to Powell's entrance. Although Will preferred studying in front of Royce, sitting on Powell's steps would work just as well. He made his way to the library and sat down on the bottom step. Tuning out the chatter around him, he grabbed the Renaissance poetry book from his backpack and opened it to a random page, which, like so many others, was filled with blue writing in the margins.

Life is just a movement toward—and then away from—one feeling.
Love.

He flipped to another page, wondering how these words found their way to the pages of a book like this.

He lets me cry.
"It's okay—it's okay to feel this way.
Don't let yourself be swallowed by silence."
So almost silently, I cry.

"What the hell," Will breathed. He flipped to another page.

"Are you *still* talking to yourself?" The voice came from behind him.

Will craned his neck and saw a familiar face.

"Hey Kim," he said, smiling. "How are you? Long time no see."

The girl standing behind him stepped down toward Will and sat next to him. Her backpack landed with a thud at her feet.

"I know," she said. "Too long. What have you been up to?"

Will shrugged. "School, mostly." His smiled morphed into a sideways grin. "I'm trying to undo some of the damage I did to my GPA during freshman and sophomore year."

Kim smiled—nearly laughing—and pushed a ponytail of long dark hair behind her shoulder. "Really? So all the craziness of the days we were neighbors in the dorms is over? For good?"

He nodded. "It sure is." He paused, his grin fading. He looked down at the Renaissance poetry book a moment before returning his attention to Kim. "So, how's Jocelyn?"

He knew the question was eventually going to come up. He figured he'd just ask and get it out of the way sooner rather than later.

Kim didn't answer right away—she just nodded for a moment. Then she fiddled with her backpack's zipper. "Good," she said. "Good." Another pause. "She recently started dating some guy she met awhile back. The other roommates and I aren't sure about him yet." She smiled and nudged her shoulder against Will's. "He's certainly no Will Chase."

"That's probably good. I wasn't the greatest boyfriend."

"No, you weren't," Kim laughed. "But you were fun to watch—in a train wreck sort of way. You drove too fast and got a fake ID too young."

Will's sideways grin returned. "That's what you always told me." He shook his head and gazed across the quad. "I don't know how she put up with it for so long. I don't know how you and your other roommates put up with it either."

"I introduced the two of you back when we were neighbors in the dorms, so I had to put up with it."

Will chuckled. "I'm surprised the rest of them are still friends with you after that." His eyes remained focused on Royce Hall across the quad. "It's been, what, seven or eight months since Jos and I broke up? Seems like a lifetime ago. I don't think I've even seen you since then."

"Has it really been that long since we've run into each other?" Kim thought a moment. "I guess you're right. Wow, nearly the whole school year has gone by. And look at you sitting here studying with the rest of the responsible students. Of all places, this is the last one I would expect to find you." She nodded toward the book in Will's hands. "What are you reading there?"

Glad to have gotten the Jocelyn portion of the conversation out of the way, Will turned his attention to Renaissance poetry book. "Check this out. It's Chris' book, but the person who owned it before him used it as a journal or something." Will shifted the book toward her and leaned in. "Look at this."

Exclamation points surrounded a circled line of poetry written by a Renaissance writer named Sir Edmund Spenser. *But let this day let this one day be mine,* Spenser had written. Next to it was the familiar handwriting Will was becoming quite familiar with.

> *I want that one day—that one special day—to be mine. But only if it's captured in all its sweetness on a Grecian Urn. I want him to reach for me, I want to feel the first excited chill of him touching me, and I want THAT feeling*

engrained on a Grecian Urn so I can have it always.

Kim finished reading and then looked at Will and pushed some stray hair behind her ears. She thought a moment before speaking. "I have a lot of questions."

"I know, me too." Will said. "Why would someone sell back a book after writing in it like this?"

She shrugged. "Maybe she didn't mean to sell it back. I've done that before with literature books. Last quarter I had ten novels for an English class, and two got mixed into the stack of books that me and my roommates were selling back. It's hard to keep track, especially when people are packing up to move home for the summer and there are piles of school stuff everywhere." She looked back at the book, eyebrows furrowed. "What's special about a Grecian Urn? What does it have to do with Sir Edmund Spenser's poem here?"

Will's mind surfed back to a class he took on Romantic poets. "Well, it doesn't really have anything to do with Spenser or Renaissance literature. The reference to the Grecian Urn is from a poem written more than two centuries later by a guy named John Keats. But maybe that doesn't matter. Basically, the Grecian Urn poem is about a bunch of pictures on a big vase. I don't remember exactly, but I think one picture showed guy chasing a girl. And it's supposed to be poignant because the picture captures the anticipation and excitement of reaching for the girl. But then there's this whole debate about it, because even though anticipation and excitement are fun, if you're stuck in that moment, you never get to see what comes next. You'd never actually get the girl and feel how great it is to have her—which, of course, is better than anticipation. But then at the same time, if you go past that moment of reaching for her, you might miss when you try to grab her. And that would be a whole lot worse than the anticipation and excitement of the chase. If you're stuck in a moment, you never risk getting something better. Or something worse, for that matter. And it's up to you to decide if you want to let things stay the same or take the risk of change."

Kim smiled. "That poem sounds like you. You're the guy chasing the girl on the vase—always going after what you want."

Will laughed. "I never thought of that." He pointed to the

blue handwriting next to the printed Spenser poem. "No, I think I'm like the person who wrote in the margins here. I don't want the chase pictured on the vase. I want the moment of getting what I want captured on the vase." He turned the page, not waiting for Kim to respond. "Look at this."

> *Wrong.*
> *He left me in shades of gray.*
> *There were no lies. Just shades of gray.*

Kim took the book from Will's hands and held it up to him. "What are you going to do with this?"

"What do you mean? I'm not going to do anything. It's not my book."

Kim gave him a look he was quite familiar with during his train wreck years. "Chris may have bought it, but it's not his. It belongs to the girl who wrote in the margins. You need to find her."

Will looked at the book and then back at Kim.

"Well, come on, Will. Why not?" she continued. "Do you really think that she meant to sell the book back?"

He shook his head. "It doesn't seem likely."

"Then this is exactly the kind of adventure you would love. You should go see the professor who teaches that class. Maybe he'll recognize the handwriting and give you some clues."

"That's a long shot. When was the last time a professor saw your handwriting?"

Kim rolled her eyes. "Okay, so maybe that won't work—but I know you will think of something." She looked at the clock tower at the far end of the quad. "Hey, I better get to class. I've got History of Religion in five minutes." She stood up and slung her backpack over her shoulders.

"It was good to see you, Kim," Will said. As an afterthought, he added, "Tell Jocelyn I said hi."

"I'll do that." She pointed to the book in Will's hands. "And *you* do something with that. Don't kid yourself—you like the anticipation of the chase as much as you like getting what you want. You couldn't have changed *that* much in the last year." She began walking backwards. "And tell me what happens. I've missed hearing about the exploits of the fantastic Will Chase."

Will chuckled. He nodded and then waved as she turned toward the far corner of North Campus.

Six

Los Gatos

Amy's parents owned a Victorian-style house. It was smallish-looking, painted white with blue trim. A knee-high picket fence encircled the yard, and two white wicker chairs sat on the porch near the front door. Potted plants grew around the legs of each chair, and planted flowers lined the yard alongside the white fence. Wind chimes, a birdfeeder, and a decorative gray stone with *welcome* engraved on it garnished the home's entrance. Amy felt its inviting warmth as she walked through the yard carrying a coffee cup filled with basil from her patio herb garden. She let herself in, knowing that neither of her parents was home yet.

She set the basil on the kitchen counter and made her way toward the backyard. Outside, white wooden patio furniture covered with overstuffed cushions sat in a circle next to a pool. Amy took her messenger bag from her shoulder and dropped it on a side table next to her favorite chair. From the bag she pulled a notebook before sitting down. She looked at the pool, took a deep breath, and thought about her day at work. Then her pen began moving across the page.

> *J—*
> *Sometimes I feel the day slip away from me. Sometimes I sit at my desk and think about all the things I let float by. All the stories that I didn't write, all the dances I didn't dance, all the music I didn't hear. I think about the people in my life whom I've missed, and I wonder how my life would be if I didn't miss any of that. It makes me sad, but before the sadness turns to anger, I realize I have work to do. So, I go on about my day, pretending it's okay and that I don't hate my marketing job.*

A breeze blew through the back yard, sending ripples across the pool's surface. Amy watch the ripples melt away as the breeze died, and she thought of all the summers that she and April spent there swimming until they were sunburned. As she touched the tip of her pen back to the paper, she heard her mom's voice.

"Hello out there!"

Amy pulled her pen back and turned toward the patio door where her mother stood. She closed her notebook and set it aside. "Hey Mom," she called, hoisting herself from the bed of oversized cushions and walking to the patio door. "I brought you some basil."

"Thank you," Debbie said. "It'll be perfect in the salad I was planning to make for dinner. Are you hungry? Do you want to stay for dinner?"

Amy joined Debbie in the kitchen where her mother was going through a stack of mail. A disconcerted look darkened Debbie's face as she read a note written on blue stationary. Amy watched, waiting for Debbie either to finish the note or to relax her face. When neither seemed imminent, she picked up the torn envelope on the counter. In the upper left corner was a pre-printed address listing Billy Strath as the sender. Amy stifled an involuntary gasp.

"Mom, what are you reading?"

"Unbelievable," Debbie muttered. "Unbelievable." She glanced at her daughter. "Put that envelope down." She took the envelope from her daughter's hand before Amy could drop it, and then she shoved the note back into it.

"What was that?" Amy asked. "What did Billy Strath want?"

"To be an eternal frustration," Debbie breathed, staring at the window as though barely aware that Amy had asked the question. Amy thought about slipping the envelope into her pocket, but before she could do it, Debbie's head snapped toward her.

"What do you know of Billy Strath?"

Amy lifted the palms of her hands toward her mother as if in surrender. "Nothing. I know his name is on that envelope."

"Oh." Debbie shook her head as though trying to rid herself of the sour thoughts associated with his name. "I shouldn't have opened it," she muttered. "It was addressed to your father—none of my business." She walked to the pantry and yanked open its doors. "Are you hungry?"

"No, I'm going to head home soon. I think April's already

got something cooking for dinner."

Debbie began slamming cabinets, tossing spices from the rack to the counter, dropping mixing bowls on the floor. Amy was unable to remember the last time such a little woman created such great noise. She bit her lip, hoping to keep words from spilling from her mouth but knowing she couldn't stop herself.

"Mom," she began, "what's wrong? Is this about Lizzie?"

Debbie froze, a knife in one hand and a cucumber in the other. Disgust colored her face. Turning her back to Amy and slicing the cucumber, she said, "I'd appreciate it if you never mention that name in my house again."

The statement startled Amy. "Mom," she said, instinctively wanting to reason with such stubbornness. "I just—"

"You just nothing," Debbie said, twirling toward her daughter and shaking the knife at her. "We will discuss neither this nor anything else regarding that woman. If you have a question about your money or the books, then," she paused, not having thought through the idea before beginning it, "then, talk to your father. I want nothing to do with it." She turned back to the cutting board and continued chopping.

Amy didn't speak. She silently slid Billy's envelope into her pocket. Then she waited until the quickness of her mother's movements slowed.

"I don't care about the money or the books," Amy said. "I just want you to be okay. And I just want to help if I can. I'm sorry."

She watched her mother's shoulders rise and fall one, two, three times. When Debbie turned back to her daughter, her eyes had returned to the kind, clear blue that Amy was used to.

"I'm sorry I snapped at you," Debbie said with a deep breath. "I'm just a little on edge lately."

Amy nodded. "I understand. Sometimes it helps to talk, and if you want to talk, plenty of people are ready to listen. Me, Dad, April, Nana, whoever."

Debbie turned back to the cutting board.

Amy tried to think of something comforting to say, but nothing came to mind.

"What is it that Grandpa always says? *This too shall pass*?"

Debbie nodded, her eyes on the cucumber. Amy approached her mother and squeezed her shoulders into a sideways hug.

"I'll see you soon."

Debbie nodded again. "Love you, honey."

As Amy walked down the front steps toward her car, she felt the blue stationary burning a hole in her pocket. It flamed with her curiosity and guilt, but she didn't dare pull it out until she was in her car and halfway down the street. When she did, her eyes flew over its words, and suddenly her head was pounding.

She drove home on autopilot, thinking about Billy's message, over and over. When she parked in front of her house, she saw Miles standing at the front door.

"Hey," he said, walking down the driveway toward her. "I was beginning to think that you got lost on your way home. Did you get any of my messages?"

Amy shook her head, grabbing her bag and sliding the blue paper into its front pocket. "No, sorry. My phone's been dead all day. Everything alright?"

Miles reached for her bag and slung it over his shoulder. Amy nearly protested, not wanting Billy's note to leave her possession, but instead she bit her lip.

"Everything's fine," he said. "April's been holding dinner for you."

"That was nice of her." They walked up the driveway together. "How long have you been here?"

"About half an hour. Long enough to wear out my welcome with your sister." Miles rested his hand on her shoulder as they approached the porch.

Amy grinned. "A bit testy, is she? Maybe she missed her afternoon nap. All kindergarten teachers need those."

"Remind me never to suggest different cooking techniques to her."

Amy cringed. "Oh, yeah. Not a good idea. The kitchen is her domain."

"Apparently she knows everything there is to know about basting barbeque ribs."

Amy reached for the front door handle but paused before pulling it open. She scrunched up her nose, almost apologetically.

"She actually does. You should know that, though—haven't you had her ribs before?"

Miles rolled his eyes.

As Amy stepped into the entryway, she breathed in the smell of espresso barbeque sauce. "April, it's smells amazing in here," she said while walking toward the kitchen. "Thank you for holding dinner for me."

Miles placed Amy's bag beside the front door and followed her into the kitchen. "Yes, it really does smell amazing in here," he said. "And thank you for holding dinner for me as well."

April looked up from the kitchen table where she was laying out silverware and napkins. Her eyes narrowed, but the faintest hint of a smile danced at the corners of her lips. "Your welcome. But I'm warning you now—I'm not in the mood for dinnertime conversation."

Amy had no problem with the idea of a quiet dinner. As they sat down to eat, she thought about the note from Billy Strath and pondered her next steps. She couldn't contact him—she knew that for sure. But maybe there was something else she could do. Idea after idea flitted through her mind, none of them solid enough to materialize into a real plan. By the time she finished eating, she still didn't know what she wanted to do.

"Does anyone want to watch a movie?" Miles asked before biting the last bit of meat from his barbeque ribs. "April, you can pick one while Amy and I clean up here."

"That sounds good," April said. She wiped her hands on a napkin and leaned back. "I'm feeling like something classic. Maybe something from the 1950s. And while we are watching the movie, you two can help me cut out a thousand stars and stripes for my kindergarten class' upcoming Flag Day celebration."

Amy raised an eyebrow at her sister and suppressed a smile. This was retribution for Miles' culinary suggestions earlier. He couldn't stand the slow pace of old movies, and helping April with kindergarten prep was low on his list of priorities. "Flag Day, huh?" Amy said. "Sounds like fun."

April winked at Amy. "You know it."

With the pots and pans scrubbed, dishes loaded into the dishwasher, and the kitchen wiped down, April announced that the night's movie would *Rebel without a Cause*.

"Who doesn't love James Dean and Natalie Wood?" she asked, flashing the DVD at Amy and Miles before walking into the family room to feed it into the DVD player.

Miles eyed Amy and threw away the paper towel he was holding. "I don't."

"This was your idea." Amy shrugged and took his arm. "Come on, let's get in there so I can grab the good construction paper scissors for you."

Like their silent dinner, Amy was glad to engage in a quiet activity so she could daydream about her long lost grandmother. Having been unable to come up with a plan involving Billy Strath, she focused her thoughts on Jean and Marie Lambert. Who were they? She wondered if she could find them. Was there an app she could download to her phone and use to communicate with them? There must be plenty of translations apps. Would she need to learn some French? And on that note, how was anyone in her family going to communicate with the Lamberts about Lizzie's will? None of them spoke French as far as she knew. Maybe the Lamberts spoke English. That would solve a lot of problems. Nana might know…

She tried to imagine what a conversation might be like. *Hello Mrs. Lambert. I'm Elizabeth Hathaway's granddaughter, and I was wondering if I could ask you a couple questions about my grandmother.*

What would come next? She couldn't find the right words.

Time slipped away, minute by minute, movie scene by scene, without Amy paying much attention.

Hello, Mrs. Lambert, she imagined again. *I was wondering if I could talk to you about my grandmother, Elizabeth Hathaway. I recently found out that…*

She didn't know how to finish the sentence.

I found your contact information in Elizabeth Hathaway's will, and I was wondering if…

Elizabeth Hathaway, she's my grandmother, and I…

"Amy. Amy, where are you?"

Miles was gently shaking her shoulder.

"Are you daydreaming? The movie is over—and I'm going to head home."

Amy looked around the family room. The last scenes of

Rebel without a Cause were fading away. April was asleep on the couch across the room. Miles was standing up. The clock on the cable box read 10:55. "Oh, okay. Yeah, good idea." She stood up and followed Miles to the door.

"That movie wasn't as bad as I remember it," he said, stretching his arms over his head.

"No, it's not bad at all. It's great, actually." Her mind was elsewhere, but the words came without thought. "What a storyline. And what a time period." Amy wasn't even quite sure what she was saying, but she didn't care. "If April were awake, she'd say 'That's when men were real men.'"

Miles reached for the doorknob, leaned toward Amy, and kissed her forehead. "And that's why she doesn't have a boyfriend now," he said. "No one can make her happy."

The comment shook Amy's mind off autopilot. *What had she said to warrant that response?* She couldn't remember, so she smiled and let it go. "See you tomorrow. Goodnight."

Miles closed the door behind him, and Amy waited a moment, listening the sound of his car disappearing down the street. She bent down toward her messenger bag still sitting by the front door and reached into its front pocket for the blue note. She pulled it out and read it again.

"Is your boyfriend gone yet?" April called from the family room.

"Uh-huh."

"He's right—that's exactly why I don't have a boyfriend right now. They don't make men like they used to."

Amy nodded, still reading. "You've never been one to settle."

April appeared in the hallway. She pushed her rumpled hair behind her ears and looked at Amy for a moment. "You're right. Goodnight." She continued on toward her bedroom.

Amy looked up from the note and then opened the front door. Stepping onto the porch, the night air pricked her skin and cooled the inside of her lungs. She sat down and looked up at the sky. The North Star glinted at her.

Why was Billy Strath so mean? she wondered. *Why did he send that note?*

Goosebumps formed on Amy's arms, and she hugged her

knees into her chest. Across the night sky, she looked for patterns in the stars. There had to be answers somewhere. In the stars, in the scraps of papers she had collected since Lizzie's death, in someone's memory—there had to be answers somewhere.

There has to be someone who can help me. Somehow.

She needed her notebook.

Seven

Los Angeles

The night was hot. Restless. Dark, warm wind rustled through the trees outside Will's window, and he wished that he were ten years old again, sleeping in a perfect tree-house where the air felt cooler and there was no need for thought provoking insights about *Paradise Lost.* He paced back and forth, casting a sideways glance now and then at his computer desk. He hated taking an entire class on John Milton. He hated writing a paper on Milton. Sure, the guy was a genius—but he was also a jerk. And both those traits came through loud and clear in *Paradise Lost.* Writing an interesting paper on a text that had already been discussed to death for centuries was hard enough; knowing that Milton died expecting generations to worship him made the paper-writing process even more painful.

Will threw his pen in the air and let it fall to the ground. Two papers and two finals were all that stood between him and summer vacation. He just needed to get through them.

He took off his San Francisco Giants hat and fell backward on his bed. He reached for Chris' Renaissance Poetry textbook, which had been sitting on his nightstand for the last couple nights. He opened it to a random page and drew his eyes to the blue handwriting in the margin.

> *Have my words already been said? I heard them before in my inspiration's voice. "Go cast your spells," he said, "And put together words with letters and love." Am I repeating him? Feigning magic? An impostor? Plagiarizer?*

He flipped the page.

> *And the back row gossip*
> *Continues.*

He eyes moved to the other side of the page.

I used to say that there was a thick layer of L.A. coating you. I used to say that as I dove into that thick layer, trying to get under it, trying to get to you. I can still feel the stickiness on my skin, the sweet-sour scent in my nose. And when I thought I cut all the way through that layer of sticky, sweet-sour L.A., my eyes were blurry so I still couldn't see you.
And then you didn't call. It was a sign.

Will dropped the book on his bed. A familiar mixture of guilt and intrigue swirled through him as he stared at the ceiling and took a deep breath. Maybe Kim was right. Maybe he should look for the book's owner. He remembered when he found a journal in his ex-girlfriend's desk while looking for some paper. He hadn't even opened it before she turned red and snatched it away. How would this girl feel about others reading her private thoughts?

And then before he could stop it, another memory of his ex-girlfriend took hold of his mind. *You can talk to me,* Jocelyn had said on the phone the day his grandfather died. *You don't have to hold it inside—it's okay to be sad. Let me drive home with you for the funeral.* He had mumbled back that he'd think about it, and then he left for home without her. He had never been able to let her in.

And then I didn't call, he thought to himself. *It was a sign.* He picked up the book again.

I've finally got all of me back together—I've picked up all the pieces, and I think they're all back in the right places. And now, I don't regret that I cared about you the way I did. I only regret that my feelings for you came out of such a deeply rooted vulnerability. Because, when you left, that vulnerability took an ugly turn—and it's that ugly turn that I regret. I'm embarrassed by my painfully obvious hurt. I should have kept it to myself better, dealt with it better, not involved you with so much of it. For that, I am truly sorry, and with the remnants of that vulnerability, all I can do is ask you to forgive me.

Jocelyn filled his thoughts again. She had ended the relationship with him—she had been the one who left—but only because he had broken her. And he left her to pick up all the pieces herself.

Who was this person describing exactly what Jocelyn must have gone through when they broke up?

He turned the page. Wedged into the book's seam was the yellow carbon copy of a receipt—probably from a hole-in-the-wall place that never bothered to update its credit card machine. Will pulled it out and examined its faint print. He didn't recognize the restaurant's name at the top, but below the smudged total, he clearly could read the restaurant patron's signature.

He held the receipt against a page of the book. The signature matched the handwriting in the margins.

"Will, get out here," Chris said from the doorway of their bedroom. Brian and Ralph appeared behind him. "We've got the water balloons ready for Midnight Yell."

Will dropped the book and pushed himself off the bed. "How long till we start?"

"About two minutes," Brian said. "Looks like the apartment across the street made a sling shot to launch its water balloons."

"We should have thought of that," Ralph said.

As the others agreed, they made their way to the balcony and each grabbed an armful of water balloons from the five-gallon buckets they had borrowed from a neighbor.

"Alright guys," Chris said. "Here we are. The night before finals begin." He caught a water balloon trying to escape his hold. "The first Midnight Yell of the week. Ready?"

As if on cue, Brian's cell phone alarm sang out, officially marking the stroke of midnight and the beginning of UCLA's long-standing late-night tradition during finals week. The roars of students frustrated by studying rose from apartment buildings across Westwood.

"Go!" Will yelled. He chucked a water balloon across the street and grabbed a second balloon. In his peripheral vision, he could see his roommates launching a rainbow of balloons in the same direction.

A balloon exploded at his feet, and another whizzed right past his shoulder, splattering against their patio door.

"Look out!" Will bellowed as the water balloon slingshot appeared on an apartment balcony across the street. His words were drowned out by hundreds of students wailing and banging pots and pans outside their homes. Will ducked just as a sling-shotted water balloon grazed his hair at double speed. He grabbed another armful of balloons and hurled them across the street.

One minute later, the choruses of midnight yellers faded, and many participants of the university tradition returned to their apartments. Will and his roommates hadn't exhausted their supply of water balloons—and neither had the apartment of guys across the street—so the fight continued. A group of girls from the apartment below stayed outside to watch the trash-talking and balloon-throwing, only retreating when the balloon sling-shot was aimed at them.

"Get 'em, boys!" The group of girls called to Will and his roommates as they ran for cover in the apartment's lobby.

"Knock it off!" a voice yelled from a different apartment down the street. Will couldn't tell exactly which apartment the voice came from, but within moments, the two apartments throwing balloons at each other shift their aim and joined forces in pummeling the building from which the voice came.

"I'll call the police!" the same voice thundered.

Will threw his last balloon and held up his palms. "I'm out!" He looked at the five-gallon buckets at his feet and saw that his roommates had also exhausted their supply.

"We're out, too," one of the guys across the street yelled.

"No need to call the police, sir," Chris called out. "We're done."

"If you'd like to join us tomorrow night," Brian added, "We'll bring you some water balloons."

The guys on both balconies waited for an answer, but none came.

"Well played," a guy across the street yelled.

"Nice touch with the sling shot," Chris called back. "And, hey, Wesley—I'll meet you downstairs at 8:30 so we can head up to Anthro together."

"Sounds good," the guy called back.

And with that, Will and his roommates filed into their apartment, dripping and covered in bits of colorful water balloon shrapnel.

"I don't feel like studying now," Brian said.

"I never do after our first midnight-yell water balloon fight," Will said.

The four roommates headed to their respective rooms to change clothes and grab whatever books they needed to prepare for upcoming finals. After pulling a dry shirt over his head, Will stood in front of his computer, staring at the screen with his hands on his hips.

"What are you doing?" Chris asked. He picked up the wet shirt Will had left on the floor and threw it onto Will's bed.

"I'm thinking about how much I don't want to write this paper."

"Then don't work on it now. Don't you have a history final before that paper is due anyway?"

"Yeah, but I'm ready for that final. I think. This paper is what's really killing me."

Chris picked up his Microeconomics book. "Well, good luck. The rest of us will be in the living room studying if you decide you'd rather join us than write."

Will nodded, continuing to stare at his computer screen. After Chris left the room, he turned around and saw the Renaissance poetry book peaking out from beneath the wet shirt Chris had thrown on it. He picked it up and thumbed through the last couple pages until he found *Appendix 5: Index of Authors.* According to the list, the anthology showcased a couple poems by John Milton. He vaguely remembered working through one of Milton's poems when taking English 151 with Professor Hollings. What had Hollings said at the time? *No need to spend too much time on Milton in this class.* Or something like that. *If you haven't already, you'll get to focus on his work throughout English 143.*

Will located a poem with a familiar title and turned to page 659. The last line of the poem was underlined in blue ink, and Will read it slowly. *I wak'd, she fled, and day brought back my night.* Then he read the handwritten words next to it. *Great line. Beautiful. But Milton was still a jerk.*

Will smiled. Finally—someone agreed with him about

Milton.

He snapped the book shut, tossed it on his bed, and sat down at his desk to write the dreaded paper.

***

During finals week, Bruin Walk looked the same: big signs advertising different clubs and organizations still lined the walk. The Taco Bell window was open for business and selling food to kids needing a study break. People filled the student union seeking coffee and a place to get out of the sun. But now, the soft hum of nervous energy filled the air, and soon that energy would melt into the silence of summer break as students went home to their families and summer jobs.

Will left Bunche Hall where he had just finished taking a final exam on the Gilded Age of America. He headed toward the center of campus, looking at his feet and thinking about his answer to the last exam question. Had he covered all the necessary points about the Robber Barons to make his argument? It seemed like he had them all. He hoped so. There was no going back now.

When Royce Quad came into sight, thoughts of Robber Barons dissolved. He climbed the steps to the Humanities building and hoped that no one was waiting in line to see Professor Hollings during office hours.

And he was in luck. As Will neared the office door, he heard no voices exchanging ideas about Renaissance literature. He peeked into the office and saw the professor sitting in his chair, reading, his feet up on the coffee table.

Will knocked on the open door. "Hi Professor Hollings," he said.

Hollings looked up from his book and smiled. "Oh, hello, Will. It's good to see you. How are you?" He dropped his feet to the floor and put his book on the coffee table.

Will walked into the office and extended his hand as he neared the seating area. Hollings leaned forward in his chair and shook his former student's hand.

"I'm doing well, Professor, thanks. How is your quarter wrapping up?"

"Very nicely. I have two more finals to give, and then it

will be on to grading. But that isn't very interesting to talk about." He chuckled. "To what do I owe this special visit?"

Will sat down in the chair designated for students and noticed that the coffee table separating him and Hollings displayed an Italian art and architecture book. The last time he came to office hours the book hadn't been there. He shook his head almost imperceptibly and looked up at the professor, reminding himself that Hollings' office decorations weren't the reason for his visit.

"I have two questions for you today. One is pretty simple, and the other is pretty complicated."

The professor leaned back in his chair. Behind him, two desks lined opposite walls. When he wasn't talking to students he turned around in his rolling chair and bounced back and forth between the typewriter's desk and the computer's desk. When students were visiting, though, the desks barely seemed to exist—all attention focused on conversations about the poetry of centuries past.

"Let's start with the simple one," Hollings said, folding his hands across his stomach. "Perhaps we can ease into the difficult one."

Not likely, Will thought, but he smiled anyway. "I saw in next fall's Schedule of Classes that you are teaching a senior seminar on Special Studies in Renaissance Literature. Have you determined the focus?"

Hollings eyebrows rose. "I was thinking of going with a class incorporating Shakespeare and the greats of the Italian Renaissance. Perhaps Michelangelo or DaVinci. Are you interested?"

"I am. Anything having to do with Shakespeare or Italy—that sounds great," Will said.

Hollings chuckled. "Well, good. I look forward to seeing you in class then. I've always enjoyed your unique readings of the world's best literature. Now, I imagine that takes care of the easy question you had. Let's tackle the complicated one."

Will leaned forward and unzipped the backpack at his feet. "Okay, well, here we go. I think I need your help." He drew the book of Renaissance poetry into the air and presented it to Hollings. "My roommate is taking a general education English class with you this quarter, and he's reading this book, right? The same book we used in English 151 last year?"

Hollings leaned forward, looking at the book's cover. "Yes, Renaissance poetry. An excellent text for any level of analysis."

Will grinned. "Certainly." His smile faded as he thought about the words to come. "My roommate bought that book used." He looked at the professor with wide eyes as he talked slowly, less sure about the words as they came. "When I was helping him with his last paper, I noticed that the previous owner had used the margins sort of like a journal. All of it was sort of poetic, and I think it was mostly about her life—but it came in bits and pieces, so it was hard to tell. None of it resembled the kind of notes people normally write in the margins of textbooks."

Hollings' eyebrows rose in agreement.

Will flipped through the book and pulled out the yellow receipt. "I also found this in there." He reached over the coffee table and handed it to Hollings.

Hollings pushed his eyeglasses higher on the bridge of his nose as he leaned forward and took the paper from Will. "By golly," he breathed, looking at the receipt. "Amy Winthrow."

Will felt his hopes rising. "You know who she is?"

Professor Hollings cleared his throat. "Oddly enough—by a strange twist of fate, perhaps—I did know Amy. Yes. You know, we see so many students pass through our classrooms every quarter, and we get to know so very few of them on a personal level. Most students listen to lectures, occasionally visit in office hours or send emails, write papers, and move on. You and Amy are part of the shrinking group of students who go beyond that and share your lives with us."

"So you really know her?" Will's hopes continued to rise.

Hollings nodded. "Yes. She was a nice young woman with lots of energy, although I didn't realize the notes she took in her book during lecture weren't notes on what I was saying." He grinned, leaning forward to hand the receipt back to Will. "Lots of really blonde curly hair, she had. It was last year, I remember, when I had her in class. She was a smart one, a talented writer. I remember her, aside from her curly blonde hair, because she came in here quite frequently to talk about what she was going to do after graduation. She was a senior, you know. Wanted to do something brilliant, just didn't know what. I think she had her eyes set on journalism. Wanted to say something—something important. Very ambitious girl. Had that glint in her eyes." He leaned back in his chair again.

"So, what'd you tell her?"

"I told her to do it. I told her to go out there and write the hell out of anything she wanted to." He chuckled again, remembering, and then sighed. "We talked about the different routes she could take to achieve her goals and make money at the same time. She was one of those people who needed to do what she loved. Some people can take jobs that simply meet their needs for survival." Professor Hollings shook his head. "She was not one of those people—that would not be enough for her."

Will nodded, letting Hollings' words sink in. After a moment of silence, he said, "I'd like to return the book to her. I don't think she meant to sell it back."

Hollings nodded slowly. "It seems unlikely that she'd purposefully put personal information in the hands of strangers."

"I agree."

Hollings continued to nod. "I see. So the task before us is finding Amy since she graduated last year. Have you tried Googling her?"

Will nodded. "And I've tried social networking sites, too. When I was looking for her on the internet, I didn't know if she had graduated or not, but I tried the alumni directories as well. I couldn't find her."

Hollings looked as though he might have been biting the inside of his lip, thinking. Will wondered if he was trying to decide whether or not it would be appropriate to give out more information about Amy.

"Professor, I know this sounds ridiculous." Will paused, wishing that he could come up with an explanation that would make sense. Nothing came, so he settled for saying, "I just don't think she'd want this book floating around from student to student. And," he paused again, looking down at the book, "I think she's interesting."

The professor nodded. "She is." After a moment, he continued. "She's from Los Gatos, up in Northern California. I know she has a sister who also went to UCLA and became a kindergarten teacher. I don't know how far that will get you, but it's all I really know about her."

Will leaned his elbows on his knees and looked at the ground as relief washed over him. *Los Gatos.* That simplified everything.

He looked up. "That is excellent news. She's not far from where I live—not at all. Thank you, Professor."

"It's not much, but it might be enough to find her."

Will nodded. He tried to gather his thoughts, but not much was coming together just yet. He needed some time.

"I really appreciate your help. I know that you have a lot of work to do, so I won't take up any more of your time." He reached forward to shake Hollings' hand and then grabbed his backpack. Standing, he slowly slung it over his shoulders, his eyes wandering around the office, still trying to process what he needed to do.

"Will." The professor's voice drew Will's eyes toward him. "It might not be easy to find her, but I think fate is on your side. What were the chances that you and Amy would take English 151—at separate times—creating a direct link through me? And then what were the chances that your roommate would end up with her book a year later? *And then* that you would pick up the book and become intrigued? Not just anyone would want to take that book back to her. I may be an old man who believes in the magic of those stories," he pointed toward Will's book, "but I say the planets are aligned, Will. It may not be easy, but fate, I think, is on your side."

Will nodded. "I hope you are right." He smiled and gave a little wave as he walked backward toward the door. "Have a great summer, Professor. I'll see you in class next fall." He turned and left the office.

Outside, Will pulled his cell phone from his pocket. He scrolled through his list of contacts and found a name he hadn't sent a message to since he and Jocelyn broke up.

Hey Kim, he began the text message. *I know how to find the girl who wrote in Chris' book. I know who she is.*

Eight

"Will, listen, this is our last night in Westwood," Chris said as he and his roommates walked out the front doors of their apartment's lobby. "We are walking straight to the bar. We're not stopping talk to someone at a coffee shop or someone in line at a movie theater or someone waiting for food outside a restaurant. Straight to the bar."

"Except we are stopping to pick up Sarah and the girls first," Brian interjected.

"Right," Chris continued, "but aside from that, we're walking straight to the bar."

Will rolled his eyes. "You make it sound like I get distracted at every corner."

"You do," his three roommates said together.

"If I stop to talk to someone, you don't have to wait for me. I'll catch up."

"If you actually managed to catch up, we might go along with that," Chris said. "But that never happens."

Will knew his roommate was right, so he didn't protest.

"We ought to get a leash for him," Ralph said.

"I'll prove to you that I can walk all the way down to Westwood without stopping," Will said. "And when I do, you each should buy me a beer for my efforts."

His roommates laughed but agreed. And with the incentive of three free beers, Will focused on getting straight to Westwood without hanging back to chat with any old friends he might see on the way down. When the group stopped in front of Sarah's apartment to meet up with the girls, Will kept going.

"I'll see you down there," he said while turning around and walking backwards. "I'm not going to risk getting distracted while you wait for those three girls to get down here." He turned around again and kept heading toward the village center.

At the edge of town, Will spied his destination and got in line so that the bouncers could check his I.D. Just as he was walking in, he heard his roommate behind him.

"Will, we'll meet you upstairs," Chris called from the end of the line.

Will nodded. "Have my beers ready for me," he called back. He waved and walked inside.

Music pulsed against his ears. Beer that had splashed across the floor clung to the bottom of his shoes. Girls with lowered inhibitions squeezed past him, most likely heading for the bathroom. Will took a deep breath of the stale air and smiled. He made his way to the bar and ordered a pint of beer. As he paid for the drink, he saw his roommates climbing the stairs toward a section of booths against the back of the bar. He made eye contact with Chris. With one hand he held up his beer; with his other, he held up three fingers. "Get me my three beers," he mouthed. Chris shrugged and smiled.

Just as Will was about to head toward the stairs, he felt a hand on his shoulder.

"Hey, Will, how are you? We haven't seen you forever!"

He turned around and saw two girls from an English class he took last year. He couldn't remember their names, but he knew they were sorority sisters. And they both hated Shakespeare.

"Hey, good to see you!" he said, extending his arms and inviting them into a hug.

After a conversation about the girls' most recent classes and sorority functions, Will wished them a good summer and turned toward the stairs again.

"Hey Will! How you'd do on that final this morning?"

He turned toward the sound of his name and saw a friend from his Detective Fiction class.

"Good, buddy. How about you?"

After they discussed the last short essay question on the test, Will gulp down the rest of his beer and ducked toward the bar to order another. Or two.

And then, two beers in hand, he put his head down and ventured toward the stairs, hoping to avoid anyone else he knew for the time being.

But then he saw her. Half way up the stairs, he finally looked up, and there she was. Jocelyn. She was standing in the middle of the stairway with Kim and some guy. He paused. Then he continued climbing upward, slower now, wondering if the guy standing there was dating his ex-girlfriend. Kim noticed Will before Jocelyn did. She nudged Jocelyn and nodded in his direction.

He stopped one step below Jocelyn. They were face-to-face, and probably a little too close for comfort under normal, daytime circumstances. In a bar, the night before heading home for the summer, the distance was probably okay.

"Hey Jos," he said. He wanted to follow up with something witty, but nothing came to him.

She forced a smile. "Will. Hi." She looked as though she were at a loss for words as well.

After a moment of nothing but music filling the space between them, Kim jumped in and said, "Hey Will, how're ya doing?"

"Hey Kim, I'm good. How about you?"

"Good, thanks. It's nice to see you." Kim turned to speak with the guy standing with her and Jocelyn. She touched his arm to get his attention, but he didn't look toward her. He continued to stare at Jocelyn and Will.

"I haven't seen you in a while," Jocelyn said.

"I know. It's been a long time." Will glanced around the bar. "What are you doing here? You hate this bar." He knew he was shouting to compete with the blaring music, and somehow he knew his volume made him sound drunk even though he wasn't—not yet. The air felt hot and thick, just as the air in bars often felt, but suddenly it was hotter and thicker.

She forced another smile. Then she leaned in and said, "I know. It's Mandy's birthday, and this is where she wanted to come. So, here we are. But now Kim and I can't even find Mandy."

She wasn't shouting. She was composed as she always was. Smelling of vanilla lotion and spearmint gum, looking calm and comfortable, she hadn't changed at all.

Jocelyn straightened up and scanned the crowd downstairs.

Will nodded. "I'll let you know if I see her."

"Thanks." After a prolonged pause, she added, "It was good to see you."

"Yeah, good to see you, too." Will nodded at the guy who had been watching the conversation, and then he continued up the stairs, concentrating on keeping the beer in the glasses.

Upstairs he found his roommates and the girls sitting in a

booth, talking and laughing over the music. Will stood at the end of the table and downed one of his beers. Then he squeezed into the booth and dropped the two glasses on the table with a thud. Beer from the full one splashed across the table. Chris eyed him but didn't say anything.

"I can't believe you made it," Brian said.

"What do you mean?" Will grumbled.

"We knew you got to the bar first, but we figured you'd never make it upstairs."

"Well, I did. And you all owe me a beer." Will picked up the second glass he had been carrying and poured its contents down his throat.

Before Will could drop the empty glass on the table, Kim appeared next to him.

"Will, don't worry about it. That guy is…" she trailed off, noticing that everyone at the table was looking at her. After a moment, she reached in her purse and pulled out a pen. Snatching the only dry napkin on the table, she crouched toward it and wrote something down. "Remember this," she said, handing the napkin to Will and then headed back toward the stairs.

"What was that?" Chris asked.

Will looked at the napkin. *Forget about Jos and that guy.* Kim had written. *Remember what Hollings said. The planets are aligned. You are going to find Amy tomorrow!*

He looked up and toward Chris. "Nothing." He folded the napkin and put it in his pocket. "I'll tell you later. Go get my beers."

Chris got up and pulled Brian out of the booth with him. They headed toward the bar together. Will tried to focus on the conversation that Ralph was having with the girls. Nothing they said seemed to penetrate his brain; their words slid right over him and evaporated into the thick, stale air. *Forget about Jos*, he said to himself. *No problem. She's forgotten already. It's that idiot she's with—he's the hard one to forget.*

When Chris and Brian returned, Will drank his beers just as quickly as he had the others. He continued listening to the conversation, and the words spoken continued to pass him by. After the third sideways glance from Chris, he stood up.

"I'm hungry. I'm going to get some pizza."

Everyone sitting at the table looked toward him, but he walked away before they could answer.

Outside, the night air cooled Will's arms and neck. Finally he could breathe. He walked down the street toward his go-to late night pizza place. *Forget about Jos and that guy*, Kim's note had said. *Forget about them. Why shouldn't he forget about them? Jos had been forgotten for months. Well, she had been completely forgotten until Amy's book resurfaced some memories of her. But that guy—he was the hard one to forget. There was something about that guy.*

Upon arriving at the pizzeria, he ordered a slice of pepperoni and sat down at the counter next to the shop's front window. He stared out the glass at the passersby enjoying Westwood's nightlife and swallowed half his pizza in one bite.

"Will, hey!"

He turned around in his stool and saw three girls from his days in the dorms walking toward him.

"Hey," he said with a mouth full of pizza and a smile. "Haven't seen you all in forever—how are you?"

The girls approached and began chatting rapidly about their last finals, their time living together in an off-campus apartment, their boyfriends, and their last trip to Lake Havasu for spring break. Will continued eating. He nodded, smiled, and chuckled whenever their facial expressions indicated that a chuckle was appropriate. He wasn't sure if all the beer had kicked in or if he just didn't care about what they had to say, but concentrating on their words was getting harder and harder.

Just as one of the girls squealed and the other two laughed—something about a missing bathing suit being found—Will eyes caught sight of Jocelyn walking past the pizza shop. His head snapped toward the window. She wasn't alone; the guy from the bar was accompanying her toward the apartments at the north end of Westwood. Jocelyn didn't see him sitting at the front window, but her companion looked into the restaurant. His gray eyes locked with Will's for a moment. Then he grabbed Jocelyn's hand as they continued on their way.

Something clicked.

A memory from the beginning of the school year burst into his mind. It was night. He was walking into a bar. He was seeing

Jocelyn talking to some guy against the back wall. He was watching them laugh.

Who the hell is this? Will had said, approaching his girlfriend and the stranger.

Hey Will, this is my friend from Econ, Jocelyn had answered. *Will, meet—*

Let's go. He grabbed her hand and pulled her toward the front of the bar.

What are you doing? What's wrong with you?

Don't you see that he's hitting on you? Why were you even talking to him?

You're crazy. You've had too much to drink.

The scene changed. It was still the same night and the same place; only now he stood outside with his roommates, waiting for Jocelyn and her friends to get out of the bathroom.

A group of bar-hoppers walked by, and Will heard one of them say something.

There's that jackass.

He looked toward the voice. It belonged to the guy Jocelyn had been talking to earlier.

Hey, Will said. *Who are you talking to?*

The guy stopped and turned around. He smirked. *I'm not talking to you. I'm talking about you.*

Will stepped forward. Chris and Ralph immediately grabbed his arms, but he shook them off. *Is there a reason for that?*

The guy continued to smirk. *I'm just stating the obvious.*

Do we have a problem here?

The guy stepped toward Will. *We might.*

They stood inches away now, staring each other down. The guy was shorter and bulkier than Will. His eyes were steely. Sharp.

Will, what are you doing? Jocelyn's voice caught in his ears just as she appeared, pushing herself between him and the steely-eyed guy.

The scene changed again. He was back in the apartment, lying on his bed, talking on the phone to Jocelyn in the dark.

I can't do this anymore, she said. *I can't keep going on, worrying that I'll find you in a jealous rage over some random person I met in Econ.*

I didn't start it.

It doesn't matter. I can't do this anymore.

One of the girls in the pizza shop touched Will's arm, bringing him back to reality. "So," she laughed, "I looked under the couch, and there was my phone. I couldn't believe it."

Will smiled. "It's a good thing you found it." He glanced back at the front window, watching Jocelyn and the steely-eyed guy shrink with distance.

He's not just a friend from Econ anymore, I guess.

***

The following morning, Will awoke with a headache. As rocks rattled against the walls of his head, visions of the previous night danced across his mind. Making it down to the bar without distraction. Running into sorority girls who didn't like Shakespeare. Seeing Jocelyn and that guy. Getting three free beers. Reading the note Kim wrote. Leaving before anyone else to get pizza. Getting caught up talking to some girls from the dorms. Seeing Jocelyn and that guy walk past the pizza place. Arriving home after his roommates, despite leaving the bar before them.

He rolled out of bed and stretched. From the pocket of the shorts he hadn't bothered to change the night before, he pulled out the note Kim had written to him.

"The planets are aligned," he muttered.

"Are you talking to yourself again?" Chris mumbled, eyes closed and half-asleep.

"Yeah," Will said, scratching his head and then shaking it. "Remember when we saw Kim last night? Right before that, I ran into her, Jocelyn, and some guy Jocelyn is dating. It was awkward, and I guess Kim felt bad about it." He waved the napkin in the air. "She wrote me a note—like she was trying to make me feel better. Go back to sleep." Will ripped the top layer of the napkin off and stuck it into the Renaissance poetry book resting on his nightstand. He began walking toward the living room.

"Hey," Chris called, his eyes still closed.

Will stopped in the doorway and looked toward his roommate.

"You and Jocelyn broke up months ago," he continued. "Who cares?"

"I didn't say I cared. I was just telling you what happened."

Chris sat up and rubbed his eyes. "Okay, buddy. Whatever you say. Sounds good." He looked at the clock. "You want to pack up and head home as soon as possible?"

Will nodded. "The sooner the better."

Nine

Three hours later, Will and Chris were on the freeway heading north toward their hometown. Friends since junior high, they played on the same soccer teams for six years, they took the same high school classes, and when they both received acceptance letters from UCLA, they immediately knew they would live together the following four years. They met Brian and Ralph in the dorms their freshman year, and soon their duo became a foursome. But with every trip they made back home for summer vacation, the foursome reverted to a duo, and Will and Chris became the Northern California boys they were at heart.

When Will found out that Amy was from Northern California as well, he was relieved. He knew there was a good chance she was from California as most UCLA students were, but he never expected her to be so close to home. Returning the book was going to be easy.

Of course, if they made it home. With the way Chris was driving—weaving in and out of slower cars—Will wasn't sure they would make it. After a couple hours, they were past the Los Angeles traffic and past the point of being nice on empty stomachs. San Jose was still hours away, and Will was getting tired of yelling at Chris to slow down. He suggested they stop for food before they went to blows over Chris' reckless driving.

A half hour later, they pulled off the freeways and into the parking lot of their favorite fast food restaurant: In-N-Out. They hadn't spoken since Will suggested lunch, and their silence continued while standing in line, while ordering food, and while finding a spot to sit. Once in their booth waiting for food, Will grabbed his cell phone and tapped its screen a couple times to access his email.

"What are you doing?" Chris asked, finally breaking the silence.

Eyes on his phone, Will answered, "I emailed Amy's sister this morning. I'm looking to see if she emailed me back."

"You what?"

Will continued watching his emails loaded. "Professor Hollings said that Amy's sister was a kindergarten teacher. So I searched the internet for kindergarten teachers with the last name Winthrow. I found one in the Los Gatos school district. I figured there was a pretty good chance she would be Amy's sister. How many Winthrows teaching kindergarten could there be, especially in the Bay Area? Anyway, all the teachers had contact information listed on the school website, and so I sent her an email about Amy's book. It couldn't hurt to try."

"What did you say in the email?"

Will put the phone on the table. "She didn't write back."

Chris grabbed it and tapped the email icon. Under his breath, he read, "Dear Ms. Winthrow, I have a book that your sister Amy lost. I've been unable to locate Amy directly; would you mind forwarding her my contact information and letting her know I would be happy to return the book in whatever manner is most convenient for her? Thank you for your time, Will Chase." Chris closed the email and slid the phone across the table to Will. He shrugged. "Not a bad idea."

"It's a school day, so I figured she'd check the account sometime soon."

Over the restaurant loud speaker, Will and Chris heard their order number called.

"I'll get the food if you get napkins and ketchup," Chris said.

They both slid out of their booth, returning moments later with trays piled with food and condiments. The sight of burgers and French fries made Will's stomach growl.

"I'm surprised you're doing this," Chris said, continuing the conversation from before. He bit through his Double-Double Cheeseburger. "Returning the book, I mean." He chewed slowly. "I can't remember the last time you followed through with one of your dumb ideas."

Will smirked at his own cheeseburger before taking a bite. "I know. I told you that I was going to turn things around our junior year of college."

"I thought you meant you were going to get better grades. I didn't think you'd grow a conscience." Chris pushed a couple French fries into his mouth. "You owe me twenty bucks for that book, by the way."

"If you had sold that book back to the bookstore, you

would have gotten a dollar. I just bought you lunch. Let's call it even."

"Fair enough." Chris swallowed. "So what happens if Amy's sister writes you back and puts you in touch with her? What are you doing to do then?"

"What do you mean? If I get in touch with her, I'm going to give the book back. That's it."

"But what are you going to say? *Hey Amy, I'm this weirdo who tracked you down because I wanted to give you a book. Here you go, and have a nice day.* Are you going to say something like that?"

Will dipped some French fries in ketchup and shoved them in his mouth. "I haven't gotten that far."

"And what if she did mean to sell the book back?"

"I haven't gotten that far yet either." Will grinned and sucked down some iced tea. "That would be pretty anticlimactic."

"No kidding. You would have grown a conscience for nothing."

Will shrugged. "You keep mentioning my conscience, but you know, I don't see this as really being about having a conscience. This is more of like," he looked around the restaurant and took another bite of his cheeseburger, "I don't know, like doing something out of the ordinary."

Chris looked at Will through narrowed eyes. "I bet you have an ulterior motive somewhere. You think she's going to be cute or something, don't you?"

Will rolled his eyes. "Yeah, Chris. That's right. I'm doing this on the off chance that she might be cute. I figured she has cute handwriting, so why not take my chances? We *never* see cute girls at school, so this could be my only opportunity to find one."

Chris crammed the rest of his cheeseburger in his mouth and said, "That's exactly what I figured. Now stop talking and finish eating. We have to get back on the road."

Will polished off his burger in two more bites. They cleared their table and left the restaurant. Back on the road, Chris stopped cutting off cars while driving, and Will finally relaxed.

As afternoon wore on, he checked his email more frequently, thinking that Amy's sister might write back after her kindergarteners went home for the day. A little after three o'clock, a reply appeared in his inbox.

"She wrote back," Will said. "Amy's sister wrote back."

"What'd she say?"

He opened the message and read, "Hi Will—Are you from the coffee shop on the strip? Amy's been looking for a book she lost there, and she'll be happy to get it back. Her cell phone number is 408-555-9987. If you text her and let her know when you will be working next, I'm sure she'd be happy to swing by to pick it up. Thanks, April."

Will reread the message silently. "Huh."

"Sounds like she loses a lot of books," Chris said.

Will nodded. He copied Amy's phone number into a text and typed *Hi Amy—my name's Will, and I found a book you lost. Want to pick it up at the coffee shop? I can bring it by whenever.*

"What'd you write?" Chris asked.

Will read him the message.

"You're going to let her think that you're talking about the book she left at the coffee shop?"

Will shrugged.

"Probably better this way," Chris continued. "You come off as less of a weirdo. How do you know which coffee shop to go to?"

"There can't be too many there." He paused, thinking. "I can only think of one on the main strip in Los Gatos. Can you think of more?"

"I can't even think of one. The only time I've been in Los Gatos is at night when we're going to bars. Not coffee shops."

Will stared out the front windshield, still thinking about North Santa Cruz Avenue, the main thoroughfare through downtown Los Gatos. "If there is more than one, then I don't know. I'll figure it out. I've figured it out so far."

"Are you going to drop it off there for her? Or are you going set up a time to meet her there?"

"I don't know." He paused. "I kinda want to meet her."

"Of course you do. After all this, I almost want to meet her. Almost."

Will's phone beeped as a new text came in. He looked at it and smiled. "She said: *Really? Great—thank you! I can swing by there after work today. I can be there by 5:30. Do you work there? Will you be in today? If not, I can come by any day this week. Thank you again.*"

Chris looked at the clock on the dashboard. "Huh. Five-thirty. That's just about the time we'll be back in the Bay Area. You're going to want to go straight there, aren't you?"

Will grinned. He began typing, reading the message as he went. "I'll be around—it's no problem for me to get the book there by 5:30."

Chris shook his head.

Ten

Los Gatos

Amy stepped into the coffee shop, and seeing that there was no line, walked up to the counter.

"Hi Beatrice," she said to the girl at the register. "Someone named Will contacted me today and said that he had a book for me. I don't know if he works here or not, but he said he'd bring the book by. Have you heard anything about that?

Beatrice looked under the counter and shook her head. "I haven't heard anything, and I don't see anything under here for you. Not yet."

Amy looked at the oversized Victorian clock on the wall. She was a couple minutes early. "In that case, I'd like to order a non-fat chai and a large cup of whatever the most popular drink is his time of day."

"Okay," Beatrice said slowly, punching buttons on her computer screen. "A non-fat chai and a large decaf iced vanilla latte."

Amy paid for the drinks, and when they were ready, took them to the outdoor patio. She sipped her chai and looked across the street. The sun felt warm on her shoulders, and she wished her job didn't keep her inside all day. In college, she spent as much time as she could outside when studying. Something about the fresh air and laughter of passersby kept her focused. Little of that existed in her office building.

Just as she did whenever she had a free moment, she pulled two pieces of paper from her bag and read them.

> *To my granddaughters—*
> *My greatest sadness is in not knowing you. This I cannot change, but I do hope that you can forgive my absence. I have loved you from afar, and I have cherished the pictures and stories about you that Eva has shared with me. Please accept the gifts coming to you as a piece of my heart.*
> *Elizabeth Hathaway*

She set the note on the table and stared at the street, focusing on nothing in particular. Then she looked at the second piece of paper.

Dear Mr. Winthrow:
I have neither the time, nor the energy, nor the desire to retrieve the books your phone message detailed. Should you feel it necessary to carry out the terms of Ms. Hathaway's will, you may bring the books to my Monterey residence yourself. Otherwise, feel free to dispose of them by any means you deem fit.
Very truly yours,
William Strath

She laid the second note next to the first. When read separately, the messages were intriguing. Read together, they were troubling. The pain in each—sorrow in one and anger in the other—seemed to bleed across the paper, and Amy wondered if the notes were simply variations of the same bleeding pain.

She pulled out a pen and her notebook and drew circles across a blank page. Circle within circles, circles over circles—circles that began to look like figure eights, then like lopsided *j* after *j* after *j*. Two lines down, she wrote, *Why is Billy so mean?*

Inside the coffee shop, Will approached the counter.

"Hi," he said to Beatrice. "I'm returning a book to someone who comes in here often, I think. Her name is Amy—"

"She's outside," Beatrice said, nodding toward the back door. She leaned over the counter to get a better view of the patio and pointed. "There she is. Right in the middle, on the far side. The one writing in a notebook."

Will smiled. "Thanks." He walked to the door and surveyed the groups of people sprinkled across the patio. People chatted and laughed at the surrounding tables—and there she was, in the middle of the chatter and laughter, silently scribbling away. Professor Hollings' description had been right on. Her hair was light and curly; it fell halfway down her back in controlled disarray with a few bobby pins pulling it away from her face.

Will approached, suddenly feeling awkward and uncertain.

"Amy?"

She looked up, sliding her notebook over the correspondence from Billy and Lizzie. Not so casually, she dropped her pen and spread her hand across the paper she had been writing on. Will opened his mouth to say something but stopped short after noticing her fingers stretched over the notebook. He wondered what she was hiding—

"Will?" She smiled.

The sound of her voice tore his eyes off the table, and he smiled back at her. "Yes, hi."

She motioned for him to sit down. "Thank you for bringing my book back. I thought I left it here, but the owner said they hadn't found it. By the way," she pushed the vanilla latte toward him, "I don't know if you drink coffee, but this is for you. It's decaf since it's so late in the day. Thank you for going out of your way to bring the book to me."

Will sat down. "Oh, thanks. You didn't have to do that. And no problem about the book."

He took a sip of the drink and said to himself, *okay, this is it.*

"Here you go." He placed the book on the table and pushed it toward her.

Amy stared at it. "This isn't—" She paused. One, two, three seconds passed as she tried to register the picture of Queen Elizabeth on the front cover. Will watched her, reading the changing expressions on her face. Confusion came first. Then recognition. Then disbelief. "No way," she breathed, picking it up. "This is my book." She thumbed through it, and then looked at Will, disbelief still coloring her face. She snapped the book closed, held it to her chest, and leaned toward the table. "I was expecting something completely different. Where—? How—?" She paused, poised to finish her question, but no words came.

"I should explain," he said.

She nodded.

"I'm a student at UCLA. Last quarter, my roommate bought your old book for an English class—a class with Professor Hollings, actually. I'm an English major, and one night he needed my help on a paper he was writing for Hollings. When I opened your book, I saw all the notes you had written in the margins—"

Amy felt heat rush to face. She closed her eyes, cringing,

but she didn't say anything.

"And I sort of figured you didn't mean to sell it back to the bookstore. Of course I didn't know whose it was at the time, but still. Whoever sold it back, I figured, probably did so by mistake. I mean, I took Hollings' 151 class myself, and I know those weren't notes on his lectures."

"Oh God," Amy said, the heat on her cheeks increasing as she closed her eyes tighter. She dropped her forehead to the table's metal surface. Curls fell around her, covering the notebook she had so intently tried to hide when Will first approached. When she looked back up, her face had peaked in its redness. "How awful—all the awful stuff I wrote in there. I was afraid someone would see it, but I didn't think it was possible for someone to bring the book back to me." She dropped her head to the table again and groaned.

"You didn't mean to sell it back, did you?" he asked.

She shook her head, rolling her forehead across the table. "No."

Will hadn't expected her to be so embarrassed. He didn't know what he expected, but it certainly wasn't this.

"Is it okay that I brought it back? I didn't mean to make you feel uncomfortable or anything."

Amy looked up—past Will and down the street—her eyebrows high and her abashed smile wide. "Of course it's okay you brought it back. Thank you," she said. "Now, luckily, no one else will see it. I was so, ugh, I don't know. Ridiculous."

"You—ridiculous?" Will shook his head. "No. Not ridiculous." He sipped his latte and then chuckled. "What you wrote made more sense than half the poetry in that book."

Amy scrunched her nose, still avoiding his eyes.

"Do you still write?" He glanced down at her notebook.

She placed the book on the table and shrugged. "That wasn't really writing. I don't know what it was. How did you find me?" The redness on her cheeks had softened to a mild pink. She drew her eyes toward him, feeling better now that some of the color had drained away.

Will smiled. "I can't take all the credit for that. Finding you was my friend Kim's idea—"

"How many people did you show the book?" Just as

quickly the red in Amy's cheeks faded, it returned.

"Oh, just Kim. No one else. My roommate who bought the book didn't crack it open all quarter—not even to read the poetry. I'm pretty sure Kim and I were the only ones who saw it. And I only showed her because I ran into her on campus while I was reading your notes—"

Any dropped her head back to the table. "Oh my gosh."

"Hey, don't do that. C'mon. I was reading it because I was intrigued that someone would interact with the book's poetry the way you did. I hadn't ever seen anything like that. And neither had Kim. She was convinced right from the beginning that you didn't mean to sell the book back—both of us were."

Amy sat up straight again. She pressed her fingers to her temples and shook her head. Then she laughed as though there was nothing else to do but laugh.

Will continued, "So Kim told me that I ought to find you." A sideways grin crossed his face. "She said that finding you would be exactly the sort of adventure I'd like."

Thoughts about Lizzie and Billy flashed across Amy's mind. Adventure. Was that what she was trying to embark upon with her family's past? Maybe.

"Then later when I was flipping through the book again, I ran across a note you wrote about John Milton being a jerk, and," he shrugged, "you're so right. I wanted to bring the book back and tell you that." Through his sideways grin, he chewed on the straw of his drink.

Amy laughed. "John Milton *was* a jerk."

Will's eyes grew. "I know—he was a pompous ass. I just finished English 143, and it was awful. I liked the professor—I had Professor Salt—but the material sucked."

Amy tilted her head to one side and smiled. "I had Professor Salt for English 143 as well. I loved how passionate she was about Milton, but I just couldn't get into *Paradise Lost*."

"Me too. Exactly." Will paused, remembering where he was in his story. "So then I found an old receipt in the book, and that's where I got your name. Once I had that, I went to Professor Hollings and asked if he knew you. I was hoping you had English 151 with him."

Amy closed her eyes before smiling again. "Greatest

professor ever."

"I know. He's the best. I didn't show him what you wrote in the book, but I did tell him why I was looking for you. He took pity on me and my crazy idea to find you. He told me that you were from Los Gatos and that your sister is a kindergarten teacher. I'm from San Jose, so I knew I could give the book back to you on my way home for summer break. I just had to find you in Los Gatos. Nothing came up when I Googled you, so I tried looking for kindergarten teachers in the Bay Area with your last name—hoping, of course, that your sister had the same last name. There was one April Winthrow teaching kindergarten in Los Gatos, and I figured there was a pretty good chance she was your sister. So I emailed her this morning. She wrote back, assuming that the book I told her about was a book you recently lost, and she gave me your phone number to text you—"

"My sister," Amy said, shaking her head. "She's always telling me that I assume too much and trust too much, but there she goes giving away my cell phone number. Geeze."

"Well, I'm glad she did. Otherwise, I'm not sure I would have been able to get this book to you." Out of the corner of his eye, he saw Chris walking down the street toward the coffee shop. Chris pointed to his watch. Will shrugged at him.

Amy looked over her shoulder. "Who's that?" she asked. Chris waved to her. She turned back to Will without returning the gesture.

"My dumb roommate, Chris. I told him to wait for me at the park down the street. He never listens." Will stood up and pointed in the direction of the park. Chris shook his head, shrugged, and continued walking toward the coffee shop. "Go away," Will called when Chris was within earshot.

"No, I'm hungry," Chris said.

"Do I need to feed you? Go get some food for yourself."

Chris approached the table, standing just on the other side of the patio gate. "Hey Amy." He nodded at her as though they were old friends. Then he turned to Will. "Come on, I'm hungry."

"You're so rude," Will said. "You interrupt us, you don't even introduce yourself, and you expect that I get up and leave because that's what you want?"

"Yes. We've gotta go." He turned to Amy. "I'm Chris.

Sorry I'm rude. It happens when my stomach is growling."

"That happens to me, too," she said.

Will looked at Amy. His story was just about over. Maybe Chris was right—maybe it was time to go. He stood up, slowly, hesitating. He didn't want to go, yet there was no reason for him to stay.

"I guess I better let you get back to what you were doing. It was really nice to meet you."

Amy stood to shake Will's hand and thank him for returning the book. As she rose, she jostled the table, causing her notebook to slide from one end to the other. Before she could steady it, the two notes, now free, lifted into the breeze and rode through the air for a moment before settling on the ground. Amy reached for the one written by Lizzie, and Will stooped to pick up the other.

"*Mr.* Winthrow?" he said, glancing at the first line. "I imagined that you would be addressed as *Ms.* or *Miss* Winthrow." He handed it back to her.

"Oh no," Amy said, taking the note. "It's not mine. It's my dad's." She frowned and bit the side of her lip, shaking her head. Fiddling with its corner, she said, "I sort of took it. There's this whole thing going on with my family right now, and I don't really understand it, and I'm trying to piece it all together." Heat crept up her neck again, and she shook her head, avoiding eye contact, as though trying to shake the thoughts of her family out of her head.

"What do you mean? Is everything okay?"

"Yes, everything's okay. Sort of. Well, no, it's not okay. It's just this thing with my grandmother." Amy shook her head again. "I guess she's my grandmother. I didn't know she existed until recently—not until she died." Words poured from her mouth, aimed in no clear direction and with no clear focus. "And I just don't understand why I didn't know her. I don't know why it was a secret. She left a bunch of money to me, and she had all these people who hated her, including my mom, and she's just so interesting. I mean, I think she's probably interesting. I want to find out if she's interesting." Amy halfway laughed and rolled her eyes. "The whole thing is just so strange. It's strange, and it's driving me crazy, and I can't figure out a way to pull all the pieces together." She rolled her eyes, laughing through a smile, knowing she sounded absurd. She wished she could stop herself from talking so much.

"Chris, go eat," Will leaned over the patio railing and pushed his roommate's shoulder toward the street. "Come back when you're done." He sat down. "How did you find out about her?"

Amy sat down. She looked directly at Will and saw pure curiosity in his eyes. She knew instantly it matched exactly what she was feeling. With a deep breath—probably the first since learning about Lizzie—she felt some of the frustration that had been balled up inside her loosen.

Eleven

"Ugh," Chris groaned. "You're such a pain in the ass. I just want to get some food and go home." He hopped over the gate and cut through the patio toward the coffee shop. Amy watched him stalk away, but Will ignored him entirely. After a moment, she turned back to Will.

"I found out about her when I got this note in the mail." She pushed Lizzie's note across the table toward him. "We didn't know anything about her until then."

Will read the note. "I would be pretty curious if I got this in the mail."

"My sister was the one who opened it, and she immediately called our parents. Our dad came over and tried to explain, but he was more cryptic than anything. I guess Elizabeth—Lizzie—was a pretty bad mom. She abandoned her children, including my mother, and then her sister adopted them."

"What about their dad? Your grandfather?"

Amy shrugged. "He died. I don't know how, but it happened around the time that Lizzie left. That's about all I was able to get out of my dad when he came over to explain. I grew up thinking that Lizzie's sister—Eva—was my grandmother, but that's not really true. The only other thing he told us was that Lizzie left me and my sister a bunch of money to further our education and a bunch of books. Oh, and that we shouldn't mention anything to my mom because it upsets her."

Will nodded, letting Amy's story sink in. "So where did you get that other note—the blue one addressed to your dad?"

Amy pushed that note toward Will. "I found the second one at my parents' house. Also," she paused reaching into her bag and pulling out a third piece of paper, "after learning about Lizzie, I wanted to find out more. No one else was really interested, so I was on my own. My sister April didn't care, my boyfriend told me to drop it, and my dad had already said we shouldn't talk to my mom about it. One day at Eva's house—we call her Nana—I found a copy of Lizzie's will." She handed the third piece of paper to Will. "I didn't have much time, so I wrote down as much from it as I could."

He looked over the list of items from the will. "She had a house in Saratoga and in Paris. Not bad." He put the will down and then read the note from Billy. Then, placing it on the table, he looked up at Amy. "So we know a couple things. First," he held up one finger, "Lizzie made some big mistakes and wasn't forgiven—at least not by your mom. Second," he held up another finger, " Eva and Lizzie reconnected at some point—enough for them to talk about you while you were growing up." A third finger went up. "She had a lot of money and cared a lot about education. Literature especially. And," a fourth finger joined the other three, "This Billy guy meant more to her than she meant to him."

Amy leaned back in her chair and bit her lip. She reached for her chai, which was now lukewarm. "We also know that Billy isn't very nice. And that he probably has a lot of money, too, since he lives in Monterey."

Will looked at the list from Lizzie's will. "Your grandma had some strong connections to Paris as well." He looked at Amy. "Ever been there?"

She shook her head. "Nope. You?"

Will also shook his head. "Some day, hopefully." He sipped his latte. "You know, you have a couple different addresses here. If you wanted to, you could go see where Lizzie lived in Saratoga and where Billy lives in Monterey." He fell silent for a moment, working on an idea. "Have you thought about doing that? Do you think Eva would let you check out Lizzie's house—now that it's her house?"

Amy scanned the street, thinking. "I don't know. I've driven by it. All I could see was a gate and a long driveway. I didn't stop once I saw the gate because I knew I couldn't really get to the house." She turned back to Will. "I asked my dad if I could help with all this stuff, and he said no—because it upsets my mom. I think Eva might say the same." Amy's shoulders slumped. "And besides that, her sister just died. I don't know what kind of relationship they had, but no matter what, it's got to be hard. I don't want to upset her either."

Will nodded. He drummed his fingers against the table. "Okay." He thought for another moment. "Then, if you don't want to go directly to Eva, you'll probably have to be a little sneaky. And it would need to be a two-person job."

Amy's left eyebrow rose involuntarily. "What do you mean?"

"Let's figure this out." Will reached for Amy's notebook and flipped to a fresh page. "You could ask anyone to help you, but—"

"No one wants to help me."

Will nodded, continuing his sentence without missing a beat. "I volunteer myself since this is more interesting than finding a summer job, which I dread doing. And before you say no, hear me out."

He grabbed Amy's pen, and as he spoke, he took notes on his own plan. Amy's eyes widened, but he didn't see her surprise. "I think you have to go through Billy somehow. Since you can't talk to your mom, Eva, your dad—" He paused and looked up at Amy. "Are you close with your mom's siblings?"

Amy shook her head. "They live far away. I've never met them."

Will nodded and looked back down at the paper. "Right. So Billy is your only option—unless you can speak French and want to try the friends from France." He glanced up at Amy who was shaking her head. "Okay, then, I think there are two options. One, you can go straight to Billy and ask him about Lizzie."

"I don't think that will work. It doesn't look like he wants anything to do with her."

"Agreed." Will put a question mark next to what he had been writing. "It's an option, but I doubt you'd get much from him. The other option is to leverage the information you have about him." Will's hand began picking up speed across the paper. "You've got to get those letters Lizzie left to him. If you had them, you wouldn't need to talk to anyone. You'd just read the letters. And hopefully that would lead to more clues about Lizzie's life, which you could then follow."

Amy found herself nodding, trying to absorb Will's words.

"So what about this—what if we, say, forge a new note from Billy to your dad? We can say that Billy's changed his mind and he'll send someone to pick up the books and letters. We give a date for the pick up, and we say that Billy expects someone to meet his pick-up-and-delivery guy there." He tapped the pen on the paper. "Or, we say that at the very least, someone in your family has to leave the books and letters outside the house for Billy's guy. Then I show up to get them."

As Will scribbled ideas across the notebook, Amy's heartbeat quickened. Forging a note? Lying to her dad? Taking books and letters that belonged to someone else? Who was this guy sitting across the table from her?

Will continued, "You come with me, and if anyone like your dad or Eva shows up, you stay in the car. If no one shows, you come and help me. We can even take a look at the books. There must be something special about them. Maybe Lizzie wrote in the margins like you." Will looked up at Amy. She smiled at him. He continued, "We'll read the letters, see what we can glean from them, and then take everything to Billy. And while we're down there in Monterey, maybe we can ask him some questions, too. It might not lead to anything, but since we'll be down there, we might as well try."

Amy leaned back in her chair and took a deep breath.

"What do you think?" Will asked.

She nearly laughed. "Half an hour ago I thought I was picking up a book that I left here. Now we have a plan to solve the mystery of my long lost grandmother. I'm not sure what to think."

Will smiled at the notebook. He laid the pen on the paper.

What am I doing here? he wondered. *I don't even know this girl.*

"I guess we don't have to do this." He shrugged, almost as though in apology. "I know you don't even know me. I kind of got carried away here."

Amy opened her mouth, about to say something, but then stopped herself. She leaned forward. "It's kind of fun to get carried away. And I just met you," she glanced at the Renaissance poetry book on the table, "but you've kind of known me for awhile—so you probably know I'm apt to get carried away pretty easily."

Will remembered something she had written in the Renaissance poetry book.

I want that one day—that one special day—to be mine. But only if it's captured in all its sweetness on a Grecian Urn.

He winked at her. Then he pushed the notebook toward her so she could see his notes.

She looked at what he had scrawled across the page. *Write note, schedule pick up, go to Lizzie's, look around, get books and letters, deliver to Billy, ask questions.*

"This is crazy," she said under her breath.

Will didn't respond. He watched her study the notebook, waiting. The breeze lifted fly-away curls off her shoulders, and she pushed a few golden strands off her face. When she looked back up, the sun glinted in her green eyes.

"Okay," she said, "what should the letter from Billy say to my dad?"

She smiled. Will smiled back. But before he could say anything, he saw her eyes move to a point over his shoulder. He turned his head in the same direction and saw a man with light brown hair and glasses walking toward them. He was thin, dressed in tan slacks and a white polo shirt. Will glanced back at Amy. She continued to smile, but now the smile looked different.

"Hi there," she said as the guy approached.

"I'm glad you're still here," Miles said, pulling up a third chair and sitting down at the table. "April said you were swinging by the coffee shop after work but didn't know how long you'd be here."

"Miles, this is Will. He's an old friend from college passing through the area. Will, this is my boyfriend, Miles."

The two exchanged greetings and shook hands. Will didn't think twice about how Amy introduced him, but he noticed Amy's notebook and the folded papers had disappeared.

"UCLA, huh?" Miles asked. "Did you graduate before me and Amy? I don't remember ever meeting you there."

"No, he's younger than us," Amy answered. "But I knew him before I met you."

"Yeah," Will added, "We know each other through English classes."

Amy smiled. She pushed some hair behind her shoulder and rested her elbows on the table. "So what are you doing over here, Miles?"

"I was trying to get a hold of you because my parents aren't going to make it to dinner tonight. My dad's business trip was cancelled, so they aren't flying up here anymore. I know we were planning on meeting at the restaurant at seven, and I didn't want you to show up for no reason."

Amy reached into her bag and pulled out her phone. Looking at the screen, she said, "Oh, and there you are. Three missed calls and three texts." She looked toward her boyfriend. "I'm so sorry—I guess I forgot to turn my ringer back on after work."

"No problem. I'm just glad that I caught you here. Do you want to do something else for dinner? Or go catch a movie?"

Amy nodded. "Sure. That sounds good."

"Will, do you want to come?" Miles asked.

"Oh, actually I'm going to be heading home in awhile. Thanks, though."

No one spoke for a moment. Will's eyes moved from Amy to Miles to the table. He wondered if he should say something. He wondered what he should say.

"Um, Miles," Amy said, "why don't you find out what movies are playing, and I'll meet you back at my house in about half an hour. Maybe we can try that new Indian place and then see a movie around eight o'clock. What do you think?"

"Perfect," Miles said, rising from his seat. "Will, it was nice to meet you."

They shook hands again, and then Miles headed down the street in the direction he came from.

Will leaned toward the table and grinned at Amy. "Did you really just tell your boyfriend to get lost?"

Amy closed her eyes, sighing. "I didn't know what else to say. He can't know what we're doing—he'd go nuts, and I don't feel like being lectured." When she opened her eyes, the golden glint of the sun had returned. "So when do you think is the soonest we could have Billy's delivery guy pick up the letters and books?"

Twelve

Dear Mr. Winthrow:

Due to a recent change of events, I will now be able to retrieve the books willed to me by Ms. Hathaway. I will send someone to Ms. Hathaway's residence next Wednesday at 4pm. Please take the actions necessary to ensure my property will be ready for me at that time.

You may call 408-555-8792 to confirm the time with my delivery boy.

Very truly yours,
William Strath

***

Will stood in front of the gated entrance to Lizzie's massive house, eyeing it up and down. It sat atop a steep hill of impeccably kept grass and colorful perennials. Trees lined the driveway winding up toward the house, and the house, painted cream with tan trim, sprawled across the hill's peak with endless windows and a multi-level roof that gave the impression of at least three stories. Will looked down the street, through thick trees and scattered houses, feeling like he was no longer in California. He knew neighborhoods with multi-million dollar homes appeared in nearly every city, but this was a far cry from the crowded rows of identical track homes where most Californians lived. This was expansive—excessive—wealth. He wondered if Amy knew Lizzie had *this much* money. *The money spent sending each granddaughter back to school was nothing,* he realized.

The sound of a car door caught his attention, and he turned around. *There he is*, Will thought. *Amy's dad.* He remembered the conversation they had the day before.

Spenser Winthrow calling to confirm a pick up time tomorrow at four, Amy's father had said. His voice was deep, his words were fast, and his tone was light.

Hi Spenser, Will said. *Four o'clock it is. My name is Will—I'll be the one meeting you at the house.*

Fantastic, Spenser said. *I'll see you then. You have a great evening.*

Will hung up and called Amy. He tried to convince her one last time to take a couple hours off work and join him on the expedition to Lizzie's house, but his efforts failed.

I can't take a couple hours off, Will, she had said. *Plus, what am I going to do there? I can't sit in the car. My dad will see me when you're loading the books. I can't walk around the neighborhood—what if he drives by me? I'm not going to hide in the bushes.*

Will had been reluctant to let her off the hook, but now, upon seeing Amy's dad trotting across the street toward him, he realized she was right. Too risky.

"Are you Will?" Spenser asked once he was almost across the street.

"Sure am. Mr. Winthrow?" Will extended his arm to shake Spenser's hand. "Good to meet you."

Amy's dad had a firm grip; he also had the same lopsided smile and green eyes as his daughter. "Good to meet you, too," he said. "Call me Spenser, please." He nodded to the hill and continued, "Unfortunately, I don't have the gate opener, so we can't pull our cars up to the front of the house." He held up a key and then slid it into the lock on the wrought iron door standing next to the gate. "I just have this—we will have to hoof it up and down the hill. Thanks for coming out, by the way. We really appreciate your help."

"Oh, no problem at all."

"So, how long have you been working for Mr. Strath?" Spencer asked as they hiked up the hill.

"Not long. It's just a summer job."

"Oh yeah? You in college?"

"Yep. UCLA. I just got back home for the summer."

"No kidding. Both my daughters went there. They loved it."

"It's a great place."

"It sure is. I work at Santa Clara University, and I tried to convince my girls to go there, but they fell in love with Westwood the moment they saw it—and there was nothing I could do to change their minds."

Spenser unlocked the front door and swung it open.

"Wow," Will breathed, walking into the house. The enormity of the inside—with its high ceilings and two staircases—matched the outside's grandeur. The tan walls and travertine floors, punctuated with sparse, modern furniture made Will feel like he had entered an interior designer's dream home.

"I know," Spenser said, walking thorough the room toward the staircase on the right. "It's really something, isn't it?"

Will followed Spenser. "It really is." As they crossed the foyer and climbed the stairs, Will asked, "So, what do you do at Santa Clara?"

"I'm a professor of Classics."

"Oh—" Will almost said *So that's where Amy got her love of literature,* but he clamped shut his mouth.

"Are you a fan of Classical literature?"

"I'm an English major, but I haven't had much exposure to Classical lit. Most of my classes have focused on literature in the last millennium. But I did just finish a class on John Milton, and we spent some time talking about Ovid's *Metamorphoses* since Milton drew from it so much."

Spenser nodded. "He sure did. I never cared much for Milton, but he sure did know his Classics."

And that is where Amy got her distaste from Milton, Will thought.

He followed Spenser into a room filled with books. Floor-to-ceiling bookcases covered all four walls. He spotted a ladder on wheels leaning against the cases—just the kind that he had seen in old movies—and a desk in the middle of the room, solid and ornate. "Unbelievable," he breathed.

Spenser grinned. "Aside from books that you're taking, everything in here is going to my daughters." He shook his head at the walls of books. "I don't know what they're going to do with all of it—this room is probably bigger than the little house they rent." He looked down at the boxes of books that had been stacked by the door. "Now, as for the books going to Mr. Strath." He planted his hands on his hips. "The good news is that they've all been boxed up for you. The bad news is that there are a lot of them." He chuckled. "If you read Elizabeth Hathaway's will, it looks like about fifty books were left to Mr. Strath. But she had multiple editions of each title, and her will didn't specify which ones went to him. We thought it would be best to send them all. So," he chuckled again, "fifty books turned into one hundred and fifty books, and that's why we have this big stack of boxes now." He picked up a box and turned toward the door. "Oh well, right?"

"Right." Will grabbed a box and followed Spenser.

"You have the red truck in front?" Spenser called over his shoulder.

"Yeah." Will picked up his speed to keep up with Spenser's pace. "So are your daughters going to come and take the rest of these books?"

"I don't know what we're going to do with them. My youngest daughter majored in English like you, and she never sold a book back. Well, she sold her Biology and Algebra books back, but she held onto her literature books. Her house is already full of book. Maybe I'll suggest donating them."

The two men arrived at the truck and lifted the boxes into its bed. They headed back up the hill toward the house.

"I wish I could offer some of these books to you," Spenser said, "but my wife is a stickler when it comes to rules. If Lizzie wanted books to go to Mr. Strath, they have to go to Mr. Strath. The books left to my girls have to go to them. I guess they'll have to give them away if that's what they want to do. It's not my choice."

They arrived at the top of the stairs and walked into the first door. Spenser stopped abruptly and held his finger up, remembering something. "Oh, and I almost forgot." He continued walking across the room toward the desk. Will followed him. "Something else I need to do while we're here today—Lizzie's will mentioned letters that were supposed to go to Mr. Strath along with these books." Spenser opened the top desk drawer and rummaged through it. "I haven't been able to find them yet."

Will's stomach tensed. No letters? The letters were the main reason he was there.

Spenser closed the drawer and opened the next one down. He pulled out a stack of papers encircled by a blue ribbon and fanned through the first couple pages. "No, not any letters here." He took a moment to look at the top sheet, holding it out at arm's length. "This doesn't even look like it's Lizzie's." He shrugged and put the stack back. "It's not a letter, though, so it's not my business."

Will thought fast. As he watched Spenser close the second desk drawer and open the third, he asked, "Professor Winthrow, is there a bathroom in here?"

Spenser closed the third drawer and muttered to himself, "No letters in this desk. Guess I'll have to keep looking." Then he turned his attention to Will. "I'm sure there is. There's probably twelve, but I couldn't tell you where. Go ahead and look around. I'll grab another box and take it out to the truck."

"Thanks. I'll be right back." Will walked out of the library and down the hallway. He listened for the sound of the front door opening and closing. When the doorknob clicked shut, he walked back to the library and headed straight for the desk. He opened each drawer, not sure what he was looking for but knowing there had to be something worth grabbing for Amy. If he wasn't going to bring back letters, he needed to bring back something else. The stack of papers in the second drawer caught his eye. Across the top sheet, he saw the title: *Eva's Words*. He remembered what Spenser had said. *This doesn't even look like it's Lizzie's.* Eva Words. Eva. He was pretty sure that was Lizzie's sister—the name seemed so familiar. He grabbed the stack and strode across the room to the boxes where he hid it under some books. Then he heaved the box to his shoulder and walked toward the stairs.

"Find a bathroom?" Spenser asked as they passed on the staircase.

Will nodded. "Yep. Almost got lost on the way back."

Spenser chuckled. "I can't imagine how it would feel to live in a place like this."

The two continued to load boxes, and when the final one landed in Will's truck, both were winded and sweating—and happy to be done.

"Thanks for your help," Spenser said, extending his hand toward Will. "I know it's a bit of a drive out from Monterey, and I appreciate you coming to get these books. It makes things a lot easier on me."

"No problem. Oh, and if you ever find those letters, you can give me a call. I'd be happy to pick them up."

"That would be great." Spenser pointed toward the house.

"I'm going back right now to see if I can find them. In a place that big, it could take awhile."

Will climbed into his truck and watched Spenser walk up the driveway to Lizzie's house. He pulled out his cell phone, and by the time he had his key in the ignition, he had dialed Amy's number and was listening to the phone ring.

"I've got presents for you," he said when she answered. "Where do you want to meet me?"

Thirteen

Will glanced at his watch. Six forty-five. At seven o'clock, he and Amy planned to meet at the coffee shop where they first met. With fifteen minutes to spare, he walked along the street, taking in the sights and sounds of North Santa Cruz Avenue. He used to hang out there sometimes during high school on Saturday nights, but he never paid much attention to anything beyond the girls cruising the strip. Now, years later—and well before sundown—he saw that there was much more to the community. A movie theater stood in the middle of the block showing two movies he had never heard of, benches popped up sporadically in front of different mom-and-pop shops, and passersby smiled and nodded at each other as they strolled by. The surrounding foothills of the Santa Cruz Mountains were almost close enough to touch, deep green and fragrant with wildflowers, reminding Will that he wasn't in Los Angeles any longer.

A bookshop stood on the corner of one block, tall and brown with windows lit to a gleaming gold. Will went in and weaved through the compact wooden bookcases, looking less at the books than at the people and store layout. Patrons sat in deep armchairs lining the walls, drinking coffee and perusing the merchandise. Portraits of great writers—Shakespeare, Chaucer, Steinbeck, Hemingway—hung above the armchairs, reminding Will of the long list of English classes he had taken over the last couple years.

He looked at the time on his cell phone. Only five minutes until he was supposed to meet Amy. He ran his fingers across a row of books on Astronomy, thinking about the way stars hid behind a blanket of smog in Los Angeles. He pulled out a book on backyard stargazing. Unlike in Los Angeles, here, at home, he could find Venus in the sky, wishing him a good night. And on a really, really good night, he could find Jupiter wishing him a good morning. He flipped through the book, thinking about how there was so much more than just Venus and Jupiter.

He took the book to the front counter, paid for it, and headed toward the coffee shop.

***

I have a ball of nerves in my stomach, and with every passing second it seems to grow. I haven't been so nervous and excited since—

"Whatcha doing?" Will asked, tapping Amy's shoulder from behind.

She turned her head toward him and closed her notebook. "Hey Will, how're you doing?"

He nodded at the notebook. "What do you have there?"

"Nothing. Just, you know, nothing." She slid the notebook into the messenger bag resting against the table leg and ignored Will's raised eyebrow. "So," she smiled, "how'd it go?"

He sat down in the chair nearest to Amy's. "I have good news and bad news for you. And then some more good news."

She turned toward him. She dropped her elbow on the table and propped up her cheek with her fist. Her eyes shone with curiosity.

"The first bit of good news: I have a ton of books in the back of my truck. Getting those books went pretty smoothly. Your dad didn't suspect anything."

Amy nodded. "Good."

"The bad news: your dad hasn't found the letters yet. He hasn't given up looking for them, but as of right now, he doesn't know where they are."

Amy squeezed her eyes closed and groaned.

"But the last bit of good news is the really good news." He held up the stack of papers tied with a blue ribbon. "I have this."

Amy's eyes flew open and grew wide. She motioned for him to put the papers on the table. "What is it?"

Will laid the papers down in front of her. "I'm not entirely sure."

Amy ran her fingers across the words written in script across the first page. Such a simple title. *Eva's Words*. She untied the blue ribbon. The paper—yellowing with softened corners and faded ink—felt surprisingly heavy in her hands. Toward the bottom, she ran her fingers over the only other words on the page: *Paris, 1955*.

"Where did you find this?" Amy asked.

"Your dad found it in Lizzie's desk. He was looking for the letters that are supposed to go to Billy, and he ran across it. When he wasn't looking, I nabbed it. Your dad's a really nice guy, by the way."

"Uh huh," she muttered. "Eva's Words. That means Nana wrote this, right? And Lizzie had it." She looked at Will. "Did you read it already?"

"I thumbed through it, but I didn't read it. I wanted you to see it first. It's about your grandmother after all. But," he paused, trying not to grin too much, "I am pretty curious now."

A close-lipped smile surfaced on Amy's face. After a moment she said, "Thank you so much. This is amazing."

"Don't get too excited just yet. We don't know what it says." He nodded toward the stack of papers. "You start reading—and then pass me each page as you finish."

Amy's smile widened as she turned over the cover page. "Paris, 1955," she said under her breath. She picked up the first piece of paper covered in Eva's longhand.

Will watched her eyes move across the page. Shade crept across the patio as the sun began its descent into the foothills, but none of it touched Amy. Surrounded by sunlight, reading her grandmother's story, she looked so much like what Will imagined she would. Watching her, thinking about all those notes she had written in her Renaissance poetry book, Will realized it all made sense. She made sense.

Fourteen

Paris, July 1955

A chill hung in the morning air. Billy cupped his hands around his mouth and blew warm breath against his fingers. Then he rubbed his hands together, working some of the stiffness from them. He looked up from his easel. There she was, walking toward him with a cup of coffee. With the breeze lifting her nearly-black hair away from her face and swirling her skirt about her legs, she reminded him of someone. Those green eyes and wind burned cheeks—they were so familiar. Perhaps a fairy in A Midsummer Night's Dream. *He wished the coffee she carried was for him, but she walked past him, dark hair fluttering against her arms and white skin glowing in the sun, right to the artist set up on his left.*

Billy's French was poor, but he could understand what she and his artist neighbor were talking about. He had to concentrate on their words, and unconsciously, he found himself staring at them instead of paying attention to his work.

She looked at Billy and raised an eyebrow.

"This," he said in broken French and holding up a nub of charcoal, "is about to become your image."

"I don't want my portrait drawn," she responded.

"That doesn't matter."

She slung her hair behind her shoulder. "Many artists have tried to create images of me before," she said, this time in English. "Yours will be just like the rest."

"Only if you look at it the same way you've looked at the others," he responded more comfortably in English.

His fingers finally began to warm. He started to sketch, and she continued talking with Billy's artist neighbor.

The drawing was only half-finished when she stood and touched her friend's shoulder to say goodbye. She stepped toward Billy's easel and examined his progress.

"You're right," she said, again speaking in English. "Yours is different. Unfinished." She walked down the row of artists, her hair swishing behind her, her skirt snapping around her legs.

"Where are you going?" Billy called after her. She simply

shook her head, responding with the ripple of her hair. He rubbed his blackened hands on his pants and removed the dusty drawing from the easel. "Who is that woman?" he asked his artist neighbor in French.

Jean scratched his beard, looking after her. "Elizabeth Hathaway. Her sister is a student at the Sorbonne, and she visits every summer. She likes to come out here sometimes and talk to the artists."

"You know her well?"

"We are friendly. She likes stories."

"Have I seen her before?"

The artist chuckled. "If you haven't, you've been blind."

Billy's eyebrows rose. He continued gazing in her direction. "I'm blind no longer. Do you know where I can find her? If I wanted to see her again?"

His neighbor shrugged. "Go to the University. I am sure she's staying with her sister."

"The Sorbonne, yes?"

"Or, you could wait until she comes back here. It won't be long."

Billy nodded slowly. "The Sorbonne." His mind wandered over the possibilities. Then he put Elizabeth out of his mind and began concentrating on his work.

That night, he finished the sketch by memory. With the last stroke of charcoal, he stepped back and smiled. He would see her again. Somehow, he was sure of it.

***

As Will finished the second page, he felt Amy's eyes on him. He looked up.

"Everything okay?" he asked.

She was leaning back in her chair, drumming her fingers against the table. "I didn't know Nana went to college in Paris." She fell silent for a moment. "Why didn't I know that? It seems like something that would have come up."

"Maybe," Will said slowly, "you didn't know because she doesn't talk about anything that has to do with Lizzie. And going to school in Paris was connected in some way to Lizzie."

Amy dropped her eyes to the stack of papers. "There's just so much I don't know."

"Not for long."

Amy nodded at the papers but didn't answer.

"Hey, what about your grandmother there?" Will said. "Lizzie sounds like she was a firecracker."

Amy smiled, cringed, and laughed at the same time. "I'm getting that feeling too." She sat forward in her chair again. "I wonder," her voice trailed off as she began reading again.

***

And Billy was right. It wasn't long before he saw Lizzie again—in fact, it was sooner than he expected.

"So, are you going to finish that portrait of me?"

Her voice came from behind, melting on Billy's neck. The words cooled his skin, tingling down his backbone. He turned around, looking Elizabeth up and down. She wore another long, layered skirt, this time pale pink, and a white sleeveless shirt. Still, his first thought was that of a mischievous nymph in a tale told centuries before.

"I already finished it," he said, watching her eyes ever so closely.

"Oh?" The expression on Elizabeth's face betrayed no surprise, no amusement, no real interest. She sat down on Billy's stool, only a foot from where he stood at his easel. "You're not new here, are you?" she asked.

"No." Billy turned back to his work. "But neither are you."

"Before yesterday, you hadn't seen me."

Billy smiled at his painting. "What gave you that idea?"

She sighed, her voice spreading warmth through the air. "So, are you going to bring out the drawing of me or not?"

He didn't look at her as his right hand gained speed, dashing across the canvass. "What makes you think I want to show you?"

"Yesterday you bragged that it would be unlike any of the others."

Billy shook his head. "I said it would only be like the

others if you looked at it the same way that you looked at the others." He tapped his temple with the pointed end of his brush. "Our perceptions can change everything."

She sat quietly for a moment and then tapped her toes on the ground, alternating left and right. The tapping was slow at first, but soon it quickened.

"Tell me a story," she said.

"A story?" He dabbed his canvass with the tip of his brush, concentrating on the result. "Once upon a time, a beautiful girl found herself enamored by a man whose social status did not match hers. She was well-monied, and he was a soldier. In fact, he was a great soldier fighting in a tumultuous war that had been waged for many long years." He dipped his brush in a schmear of paint on his palette. With a long exhale, he continued, "These different social statuses, however, did not pose the biggest problem in their relationship. The girl's father was a traitor. He had given information to the enemy, and everyone knew—"

"So you read great literature, do you?"

Billy cocked his head to one side, still focusing his eyes on his canvass. "You know that Shakespeare play, do you? It's not exactly popular."

Lizzie didn't answer for a moment. "I was thinking of Geoffrey Chaucer's Troilus and Criseyde, *which is much better than Shakespeare's version—*Troilus and Cressida. *You know, Shakespeare did a poor job portraying the heroine, Criseyde. She is quite misrepresented and misunderstood. Perhaps that is why his is not very popular and Chaucer's is so much stronger."*

"Ah, and you know about being misrepresented and misunderstood?"

"I am too young for either, really." Lizzie peered around the corner of his canvass, trying to get a look at the shapes coming to life through Billy's hands. "But if you showed me the portrait you were working on yesterday, I may find that you've created a misrepresented or misunderstood version of me."

He never stopped painting. "My, my. It seems that you really want to see it. Yesterday you didn't want me to bother with it at all."

She pretended not to hear him. "So, will you show me or not?"

"I don't think so."

"No?"

"No."

"Then why did you waste your time doing it?"

He turned toward her, studying the thick eyelashes framing her eyes. "Are you ever going to introduce yourself to me?"

She stood up, eyes shining. "You already know who I am."

"Do I?"

She straightened her skirt, almost imperceptibly, and nearly smiled. "It was nice talking to you, Billy Shakespeare. I'm sure I'll see you again soon."

She floated down the row of artists and disappeared into the mouth of a coffeehouse.

***

Amy looked up, realizing dusk was falling on them. She felt heavy questions sinking in her chest and imminent darkness weighing on her shoulders. She sat silently, thinking. Then she took out her cell phone.

"What are you doing?" Will asked, looking up from his page.

Amy scrolled through the phone numbers on her phone. "I have to call Miles and tell him not to come over tonight." She glanced at her watch. "He might already be on his way." She held the phone to her ear and tapped her index finger on the table impatiently. "Voicemail," she exhaled, her shoulders dropping. "Hi Miles, it's me. Hey, it looks like I'm going to be stuck working late tonight, so don't worry about coming over. I'll call you later. Bye." She dropped the phone on the table.

Will watched her, one eyebrow raised.

Amy sighed. "I know, I know. It looks like I lie to Miles a lot. And lately, yes, I have been lying and hiding things from him. But before this Lizzie thing came up, I never did that. Right now I don't have much choice—unless I want to tell him about what we're doing, and that will just end in an argument." Before Will could comment, she changed the subject. "Hey, I'm getting hungry and a little cold out here. Do you want to take the books to my house and finish reading *Eva's Words* there? If we're lucky, my sister might have dinner made already."

Will felt his stomach contract. "Dinner? That sounds good. Your sister wouldn't mind me coming over and eating her food?"

"As long as you don't question her cooking methods, she'll feed you anything you like. She loves cooking."

They packed up Eva's story and headed through the coffee shop toward the exit. As Amy pushed open the door, she said, "I only live a couple blocks away, so I walked here."

Will stepped next to her on the sidewalk and pointed down the street. "I parked over there. Want to ride with me?"

Amy nodded.

"So," she said as they began walking to his truck, "we haven't gotten too far into it yet, but what do you make of what Eva wrote?"

Will shoved his hands in his pockets and halfway shrugged. "I don't know. Lizzie and Billy both seem strong-willed. And of course something is going to happen with them—but whether it's going to be good or bad, I can't tell."

Amy looked at her feet. "Why did Eva write this?" she muttered.

Will didn't answer.

The drive to Amy's house took no more than three minutes. Aside from giving Will directions, she sat quietly, staring out the window, musing over what she had just read.

As they pulled into the driveway, Amy could see her sister through the kitchen window, standing at the stove.

"Looks like April's making dinner," she said as they got out of the car.

"I feel sort of bad showing up unannounced."

"Don't." Amy went around to the back of the truck and waited for Will to hand her a box from the bed. "She always cooks enough to feed the entire block."

Will put a box in Amy's hands and grabbed one for himself. As they walked up the driveway, Amy said, "But just a warning—my sister doesn't always think before she speaks."

Will grinned. "Neither do I."

Amy dropped her box at the front door step and fished a key from her pocket. She unlocked and pushed the door open.

"Hi April," she called, grabbing her box and moving through the entryway. "Smells good. What are you making?"

Will followed her into the kitchen and set his box on the table next to where Amy put hers.

April turned from the stove and eyed Amy and Will. "Who are you?" she asked Will.

"I'm Will. The one who emailed your sister about the book she lost."

She turned back to the stove and stirred the contents of a Dutch oven. "We're having a shrimp boil tonight."

"That sounds great," Amy said. "Do you want to help us with some boxes?"

"Nope."

"Please?"

April stepped away from the stove and followed Amy and Will as they moved toward the front door. "What are these boxes anyway?"

"They're Billy Strath's books," Amy threw over her shoulder. "The ones that Lizzie gave him."

"Really? You really did it? I can't believe you actually went through with it."

Amy gave her sister the details as they hauled boxes from the truck to the house. Will watched and listened to the girls as they moved back and forth across the driveway. April clearly wasn't interested in a long-lost grandmother, and she clucked and shook her head throughout Amy's narrative. In the falling darkness, he had to pay attention to each girl's words to tell them apart. They looked almost like twins in the shadows of evening with their curly blonde hair and green eyes. Only when they finished unloading the boxes and returned inside could Will tell that April's skin was darker and her face was thinner. Unlike Amy, she had a sprinkling of freckles across her nose and cheeks.

"Do you want to read this with us?" Amy asked her sister, holding up the stack of *Eva's Words*.

"Not a chance. I want to finish making dinner. Then I want to watch some mindless television and fall asleep."

"Sounds like a pretty good night," Will said as he followed Amy into the family room.

"I know," she called after them, retuning to the stove.

"Call us when dinner is ready," Amy said.

"You've got it."

Amy sat down on the couch and placed *Eva's Words* on the coffee table. She picked up the piece of paper Will had been reading and handed it to him. "Here you go." Then she picked up another piece of paper and began reading.

Will sat down on the other side of the couch and began reading as well.

Fifteen

Billy seated himself at the table a few feet from hers. He opened a menu and held it high enough to shield most of his face. Over its top, he watched her talking to a male companion. He waited. When the waiter came by, he ordered a cup of coffee. And when the waiter delivered the order, Billy sipped the coffee slowly, still waiting.

Minutes had lapsed when Lizzie took the napkin off her lap and placed it on the table. Billy set his coffee cup down. He watched her stand and turn around. She didn't notice him sitting just one table over as she stepped away from her company.

"Excuse me, Miss," Billy said, reaching to touch her arm. Lizzie stopped. "Can you give me one moment, please?" he continued.

She nearly gasped, surprised, but stifled it. "You!" she said, barely aware that his hand was still on her arm. "What are you doing here?"

"Looking for you." Billy glanced at the man sitting at Lizzie's table. "But maybe I shouldn't be. Your gentleman-friend doesn't seem too happy that I'm talking to you."

Lizzie's eyebrows rose. "Why would he be?"

Billy's hand slid down Lizzie's arm until his fingers met hers. He lifted her hand to his lips and kissed it.

Lizzie laughed. "Is this really why you came here? To make my friend jealous?"

"I came to see you."

"Well, you see me, don't you?"

"I do." He continued holding her hand.

She smiled. "All right. Now, if you'll excuse me—"

"Where are you going?"

"To the ladies room, if you ever give me my hand back."

"And if I don't?"

"I will call my friend over here," she said, "and he will force you to give it back to me."

"No one forces me to do anything."

She smiled. "That may someday change."

Billy dropped her hand and watched her float away, dark

hair swaying behind her.

Time ticked by as he waited for her to return. He finished his coffee, still waiting. He left some money on the table and headed toward the door.

On the way out of the restaurant, he heard a voice calling after him. "It took you long enough," she said.

Billy turned around. Lizzie was walking toward him.

"What do you mean?" he asked.

"I've been waiting here for you. I was just about to give up and go back to having dinner with my friend."

Billy continued his walk out of the restaurant. "Are you saying that since you've been to the ladies room you've been waiting here for me to come out, intending to leave with me instead of finishing your meal with that man?"

She reached to his side. "Yes."

"That's not a very friendly way to treat a friend, now is it?"

She shrugged. "What do you care?"

"I don't."

They walked down the street in silence.

"So why did you come looking for me?" she asked.

"I came to give you the portrait from the other day."

"I don't want it."

"That's fine. Then I won't give it to you."

They slipped into silence again. Billy didn't know where they were going. He wasn't familiar with the Latin Quarter of Paris, which was largely populated by students. Lizzie seemed comfortable with their direction; he followed her lead.

"Do you have it with you?" she asked.

"Have what?"

"The portrait."

"Oh." He shook his head. "No."

"Then why—" Lizzie cut herself off, deciding to keep her thoughts to herself. She watched her feet moving on the concrete. "You should meet my sister," she said.

"Why is that?"

"She's an artist. Like you."

"Is that what she does for a living?"

"No. She's in school right now."

Billy nodded. "And you? Are you an artist? Or are you in school right now, too?"

"I am both, but right now I am neither."

"I see."

"I am on my summer break for school. I'm just out here to visit Eva—my sister. I'm supposed to go back in a couple of weeks—to school, I mean."

"And, how is it that you are an artist, but not at the moment?"

"I am not the same kind of artist that you are. I don't draw or paint. I'm an actress."

"But you're not acting right now?"

She shook her head.

"And are you looking forward to your return to school?"

She shook her head again. "It bores me."

A cigarette appeared in Billy's hand, and he lit it. "What are you studying in school?"

"My parents think I'm studying English, and I am a little bit. Enough to keep them fooled. But really, I'm studying theater."

Billy exhaled smoke. "You're lying to your parents about what you're studying?"

"I am." She took the cigarette from his fingers and brought it to her lips.

"Why are you tired of school if you're studying what you love?" He took the cigarette back.

"Because school is not making me famous."

"Where is this school? This school that isn't making you famous?"

"In Northern California."

Billy's eyebrows rose. "Well, California is certainly a good place to be if you want to become famous."

"Not Northern California. I need to be in Los Angeles."

He nodded. "You do."

Lizzie pointed across the street and stepped off the sidewalk. "Do you feel like having a drink?"

Billy's eyes followed her finger and caught sight of a building permeating music and lights. "Sure." They walked toward the bar. "Do you dance as well?"

"I do." Lizzie twirled across the street, her skirt whipping around her legs and her hair crisscrossing her face. "The question, really," she said "is do you dance well?"

***

Will leaned back against the couch, and in a sing-song voice said, "I know what's going to happen next."

"What?" Amy looked up from the page she was reading and pushed some hair behind her ear.

Will squinted at her. "C'mon, really? They're going to a bar, Lizzie asked him to have a drink with her, she wants to dance…" His voice trailed off.

Amy looked down at the piece of paper in her hand and then back at Will. "I'm a bit ahead of you in reading, and I still don't know what you mean."

"Dear Amy," April said, carrying two plates piled high with shrimp boil. "He's saying your grandmother's easy and that Billy's probably going to get lucky."

Amy's eyes darted back and forth between Will and her sister. "Why would you think that?"

April set the plates on the coffee table and looked at Will. "She's serious, you know. She really doesn't know why we would think that." April winked Amy. "She's always been a bit naïve."

"This is amazing," Will said, his attention focused on the food. "Thank you, April." He stabbed a piece of sausage and shifted his body to look at Amy. "Listen, Amy," he pushed the food into his mouth and began chewing between words, "Bars are only for two things: getting drunk and hooking up. I know things have changed in the last fifty or sixty years, but I bet things haven't changed that much. They're going home together."

Amy picked up a shrimp and bit into it. "I don't know. You two really think bars are just for drinking and hooking up? You can't go to a bar just to hang out?"

April and Will shook their heads.

"You might end up *just* hanging out," Will said, talking through a mouthful of potato. "But who wants to do that?"

Amy's eyebrows furrowed. "That would be fine with me. And here in this story, I just don't think that's what's going to happen."

"There is zero evidence to support your conclusion," Will said. "They've been flirting constantly. This is headed somewhere."

"Okay Mr. English major, settle down. We're not writing an argumentative essay here."

April grinned, watching her sister. "It'll all be okay in the end, Amy. Don't worry about it."

"But it's not all okay in the end." The volume of Amy's voice began to increase. "That's the problem. That's why we're sitting here decades later trying to piece together what happened."

April walked toward the kitchen. "Details," she said over her shoulder. She stopped in the doorway. "Oh, and by the way Will, I like your truck."

Will swallowed his food and answered, "Oh, thanks."

"Have you had it a long time?"

He nodded his head. "Yeah, I got it when I went away to college—so three years."

"Hmm," April said, thinking. "Okay, well, goodnight."

"Thanks again for dinner," Will said.

As she headed toward her room, Amy and Will exchanged sideways glances. "Is your sister a fan of old trucks?" Will asked.

"Don't know, don't care," Amy replied. She picked up a piece of corn on the cob and then leaned toward the paper she was reading.

Will continued looking at Amy for a moment. "This thing with Lizzie—you do know that it's going to be okay in the end, right? In it's own imperfect way, it will be okay. It is okay. You and your sister, Eva, your mom—you're all proof that it is okay."

Amy nodded, chewing slowly, unable to think of an answer. She kept her eyes on the paper.

***

Morning crept over the horizon without the slightest warning, drowning shadows with its light and rousing people from their dreams. Eva opened the windows in the living room of her apartment. She spent a few moments staring out the window and across the courtyard, breathing in the warm, quiet air. Then she turned around and pursed her lips, taking in the sight of her sister sleeping on the couch. She walked to the couch and thought about pouring her cup of tea directly on Lizzie.

Instead, however, she said, "Liz, the next time I arrange a date for you and a friend of mine, I'd appreciate it if you didn't leave him at a restaurant all night long."

Lizzie opened her eyes. The light flooding through the window blurred her vision. "Huh?" She lifted her head off the couch pillow and then dropped it back down. Pain pulsed through her temples.

Eva stripped a blanket off her younger sister. "Get up. It's time to go."

Lizzie moaned. "No." She reached for the blanket rumpled at her feet. "Leave me alone."

"We have to go. The day's already wasting away, and we're supposed to meet Rob for lunch."

Lizzie's eyes remained shut, but her eyebrows furrowed. "Who's Rob?"

"Lizzie! Get up!" Eva sat down on the couch and shook her sister's shoulder. "What happened to you last night? I don't remember hearing you come home."

Lizzie tried to open her eyes. They felt like rocks pressed into her head. "I came home last night? I don't remember that either. Who's Bob?"

"Rob—not Bob—is the man that you left at the restaurant. He came by late last night wondering what happened to you. I didn't know what to say. I didn't know where you were either. So I told him we'd have lunch today to make up for your rudeness."

"Oh." Lizzie licked her lips. "Eva, could you get me some water, please?"

Eva walked toward the bathroom. "How much did you drink last night?"

The tap water ran in the bathroom for a few seconds before Eva reappeared at Lizzie's side with a cup. Eva smiled as Lizzie reached for the water.

"I have no idea," Lizzie said. She brought the cup to her lips without propping herself up. Water spilled down her neck as she drank. "I can't go anywhere today. I'm going to die if I go anywhere."

Eva sat down again. "What happened last night?"

Lizzie drank more water and then held the cup out to Eva. "More?" She closed her eyes. "I don't know what happened. I can't remember."

She felt the couch move as Eva got up for more water. Lizzie tried to think. Out of the fogginess in her mind, she began to extract memories of the previous evening.

"Eva, you said that I left—what's his name? Bob? I left Bob at the restaurant? Why did I do that?"

"I don't know." Eva called from the bathroom. "Why did you do that?"

Billy's face flashed across Lizzie's mind. "Oh, I remember. I met a guy last night."

Eva tapped Lizzie's shoulder with the dripping cup of water. "You met a guy? While you were out with another man?"

Lizzie wasn't sure. "Yes?" Her voice was small. "Maybe? Wait, no. I met him before last night. But I saw him last night. And since he was a whole lot more interesting than your friend, I decided to spend my time with him."

"He must have been quite interesting. You can't remember what happened."

Lizzie poured water down her throat. "I hope I didn't do anything stupid."

Eva smiled. "Oh, I'm sure you did."

Lizzie's eyebrows rose over closed eyes. "Probably." Talking was becoming difficult as her head pulsed harder. "I'm going to have to find out. But not now, not tonight, not tomorrow, not for a really long time." She pushed the cup at Eva's arm. "Tell Bob that I'm really sorry. And go now. Leave me alone to die in peace."

Eva stood up. "His name is Rob."

"I don't care. And don't send me on a date with any of your boring friends again. This is all your fault."

Eva smiled and walked out of the room. "It's always my fault, isn't it?" she said. "I've been blamed since the beginning of time."

***

Will cast a sideways glance at Amy as she passed him the next page. He suppressed a smile.

"We still don't know what happened," she said, keeping her eyes down. She tried to hide the smile teasing the corners of her mouth. "Plus, all we are getting here is fragments, and they were written by Eva, who wasn't even there most of the time. She probably was writing from fragments that Lizzie told her. We don't know how reliable any of this is."

Will couldn't suppress his smile any longer. "You're right," he said, taking the paper from Amy.

***

A week later, Lizzie walked up to Billy's easel and sat down on his stool.

"Hello," she said when he looked at her.

Billy studied her a moment before turning back to his work. "You again," he breathed.

"Me again?" She pointed to herself. "What do you mean by that?"

"I mean exactly what I said. "You again."

Lizzie's voice left her momentarily. When it returned, she stood up and said, "Well, if that's all you have to say, I can certainly go."

He reached over and touched her elbow before she could step away. "No. Don't go." His voice was soft. "Sit down."

She obeyed. "I'm sorry that you're not happier to see me."

He studied his canvass. "I would have been happier to see you sooner."

"You could have found me earlier if you wanted to."

"Is that right?"

"Absolutely."

Billy set down his paintbrush and turned to her. He crossed his arms and stared directly into her eyes. Lizzie stared back. She stood up so that they were closer to the same height. The urge to ask 'what?' tickled the back of her throat, but she swallowed it.

"I don't remember what happened that night I was with you," she said, forfeiting the contest of silent staring.

Billy's eyebrows rose. He continued to study her eyes. "And you want to know what happened?"

"I wouldn't mind knowing."

"Have you ever done that before? Drank so much alcohol with a man you don't know? So much that he has to find out where you live and carry you home over his shoulder?"

Her eyebrows furrowed and she looked past him at a coffee shop, thinking. She pursed her lips together. "I don't know. It is a possibility—after all, if it has happened before, I wouldn't remember it, right?"

"How old are you, Elizabeth?"

"Call me Lizzie. I'm twenty."

"You don't drink often, do you?"

"Why do you say that?"

Billy turned back to his painting. He didn't answer.

"No. I don't drink much." She sat back down on the stool and watched him paint. After a while, she asked, "So, are you going to tell me what happened that night?"

"Well," Billy said, dipping his brush into some paint. "You and I drank a little, then you tried to get me to dance but I wouldn't. Then we drank some more, then went for a walk and screamed at the moon. Then you got sick, then you passed out, and then I had to carry you around the Latin Quarter, asking if anyone knew you and where to find your sister's place. When I finally found someone who knew you and your sister, I took you home. It's a good thing your sister doesn't lock her door."

Lizzie's eyes narrowed. "That's what happened? Really?"

"That's exactly what happened." Billy continued painting.

Lizzie watched his hands fly over the canvass. Her eyes were still narrowed, and they remained that way until she said, "You wouldn't dance with me?"

"Is that the only part of the evening that concerns you?"

"Well, that's definitely what concerns me most. If you'd scream at the moon, why wouldn't you dance?"

Billy put his paintbrush down. "I will dance with you tonight, at eight, at the same place, if you like. "I will dance with you, sober, if you leave me to my work now, and if you show up at eight."

Lizzie stood up. She examined him for a moment and then

walked down the row of artists without saying anything.

***

Amy waited for Will to finish reading. When he looked up, she smiled. "See. My grandmother wasn't easy. A little bit of an idiot, but not easy."

Will winked at her. "There's still a lot left in this story."

"We'll see." She turned back to the papers.

Sixteen

The thick moan of a trumpet hung in the air, darkening the club's already dim atmosphere and invoking dancers to sway across the dance floor like zombies in a trance. Behind the powerful voice of the trumpet hummed a choir of piano, bass, and saxophone, but behind the musical lament was an unmistakable silence throughout the club. No laughter or conversation challenged the instruments' voices. Only the shuffling feet of dancers could be heard every now and again when the musicians gasped for breath between notes.

Billy sat at a table near the back of the bar. He watched the dancers circling the floor in front of his table, and he watched the band playing on the other side of the dance floor. He sat there, waiting and watching. He waited, comfortable, listening to music with a thin smile.

Eva walked into the bar and went straight to Billy's table, weaving gracefully through the unaware dancers. She set her purse on the table and sat down.

"Hello," she said.

He smiled at her. "Hello."

"Lizzie's running a little late," she said. "So I came to entertain you until she gets here. I'm her sister, Eva." She extended her hand. He took it.

"Nice to meet you," he said. "How thoughtful of you to come by. How thoughtful of you—and of her."

"Oh, well, if there's one thing Lizzie and I are not, it's rude."

"Is that right?"

"Well, I'm not rude, and Lizzie, well, you know Lizzie." She smiled and placed her elbows on the table. Her eyes wandered around the room as she dropped her cheek against her fist. "So, tell me, how is it that you met my sister?"

She noticed that her voice was the only one in the club full of drinkers at tables and dancers on the floor. She continued smiling.

Billy lit a cigarette. "Hasn't she told you already?'

"I want you to tell me."

"Well," he said, looking past Eva to the exit, "your sister walked up to me and demanded that I draw a portrait of her. So I did."

Eva smiled. "She demanded it? Sounds like her."

"Oh yes." Billy nodded and blew smoke toward his shoulder. "Not with words. But with those eyes and that breezy way of hers. He nodded again, looking at Eva. "Surely you know this already."

Eva took his cigarette and sighed. "She does tend to demand what she wants."

"And you don't?" He watched Eva draw on the cigarette, remembering the way Lizzie had helped herself to his cigarette the night he carried her home over his shoulder.

"Sometimes." She ashed the cigarette and handed it back to him. "So, you're an artist?"

"I am. I hear you are too."

"I'm not."

"Lizzie told me that you were."

Eva smiled. "She thinks everyone is an artist. When we were in middle school, our family visited Monet's home. I fell in love with the gardens there, and I tried to draw the little bridge in that one very famous painting—you know the one, I'm sure. Water Lilies, *I think. It's a rather poor drawing, but I've hung it in my room—a reminder of a simpler time." She shrugged. "That's just about my only foray into art. I do like looking at art though."*

"So, is she a real artist then, if she thinks that everyone is an artist?"

"Lizzie? You mean as a dancer? Or an actress? Oh yes. She's quite talented. Always has been."

A couple blocks away, Lizzie plunged her dirty arms into a basin of cold water. She scrubbed them, splashing water across her blouse and skirt, but not minding the water because her clothes were as dirty as her arms. She whipped her head around to see the clock hanging on the wall. Eight-ten. She shook her head, going back to washing her arms and wondering how she could have spent the whole evening planting flowers on Eva's balcony without noticing the movement of the sun toward the horizon. If only she had asked Eva to call her in at seven instead of relying on herself.

She shook the water off her clean arms, rushing toward her collection of clothes where she found a yellow skirt and a matching pair of shoes. Changing her clothes, she noticed dirt rubbing off her face onto her hand. Sighing, she snatched her dirty skirt off the floor and wiped her face with the fabric. In her high heels, she wobbled to a mirror in the wardrobe. Her hair hung about her face, tangled and unbrushed. She shook her head at the ceiling and groaned with frustration. Her shoes banged against the wardrobe door as she kicked them off and headed back toward the basin. Her stomach growled, but she barely noticed as she brushed her teeth and washed the remaining dirt off her face. At the last glance of the clock, it was eight-seventeen. Without makeup, brushed hair, or shoes, she left her sister's flat, moving quickly toward the club. The evening was warm and felt nice on her neck. She smiled, her breath and composure coming back to her.

"Ah—I'm here!"

Eva and Billy looked up to see Lizzie standing next to their table.

"Your sister told me you were running late," Billy said. "You could have taken an extra moment to put shoes on. I would have continued to wait." He remained seated.

"Well, what's done is done, and I'm here now." Lizzie sat in the empty chair and turned to her sister. "So, you didn't have any problems finding him?"

Eva shook her head. "Your description was perfect." She turned to Billy. "The second I saw you, I knew. Rhett Butler, just like Lizzie said."

Billy's right eyebrow rose. "I beg your pardon, but I don't believe I look anything like Clark Gable."

"I didn't say Clark Gable," Lizzie answered. "I said Rhett Butler."

"Tremendous difference," Eva added.

Billy sat back in his chair and gazed at the sisters, his right eyebrow still high. "And my twin Scarlet O'Haras, do you describe everyone in terms of characters in books?"

"Only when it fits," Lizzie said.

Billy smiled at the sisters. "Quite a duo you two must be. You, young American beauties, frolicking about Paris, boasting your education with the rest of the American-in-Paris snobs."

"My now, American-in-Paris snobs?" Lizzie said. "I never thought of us quite like that. Did you, Eva?" Lizzie turned to her sister.

"Of course I have, Liz. Why else would I choose a school in France? So that I can frolic with my sister every summer like an educated American-in-Paris snob."

Lizzie sighed, gazing across the bar. "Well, yes. I suppose it's the only rightful way to waste the family's money. And I suppose we are American-in-Paris snobs—is that the right term, Billy? That must be why I go to Montmartre and beg artists to draw portraits of me."

"No, no dear," Eva said. "You demand them to draw portraits of you. Ask Billy. He'll tell you."

"That's true," Billy said, lighting a new cigarette. "Demanding is your way."

Lizzie smiled. "Yes. I've probably been going about it in a rather round-about manner then. If it's my way, maybe I should just forget the act and go around telling everyone, 'I demand you to do this for me,' and 'I demand you to do that for me.' I hate wasting time, you know."

"But as an American-in-Paris snob, dear, you can't be too forthright," Eva said. "That would make you an American-in-Paris bitch."

Lizzie smiled at Billy. "I think I like that title better. What do you think, Billy?"

He pulled the cigarette away from his lips. "I don't think anything."

"All the better." Lizzie leaned forward and stared into Billy's eyes. "I demand that you get me a drink, Rhett Butler."

"I'd prefer not. But if you'll excuse me," he said, slowly rising and nodding at them.

"Oh fine, go, if you must," Lizzie said, waving him on.

He walked away from the girls. They watched him go.

"How strange," Eva said when he was out of earshot.

"I know," Lizzie said, looking after him. "Strange, but so much fun. Where do you suppose he's going?"

Eva shrugged. "Bathroom?" She shrugged again. "Don't wonder too much about it. He'll be back."

Lizzie shrugged. "Maybe." After a few moments, she

leaned toward her sister. "How long are you staying, Eva?"

"Tonight? Not long. I'm supposed to meet Jack for dinner."

"Oh. I wish that you'd stay longer."

"Jack calls."

Lizzie looked back to the crowd. "And no one calls quite the way Jack does."

"Really?" A male voice wafted toward them from behind.

The two girls slowly turned toward the voice. Lizzie sighed, looking at Billy. "That's right. No one calls quite like Jack. So you're back. I didn't think you'd be back."

"What, and deny myself the privilege of spending an evening with two Scarlet O'Haras? I'd never dream of it."

"One Scarlet O'Hara." Eva rose. "I am going to meet the call of Jack, which we just established was quite like no other. It was very nice meeting you, Billy." Eva extended her hand.

"Likewise." He kissed her knuckles and bowed.

"My Rhett, I didn't expect you to be such a gentleman." Eva smiled and batted her eyelashes.

"Oh, just go, Eva," Lizzie said. "He already thinks too highly of himself."

Eva smiled at her sister. "Goodbye, dear." She kissed Lizzie on the cheek.

"You have fun tonight," Lizzie said.

"You too. Goodbye, Billy."

"Goodbye."

Eva turned to leave, but neither Billy nor Lizzie watched her go.

"Are you just going to stand there?" Lizzie asked after staring at him for a moment.

Billy's eyebrows rose. "Shall we dance?"

Lizzie's eyebrows rose also. She glanced toward the band, noticing that they had switched to a lively composition. "I imagine we shall." She took his extended hand and rose from her seat. "I hope that you don't dance like an American. I hate the way American boys dance. It is as though they don't hear the music."

"Do you hear the music?"

"The good music, yes."

"You're missing out on all the bad music then. A loss you

don't even realize."

They walked toward the dance floor.

"I'm serious about you dancing like an American," she said turning to him upon reaching the dance floor. "If you dance that way, we will have to stop."

"Fair enough," he said, sweeping her into a turn before she expected.

Lizzie felt her feet respond to his strong lead and a laugh rising to her throat. Music permeated her skin and rushed through her veins. As she looked at Billy once their rhythm was established, she felt like she was flying.

***

Amy's cell phone rang. She jumped, startled.

"Miles?" Will asked as she grabbed it from the table.

Amy nodded, answering the call. "Hey Miles," she said. "Yeah, I'm home now. It's been a long day. I'm pretty tired. How are you doing?"

Will watched her lean back on the couch and close her eyes. She rested her elbow on the couch's arm and propped up her head with her hand. Prior to telling Miles that she was tired, she hadn't looked it. Now she did. Will wondered if he just hadn't noticed.

"Oh, that sounds great—but you must be tired too. Yeah? I'm going to call it a night soon myself. Okay, well, sweet dreams. See you tomorrow. Me too."

She put her phone on the table and looked at Will. She sighed. "I didn't know what to say."

Will shrugged. "That's okay. It's just weird that you have to hide this from your boyfriend. It seems like he should be the one sitting here with you reading this stuff. Not me."

Amy pursed her lips and tilted her head to one side. "He's not that kind of boyfriend. He's wonderful and supportive in his own way, but he's not that kind of boyfriend."

"Well, that's fine with me. Because if he were, I couldn't be here right now." Will lifted the final pages, feeling their weight. "We only have a little left here. Ready to keep going?"

Amy nodded, looking at the pages hesitantly. "The story

couldn't be wrapped up in those final pages, could it? I feel like we're still only at the beginning."

Seventeen

"How long are you going to be here?" he asked, his eyes darting back and forth between his canvass and the woman sitting next to his easel.

"Another two weeks." Lizzie glanced toward the easel, continuing to tap her toes the way she had for the past thirty minutes.

"And then back to the States?" His eyebrows furrowed toward the canvass and then relaxed as they moved toward her again.

"Yes."

"And then back to school."

She did not answer right away. "I might not go back to school this year."

"Hmm? And how are you going to manage that?"

"I haven't thought about it fully yet, but I know there is a way."

"Defy the parents? Betray their love and support?"

"They offer us neither love nor support. Just money. Why do you think Eva is in France for school? You're right about us being rich, educated, American-in-Paris snobs. But it is not by choice so much as it is by a need to run away."

"So is that what you are going to do next year? Run away? Instead of going back to school?"

"I don't know yet."

Billy glanced at her tapping toes. "Are you bored sitting here?" he asked.

Lizzie held her feet still.

"I suggest," Billy continued, "not going back to school. You could make money as a street performer." He looked over at her again, and a smirk formed on his face.

Lizzie fought to hide a scowl. Her toe began tapping again. "I know that you only say that to demean me. You don't think that I could live without the luxuries that my parents provide for me, and you think that I see myself as above street performers."

"I do. You are right. It's sweet of you to come to Montmartre with your coffee to talk to artists, but you, working as

an artist? Lowering yourself to the line of poverty, where the books you read are not a status symbol but just books? Where no one is impressed with literary illusions, and you only make them because you enjoy doing so? You, working as an artist? You wouldn't wear shoes, and not because you did not want to, but because you wouldn't have any. You would be cold in the mornings, and you would not be able to afford coffee to warm you. And you would have to listen to people's complaints and insults, finding compliments buried deep beneath American snobbery. You, as an artist? Maybe in the States, but certainly not here."

Lizzie kept her face still. "And so why would you suggest such a course of action if you don't think I could follow it?"

Billy shrugged. "It is still a possibility. A possibility that you could choose—with a couple of modifications."

"But why would you suggest such a possibility when you don't think I could follow it unless modifications were made?"

"I think you should go back to the States and—"

"Why?"

"Get a job there as—"

"Why?"

"Waitress and try to—"

"Why? Why would you make a suggestion like that?"

Billy looked over at her, one eyebrow high.

"Why?" She asked again. "I am not going to sit here and let you go out of your way to insult me. I am fond neither of unnecessary unkindness nor of points driven into the ground. Do you wish for me to leave now?"

Billy's other eyebrow rose while the first one dropped. He nodded, his eyes cast low for a moment. "I apologize for the insult. You are right. It was unnecessary and unkind."

"If you find faults in my character, we can address them as adults, directly."

He nodded. "Again, my deepest apologies."

"As a matter of fact," Lizzie began, twirling her hair around a finger, "I don't think that I will go back to school next year. I rarely speak to my parents while I'm away, and I'll just continue calling them once a month when I need more money. I'll take the money that they send me and move to Los Angeles. I'll find a place where I can settle down, and then I'll work on getting

myself involved in the business."

"Ah, I see. Exploit the parents. It is another option."

"They have exploited me and Eva all our lives. We were puppets to them from the time we could talk. I would not feel bad in the least if I did this."

Billy continued to paint, his head tilting slightly to the right. "I'm sorry to hear that. How much longer to you have in school?"

"Two years."

"And the money runs out after that? Provided your parents do not find out about this plan of yours?"

"I suppose." She shrugged. "It should be enough."

"What will Eva say?"

"She won't say anything."

"Despite your relationship with her? She won't worry?"

"Because of my relationship with her, she won't worry."

"Fair enough."

"In fact, it's time for me to tell her about this plan so she can start the process of not worrying about me." She slid of her stool. "Goodbye."

Billy did not respond, nor did Lizzie expect him to.

She spent the entire walk home formulating her plan. By the time she arrived at Eva's flat, her excitement had risen, and she had made up her mind about the following school year.

"I'm not going back to school, Eva," Lizzie said as she opened the door to the apartment and spotted her sister lying on the couch, reading a book.

Eva closed the book and laid it on her stomach. "No?"

"No." Lizzie skipped into the room and sat on the coffee table in front of her sister.

"What are you going to do then? What are you going to tell Mom and Dad?"

"I'm not going to tell them anything. They don't need to know. I'll leave as I always do for school, but instead of actually going to school, I'll go to Los Angeles instead."

Eva smiled. She studied her sister, noticing a lightness in the lines of her face. "And, since you're going to pretend that you're back at school, you'll have the money they send you for tuition and living expenses to finance the move to L.A."

Lizzie nodded. "I can't believe I didn't think of this before."

"And then when it takes an additional year of school to make up the one you missed, you'll tell them that you decided to change your major?"

"I don't plan on ever going back. I don't think it will take me that long to get started in Los Angeles. A year, maybe. If it takes longer, then it takes longer. I have two more years of tuition money from them to spend."

Eva shook her head. "Can I visit you in L.A.?"

"Of course. You should come out and live with me after you graduate this year."

"That would be something."

"It would be wonderful. You and I could—"

"Did Billy put this idea into your head? This whole moving to Los Angeles bit?"

"I don't know," Lizzie said softly, looking at the clock behind the couch. "Maybe. It's hard to tell who says what in our conversations now. It's all a blur. He talks and then I talk back. I talk, then he talks back."

"Sounds wonderful."

Lizzie looked at her sister and smiled. She shrugged. "Who knows?" She leaned her elbows on her knee and rocked forward on them. "Let's do something today, Eva. Let's go somewhere. Now."

"Where do you want to go?" Eva craned her neck to see the clock behind her. "What time is it?"

"It doesn't matter. Let's just go. Anywhere."

***

Amy leaned back on the couch and stared at the ceiling.

"What's wrong?" Will asked.

Amy handed him a piece of paper. "Lizzie's kinda...*wild*, isn't she?" she asked.

"She's completely wild. She's awesome."

Amy pushed a curl behind her ear. "She wanted to steal from her parents so she could move to Los Angeles."

He shrugged. "A bit scandalous, yes, but it sure makes for

a great story."

Eighteen

"Why are you here?" They walked through the Latin Quarter slowly, paying little attention to the sun setting behind them.

"Why am I here?" he repeated. "Are you asking how I came to be an artist in Paris?"

"Yes."

"Well," he began, squinting at the sun. "I was born in America. Florida, to be more precise. My parents owned a pharmacy. When I was fourteen, they died in an automobile accident. I lived with my grandfather for about two months. He despised me, and I despised him. So I left."

Silence lapsed between them.

"And does that bring us up to the present day?" Lizzie asked.

"Pretty much. I left at fourteen and have been wandering ever since."

"You make it sound so simple. Surely it was harder than that. You must have an education."

He shrugged. "Not like yours. I didn't have money when I left my grandfather's home. But when I left, there was room in my knapsack for four books. So I stole four books from my grandfather's library. And that was the beginning of my education."

"What books were they?"

*He watched his feet as they continued their walk. "*Huck Finn, The Odyssey, Canterbury Tales, *and* The Inferno. *It wasn't much, but my grandfather did not display many of his books. I took what I could get, and they meant everything to me." Billy sighed. "So, that's what I did. I wandered across America for a while, offering my services as a handyman and as a street artist. And, when I met nice people, I traded books with them. I've had a constant flow of literature in my life because I always had something to trade. Over the years, I read many books that were old college texts. They were marked up with comments in the margins and underlining. Those were my favorites. They taught me how to read. They taught me what to focus on and what to look* *for." He paused. "That was one side of my education. The other side was what I learned on the road. Out in the open."*

"How did you get to Paris?"

He shrugged. "I don't know."

"Do you like it here?"

"I have liked it, yes. But I won't be here forever. It's important never to over-stay one's welcome."

"How do you know when you've stayed too long?"

They walked in silence for a moment. "The restlessness comes."

Lizzie looked at him and nodded. "Have you ever been to jail?"

He smiled at her. "Ah, the stereotypes. No, I've never been in jail. Not all wanderers are beggars who must steal to survive."

"Then how did you make it?"

Billy grinned at the setting sun and shook his head. "You must stop believing everything you read. Naïveté is only so attractive."

Lizzie's eyebrows rose. "If I've insulted you, forgive me."

Billy didn't acknowledge her apology. "Some people can master the art of wandering. They rely on their skills, and they love the freedom of the open land enough to wander honestly their whole lives. I didn't mind the weight of four books in my knapsack. I was not afraid of a little weight on my back or in my mind. That's how I did it. How I'm doing it." He shrugged. "And, people love mystery in art. So, I add a little of that in my work, which is how I've become marginally successful."

"Beg your pardon?"

"People love to look at art and wonder. Think about the Mona Lisa's smile. There's something about it that no one can really explain." He looked at Lizzie and smiled. "We all like a little mystery, don't we? That's why we push forward. Our curiosity drives us forward. I create art by adding a couple details that don't quite fit. Facial expressions, colors, the direction of the wind, that sort of thing."

"You've created a formula out of something that isn't supposed to be formulaic."

"Everything has a formula. Every feeling, every event,

every conversation. Identifying the ingredients and their amounts is what makes formulas so difficult to crack. No one bothers to identify the 'why' part of the equation. They just try to identify the result. Life makes sense, though, if you understand the why."

"That's not fun."

"Sometimes it's not."

"So what comes after Paris?"

"I don't know."

They walked along in silence. "I don't know how much of your story I believe."

"Why is that?"

"I think you leave things up to chance more than you analyze formulas."

He considered her words. "It's possible to do both. There is a time and a place for everything. The beauty of knowledge is that I can choose when I want to understand and when I want to leave it up to chance. Understanding is a powerful tool."

They continued walking in silence. Lizzie wanted to ask Billy so many questions. She wanted him to teach her about wandering, about reading people, about understanding the world. She, however, knew she couldn't. So she remained silent.

***

Amy passed Will the last sheet of paper and waited. When he finished, she said, "I don't know how that could be it. How could that be where it ends?"

He shrugged. "This isn't the end of the story. We just have to find the rest."

Amy leaned back on the couch and crossed her arms. "I can't believe that's it."

"It's not the end. C'mon, we just have to figure out how to get the rest of the story. We know there's more." Will stretched his arms over his head and yawned.

"I know. But where is it? Did Lizzie really take her parents' money and run? Did she become an actress? And what happened with Billy? How did he go from a starving artist in Paris to a grouchy old man in Monterey?" Amy sat forward and straightened the stack of papers they just read. "Tomorrow I'm going to Nana's after work. I'm going to ask her what happened."

"Good." Will stood up. "That's a good idea." He picked up both his and Amy's dinner plates and carried them into the kitchen. Amy followed.

"Now that you have a basic idea of who Lizzie was," Will continued, "when she was younger at least, you can think about the best way to approach Eva about her."

Amy stood at the kitchen table and watched him put the dishes in the sink. When he turned around, she nodded and then looked at the boxes on the table.

"What do you want to do with those books?" Will pointed to them as he walked toward Amy. "Do you want me to take them to Billy tomorrow? Do you want to take a look at them first?"

Amy opened a box and picked up a book. Leafing through it, she said, "I don't know." She put it back down.

"Why don't you sleep on it? I know you have a lot to think about right now."

Amy nodded.

"Okay, so here's the plan," Will continued. "Tonight and tomorrow you think about whatever you have to think about. Then after work, go talk to Eva. I'll meet you back here tomorrow night, and if you want me to take the books to Billy, I will. If you want me to do something else, I'll do that." He picked up a book and flipped through a couple pages. "We probably should look through these before they go up to Billy though—just to see if there are any letters or notes left in them, but," he put the book back in a box, "that's up to you."

He winked at Amy and then turned toward the front door. She followed him.

"Thanks, Will," she said. "It's really nice of you to do all this for me."

He reached for the doorknob. "It's much more interesting than looking for a job."

Amy smiled. "See you tomorrow. How does seven-thirty sound?"

"Perfect. Good night, Amy."

She closed the door behind him and walked to her room. The clock on the nightstand reminded her that it wasn't that late, but she threw herself across her bed, exhausted, wishing she didn't have to change her clothes or brush her teeth.

Eva's words flowed through her mind over and over, over and over. Over and over. She stared at the ceiling, wishing they would stop.

From the corner of her eye, she could see the book of Renaissance poetry sitting on the nightstand. She rolled over and reached for it. Since Will returned it to her, she hadn't brought herself to open it. As she fanned through the pages, a flash of white caught her eye. She flipped back and realized it was the top layer of a napkin that had been torn away and folded in half. She pulled it out and opened it.

Forget about Jos and that guy. Remember what Hollings said. The planets are aligned. You are going to find Amy tomorrow!

Amy refolded the napkin and tucked it back in the book. She thought about Hollings and what it felt like to sit in a lecture hall, listening to him recite poetry that had been scrawled across parchment hundreds of years before. She remembered how hearing those words had caused her breath to catch in her chest—how those words had pricked her skin and consumed her imagination. She hadn't felt that way since college. Not until tonight.

And then there was Will. Who was this guy? Where did he come from? How did he find her?

And who was Jos?

She reached up to the lamp on her nightstand and turned it off.

Nineteen

Amy sat in the recliner across the room from Eva and Aidan. She traced the edges of the armrest with her fingers, listening to the evening news on the television. When she stopped by after work, she hadn't intended to stay for dinner, but Eva insisted. Throughout the meal, she had tried to bring up Lizzie but couldn't think of a good way to do it. Now that the dishes were done and put away, Amy knew there wasn't much time. There wasn't a way to ease into the conversation. She just had to jump in.

She looked toward her grandparents. Aidan sat at one end of the couch reading the paper while Eva sat at the other end, her legs tucked beneath her and her fingers flying around a needlepoint design. Amy took a deep breath.

"Nana?"

"Yes, honey?" Eva's eyes remained on her needlework, but her chin lifted toward her granddaughter.

"I think I did something that's going to make Mom mad."

"What was that?"

Amy glanced at her grandfather. He continued reading the paper. "I took Lizzie's books," she said. "The ones that are supposed to go to Billy Strath. They're at my house right now."

Eva continued to work her needle. "How did you do that? I thought your dad said the books were picked up yesterday."

Amy cringed. "I know. They were. But I have them now."

Eva waited a moment before responding. "Should I ask how you know about Billy Strath? Or how you got those books?"

"Probably not."

Eva nodded. She didn't lift her gaze toward her granddaughter, and Amy wondered if she was engrossed in the needlepoint or avoiding eye contact.

"I think I know who Billy Strath is," Amy continued. The words were slow and seemed to fill the air longer than she would have liked.

"Oh honey, you don't know who he is. And it's better that way."

"He's someone you and Lizzie met in Paris over fifty years ago."

Eva's eyes rose toward her granddaughter. Aidan lowered his newspaper and looked in his granddaughter's direction as well. Amy's cheeks burned.

"Honey, you don't know who he is, and it's better that way," Eva repeated. She dropped her eyes back to the needlepoint.

"Nana," she sighed. "Please tell me about your sister. Please. Did you know that she was going to die? Did you know that she lived so close?"

Eva nodded. "I did. I knew that she was dying." She reached over the end table and switched on a lamp. "I knew the cancer had spread too far, too fast. And I went and saw her everyday for a long time."

"Cancer?"

Eva nodded.

"Were you sad?"

Eva nodded again. "I was heartbroken. I am heartbroken. She was my sister." She pursed her lips. "She is my sister." Eva continued to sew, silently, for a moment. "Where's Miles tonight? I thought that you'd bring him with you."

Amy leaned back in her chair and stared at the ceiling.

Lizzie died of cancer.

Eva wanted to know about Miles.

Amy's focus was fading—she couldn't think about Lizzie and talk about Miles at the same time. She closed her eyes, trying to untangle the competing thoughts. "Miles. I didn't want to bring him over. I knew he'd get mad if I brought up Lizzie in front of him."

"That Miles boy is a goofball," Aidan said over his newspaper, turning the page.

Amy lifted her head toward grandfather. "Grandpa! What do you mean?"

"Exactly what I said. He's a goofball. Doesn't he know that you're only young once? He's so darn serious all the time. Where's his energy? He should be running around and having fun. Not working so hard. You want to hear something about Lizzie? I'll tell you something. She was a wild woman, kicking and screaming until the end."

"Aidan, stop now," Eva said. "Read your paper."

Amy grinned at her grandfather, watching his eyes crinkle into a smile behind the newspaper.

Eva looked at Amy. "Lizzie," she paused, choosing her words, "She took a lot of chances in her life, and she paid dearly for some of them. Your mother paid for some of Lizzie's choices as well—and for her sake, let's just let this go."

But I don't want to.

Amy felt the words rise to her throat, but she stopped them from coming out.

Upon seeing Amy's fallen face, Eva continued, "Honey, just give it time."

Amy looked at the clock on the far wall and jumped out of her chair. "Oh no—I'm supposed to meet a friend, and I'm going to be late." She walked to her grandparents and gave each a hug. "I'm sorry to run out of here, but I better get going. I can't believe I lost track of time like that. Thank you so much for dinner."

Eva and Aidan stood up and followed Amy to the front door.

"You are welcome any time," Aidan said, "with or without that goofball boyfriend of yours."

Amy laughed as she walked to her car. "Goodnight, Grandpa. Goodnight, Nana."

Aidan and Eva stood in the doorway watching Amy as she backed her car out of their driveway.

"Do you think she'll give up?" Aidan asked.

Eva shook her head. "No."

"Me neither."

Amy put the car into drive and waved to her grandparents before heading down the street.

"I'm proud of her," Eva said. "She's figured out more than I expected in such a short period of time. And I've barely had a hand in it."

"It seems like something is waking up inside her."

Eva nodded and watched Amy's car shrink with distance. "We just have to keep her going." She thought about Lizzie, wondering what exactly Amy knew and how she figured it out. "History is a terrible thing to repeat." She turned and walked back into the house. "I'm going to call April."

***

Will pulled up to Amy's house, glancing at the time displayed on his stereo before turning off the truck. He was fifteen minutes early, but he jumped out anyway and walked up the driveway.

He knocked on the front door and waited. Then he knocked again. He couldn't hear anyone moving around inside the house. Impulsively, he turned the doorknob; it clicked open.

"Hello? Amy? April? Didn't your mom teach you never to leave your house unlocked?" He stepped through the door and into the entryway. "You guys are home, right?" He was answered with silence.

In the kitchen he saw the boxes of books that he figured he would be taking to Billy Strath the following day. He sat down at the table and thought about opening up a book or two—just to see if Lizzie wrote in margins the way that Amy did. He decided against it.

"No one's really here?" he said out loud, looking around the kitchen. "Really? You're not in a back room, are you?" He stood up, looking at his watch. Seven-twenty. "Okay, I'm walking to the back, just to see if anyone's here."

At the end of the hallway stood a room on either side, both their doors open. The room on the left was neat and clean; the bed was made and the desk was lined with perfect stacks of papers and books. Will assumed from the crayon drawings hanging on a bulletin board that the room was the resident kindergarten teacher's.

Through the other door, Will could see that Amy was clearly the messier of the two sisters. He walked in, feeling like he just walked into his cluttered, disorganized Westwood apartment. A ball of sheets lay at the end of her bed, clothes spilled out of a laundry basket onto the floor, and fallen over stacks of books covered her desk.

"Amy? Are you in here somewhere? Under all these clothes or something?"

The bookcase next to the closet was the only neat part of the room. Each shelf displayed a different genre of books alphabetized by author. He noticed a few empty spots on the bookcase and guessed they were for the books strewn about on her desk. He walked over to them. *Marketing for Dummies*, *Harry Potter and the Sorcerer's Stone, A Guide to Italy's Northern Coast*. Will sifted through the top layer and wondered if she was reading them all at once. Below *The Poetry of Langston Hughes* and *The Tales of Sir Lancelot,* he saw a notebook. He picked it up, knowing that he had seen her writing in it before. He opened it. In short sections across the first page he saw her familiar handwriting.

> *Last night, I had a dream about you. You were standing in a courtyard, smiling at me. That was the whole dream. And then when I woke up, my alarm clock was playing that song from our first date. It reminded me of you. I don't know if that meant today was supposed to be a good day or a bad day. And I don't know if today has turned out the way it was supposed to either. I miss you.*

> *Wasn't it John Milton who wrote, "What hath night to do with sleep?"*
> *Here I lie silently, the dark my companion, and I realize that night once held so much more than sleep for me. But now, sleep is all I hope for. A break from being awake.*
> *I hate Milton.*

> *J,*
> *The hardest part of last year was that when we were together, I felt like I could share my whole life with you. I felt like you were there listening and understanding. But then, you left.*

> *I hear people talk about having ideas for stories—they say these stories are bursting out of their heads. But they never write them down. And me, I don't have stories bursting out of my head. But I write anyway. Am I jealous? Or are they liars?*

Will turned the page.

J—
Sometimes I think you're near me. If I turn around, or look to my left, even if I look down the path, you must be there. Sometimes I scan a crowd, knowing, feeling your presence. But somehow, my eyes can't find you. Still, it's okay, because I know you're there. Somewhere.

"Do you really think you should be letting yourself into our home and going through our stuff?"

Will whirled around.

"God April, you scared me," he said.

Her eyebrows furrowed. "Says the guy found breaking and entering."

"I didn't break anything—the door was unlocked, and I thought you were home but couldn't hear me knocking." He dropped the notebook on the desk. "Hey, why don't you lock your door anyway?"

April turned and headed for the kitchen. "Talk to your friend Amy about that. She's always forgetting to lock the door after herself. It's a trait she picked up from our mother, unfortunately. Are you hungry, by the way? I can grill up some onions and make you a sandwich with the leftover sausage from last night."

"I already ate, but thank you. That sounds better than what I had." Will looked through the kitchen to the front of the house. "Where is Amy anyway?" He looked at the clock on the kitchen microwave. "She was supposed to be here by now."

April glanced at a teapot that she had placed on the stove before finding Will in the back of the house. "You never know what you're going to get with her. She could be a half hour early or an hour late. There's no rhyme or reason to how she keeps her schedule."

"Messy, late, and absent-minded about locking doors. I never would have guessed that about her. She seems so put together."

April pulled a mug from a cupboard and made a face.

"Have you met my sister? Miss Head-in-the-Clouds?"

Will grinned. "Barely, I guess." He sat down at the kitchen table and pushed a box of books aside so he could see April standing by the stove. "Hey—I thought she was going into journalism or something. But I saw a book on her desk about marketing. Is that what she's doing now?"

April nodded. "How do you know about the journalism thing?"

"A professor told me. It's a long story. What happened there—why is she in marketing?"

April grabbed a small, yellow box on the counter and pulled a tea bag from it. "Want some tea?"

Will shook his head. She poured hot water into her mug and laid a teabag across the top, watching it sink to the bottom. She walked to the kitchen table, her eyes on the mug.

"I don't know." She sat down across from Will. "I get the feeling she didn't like having to pay her dues."

"Really? Our professor made it sounds like she was a really hard worker."

April sipped her tea. "Again, have you met my sister? She doesn't seem like the kind of person who wants to jump right to the top without looking back?"

Will considered this. "Well, when you put it that way, okay."

"She went to New York right after college. She got a job working at some newspaper as a copy editor over there. Miles had to finish up his last quarter of school in the fall, and the two of them made a pact. Amy moved to New York in the summer and was going to stay there, working, through the fall. At the end of six months, she was going to decide whether or not she wanted to stay. If she decided New York was right for her, Miles was going to join her. If she didn't want to be there, she would come home and Miles would come here."

"He was going to follow her wherever she went?"

April nodded.

Will looked over the pictures hanging on the walls of the kitchen, formulating his thoughts. As though rewinding through his memories, images of Jocelyn and their time together flowed through his head. "I don't think that I could follow a girl across the country like that."

April raised an eyebrow at him. "No? But it's okay to look for a girl on the other side of the state because you have her book?"

"That's different."

"Oh, I see. Well, you're obviously not Miles."

"It certainly seems that way." Will leaned forward in his chair and rested his forearms on the table. He nodded toward Amy's bedroom. "So, why did she leave New York? Didn't she like the whole journalism thing?"

April shrugged. "I don't know. Maybe. She doesn't talk about it." April sipped her tea and then smiled, barely, her eyes on the hallway behind Will. "She doesn't talk about any of it. I think," she paused, dropping her eyes to the mug in her hands, "I think it had to do with something else."

Her eyes rose to the boxes of books on the table. A long moment passed.

"Okay, so listen," she said. "You voluntarily threw yourself into Amy's world, bringing her that book and helping her with this Lizzie stuff." Her eyes narrowed. "That doesn't entitle you to know everything about my sister, but I think there are some things you should know."

If Will could have leaned forward any further, he would have. "Like what?"

April's eyes returned to her tea. "For years, Amy had dreamed of going to New York after college. It was a dream she and her ex-boyfriend shared. She had been dating a guy named Jason—"

"Jason?" Will pointed toward Amy's room. "Is that the guy in the notebook? J?"

"Probably. I don't go around reading her notebooks like you, but she did call him J sometimes. He was a good guy. I even liked him. Together they concocted all sorts of plans for the future, like moving to New York. He was a musician, and she was a writer. It was all very bohemian. But then he broke up with her at the beginning of their senior year. I don't know why. I don't think Amy knew why either. And that was hard for her—not knowing why things turned out the way they did. But not long after they broke up, Amy started dating Miles." April's eyebrows furrowed. "It seemed strange at the time because I didn't think she was over Jason. I don't know how she could have been."

April thought for a moment. She sipped her tea.

"Anyway, Jason went to New York as planned. Even though he and Amy didn't talk anymore, they had the same circle of friends, so they always knew what the other was doing. I often wondered if Amy also went to New York hoping that she and Jason would cross paths."

"She was dating Miles though."

"I know." April shrugged. "This is just my theory."

"So, do you think she came home because she and Jason never crossed paths?"

"I think she was all alone in a tough city. And she was working as a copy editor—not a writer. What did she have going for her? She is a hard worker, but she's soft. She shatters easily." April stood up. She carried her mug to the counter and poured more hot water in it. "Do you know why I'm telling you all this?"

Will grinned. "Is it because you find me irresistibly charming and easy to talk to?"

April smirked as she walked back to the kitchen table and sat down. "Close. Because I recognize your truck. You have that stupid little surfboard hanging from your rearview mirror and that retro UCLA sticker on the back window. You were a freshmen in college when I was a senior. And you used to go tearing down the streets of Westwood to pick up your girlfriend after work. Remember that? She worked at *Jerry's Famous Deli,* right?"

Will stared at April. Slowly, he answered, "Yes."

"So did I." April cocked her head to one side and smiled. "I heard lots of stories about the disastrously reckless Will Chase." Her eyes wandered across the wall behind Will before settling on him. "I didn't recognize your name when you emailed me about Amy's book. But it clicked when I saw your truck and you get out of it."

Will slumped in his chair. "Oh," he said, remembering exactly what April described: him tearing down the streets of Westwood to pick up Jocelyn. "So were you the one always telling Jocelyn to break up with me?"

April shook her head. "Nah. The younger girls who worked there thought she should break up with you. I figured your ridiculous relationship was part of growing up. We all need a couple bad relationships so that we can recognize a good one when it comes along. And who am I to judge?"

Will raised an eyebrow at her. "So I guess you really don't find me irresistibly charming."

April chuckled. "I didn't back then, and I don't now. But I need you to remember what I told you about my sister. She shatters easily. You've come swooping into her life with a treasure she lost, and now you're indulging her in this game of family mysteries. It's straight out of one those three-hundred-year-old love stories she reads."

Will kept his eyes on the boxes of books on the table. "Okay. I don't really understand why you are telling me this."

"She has a boyfriend who has filled a void for a couple years," April continued. "He's nothing like her, and I'm not convinced he really knows who she is. But you," she shook her head, "I heard you and Amy talking last night about that Lizzie stuff. You barely know my sister, but you understand her. More than Miles." Her voice dropped, and her words slowed, punctuated with long pauses in between. "Don't shatter her."

Will stared at his hands folded on the table and tried to gather his thoughts. He wanted to tell her that he wasn't that reckless kid anymore, and he wanted to tell her that he had no plans to shatter anyone. Before he could say anything, the front door swished open.

"Sorry I'm late," Amy said, smiling breathlessly as she rushed around the corner and into the kitchen. "I went over to Nana's after work and lost track of time." She fell into the third chair at the kitchen table and blew a stray curl off her forehead.

April raised an eyebrow at Will. Then she turned to her sister and said, "You're in a good mood."

"I am. I'm finally home." Amy lifted her messenger bag onto the table and opened it, fishing through its contents. She pulled out the book of Renaissance poetry, smiling. "There was a note in here. Do you remember it?" She glanced at Will and then fanned through the pages of the book until she saw the napkin.

Will shook his head, thinking. "A note?"

Amy pulled out the napkin and began reading. "Forget about Jos and that guy. Remember what Hollings said. The planets are aligned. You are going to find Amy tomorrow!" She smiled and put the note back. Tossing the book on the table, she said, "I'm guessing your friend from Powell wrote this. What was her name? Kim? Kate? It's too funny—I think if I had known her, we would have been friends. I kept reading it today at work. It took my mind off my stupid job."

"Yeah," Will said slowly, feeling the eyes of a protective older sister on him. "You and Kim would have been great friends."

Across the kitchen, April's cell phone rang on the counter. She rose from the table to answer it.

"See you later," she said, picking it up and heading toward the back of the house. "Hey Nana…" her voice trailed off as she approached her bedroom.

"Want to look through these books?" Will asked, pointing to the boxes on the table.

Twenty

"I was hoping that Nana would tell me something about Lizzie tonight," Amy said. "But all I could pull out of her was that Lizzie died of cancer. I guess that means I don't have much to report." She nodded toward the boxes on the table. "I think we should just get these to Billy Strath as soon as possible and see if he'll tell us anything about Lizzie. Do you think he might?"

Will shrugged. "I don't know. But at this point, I think we need to try talking to him. It doesn't hurt to try. Let's take a look at the books before we haul them out to Monterey though." He started unpacking a box. "There must be a reason she left the books to him. Maybe she wrote notes to him in the margins or something."

"Okay." Amy followed his lead and began unpacking books as well. "Maybe."

The books were just like the literature Amy and Will each studied in college. Shakespearean plays; compilations of Medieval, Renaissance, and Victorian poetry; and translations of Ancient Mythologies. Copies of *The Canterbury Tales* by Geoffrey Chaucer and *Paradise Lost* by John Milton. The great American writers: Hemmingway and Steinbeck and Fitzgerald. There was no single thread that connected them—no reoccurring theme, and no obvious significance. But Will was right about Lizzie writing in the books: black pen underlined passages copiously, and the margins next to the underlined passages were littered with cryptic notes in shorthand.

"It would help if the notes made sense," Amy said under her breath. She flipped through the pages of *The Great Gatsby*. "There's nothing I can understand in here." She picked up *The Sun Also Rises* and flipped through its pages. "Nothing in here either. I think we're wasting our time."

"Amy, don't be so impatient. If I hadn't run across that tiny receipt in your book, I wouldn't have figured out who you were, and I wouldn't be standing here now. Let's not be careless and miss something."

She exhaled loudly. "I know. I just want to find something helpful."

Will continued unpacking. "Of course. Me too." Will smiled to himself, remembering the bookcase in Amy's room. "And if we don't find anything, I'll help you organize all the books according to genre before packing them up. That'll be fun, right?"

Amy tried to suppress a smile. "I love organizing books."

"Who doesn't? After hitting the bars in Westwood, I always come home and organize my books." Will picked up *The Adventures of Huckleberry Finn.* "You know, I'm not sure why Lizzie—"

Something wasn't right about the book in Will's hand; its lightness caught him off guard. When he didn't finish his sentence, Amy looked toward him.

"What? What'd you find?" she asked, watching him flip the book over and weigh it in his hands.

Will lifted the front cover. A moment later, he snapped it shut.

"What?" Amy said again. "What'd you have?"

"Oh Amy," he said, grinning. "You thought we were wasting our time." He rattled the book next to his head and said, "This isn't a book." He tossed it to her, continuing to grin.

Amy opened the front cover, and immediately her heart beat faster. Inside was a folded stack of papers. She drew out the top one and unfolded it. "It's a letter from Billy," she muttered, scanning it. "These must be the letters Lizzie left to him."

Will scooted his chair toward her and looked over her shoulder at the letter.

September 1, 1955. Miss Hathaway, I hope this note finds you well and content in pursuing all your Hollywood dreams.

"You might want to find the rest of the fake books before reading any letters," April said, walking through the kitchen to the pantry. "There are three more."

Will and Amy looked toward April. Then they looked at each other.

"What?" Amy said.

"I'm not telling you which ones." April grabbed a snack-size bag of cookies from the pantry's top shelf and headed back toward her bedroom.

"How do you know that?"

Will and Amy saw April's shoulders shrugging as she turned the corner into the hallway.

"Let's look for the others then," Will said, reaching into a box and pulling out a stack of books. He shook his head as he opened the top one. "Your sister is something else."

"Don't I know it," Amy breathed.

They shuffled through the boxes, looking for books that felt oddly light in their hands. When they sifted through all the literature, they did indeed have four hollow books: *The Adventures of Huckleberry Finn, The Divine Comedy, Canterbury Tales, and The Odyssey.*

Amy looked at the books and then at Will. She smiled. "I guess this wasn't a waste of time." She picked up the top letter and slid it halfway across the table so that she and Will could read it at the same time.

***

September 1, 1955

Miss Hathaway,

I hope this note finds you well and content in pursuing all your Hollywood dreams.

Life is all that it has been here in Paris. I continue to paint and draw in Montmartre, making enough money to keep myself fed and clothed. I continue to meet people everyday, most of whom are boring American tourists. I must say that none are as lively—or interesting—as you. Although I didn't expect it, your absence has left a small hole in my being. I sometimes forget that you are gone and find myself waiting, irritated, that you haven't come, coffee in hand, to keep me company. Even after this length of time, I still forget that you are gone.

Will you be returning? Perhaps after you wrap production on your first major movie project? Perhaps that first major project will be set in Paris and you can return then? I am certainly not the only one who misses you. The city itself seems a little darker, quieter, slower without you.

Ever yours,

Billy

Amy looked at Will. "I didn't know he could be so nice. He's acting like he actually cares about her."

Will nodded. "It's easier to write how we feel than it is to say it. Right?" He grabbed up the next letter and angled it toward Amy so she could read it with him.

October 4, 1955

Oh Billy,

I would be lying if I said that your kind letter didn't lift my spirits. I don't believe you've ever said anything nice to me directly, but I won't linger on the subject for fear that I'll never hear such words again.

Los Angeles is, well, invigorating. The pace is swift, and the air is filled with energy. It's beautiful here. Breathtaking and beautiful. I wish you were here. I do.

The weather is probably turning cold in Paris, is it not? I've never spent fall in Paris with Eva; I've always returned to school in California once summer ends. She tells me that the city is beautiful in the fall. Is it? I believe Paris is always beautiful.

Tell me more about the boring American tourists. Not one has caught your eye? Not even one?

Your Lizzie

November 10, 1955

My Dear Lizzie,

The American tourists have not caught my eye. Not even one. However, your sister has come to visit on occasion. She's not entirely happy with me, nor with the letters you and I write back and forth. In fact, I believe her exact words were, "Lizzie sees something in you that I don't understand. I suggest you leave her alone. My sister does not need a broken heart." It seems that she thinks you are fragile in ways I am unaware of. I asked her why she thought I had the power to break a heart, but in true Hathaway fashion, she turned on her heal and left.

Might you be able to shed some light on this matter?

Paris is cooling down, yet the city does remain beautiful.

Billy

Will looked up from the letter and shook his head. When Amy noticed, he looked away from her inquisitive eyes.

"What?" Amy asked. "What are you thinking about? You look like you just got bad news."

"Your sister reminds me of Eva as a girl. Don't you think? Smart—maybe too smart. And protective, but quietly protective."

"Really? I always thought I was more like Nana."

Will shook his head again. "Oh no, Amy. You're not the Eva of this generation." He nodded to the next letter. "This one's next."

December 13, 1955

Billy,

I'm sorry about my sister. Sometimes she jumps to conclusions. Sometimes she thinks she knows more than anyone. She doesn't.

Los Angeles continues to intoxicate me. I took a small part in a play running in West L.A. I'm on stage no more than three minutes, but I love every second. I continue to audition for commercials, and I met a lovely woman who said she'd get me a meeting at RKO. Maybe I'll be the next Ginger Rogers or Katharine Hepburn. I do hope she can set up that meeting.

How long do you plan to be in Paris?

Ever yours,

Lizzie

December 13, 1955

Eva,

I cannot comprehend why you would talk with Billy about me. You are my sister. You are not my mother, nor my keeper. Perhaps our parents' ambivalence toward us has made you somehow feel responsible for me. I prefer, however, that you do not. It does no good—not for me, not for you, and not for Billy. So in the future, please keep your thoughts to yourself.

After all, you are wrong about Billy and me.

I miss being in Paris with you. While Los Angeles fills me with energy and strength, a piece of me is always missing when you are not around.

I love you (especially when you aren't meddling),

Lizzie

January 17, 1956

Lizzie,

I see that Billy wants to get me in trouble. Well, that doesn't change the truth, so I will say to you what I said to him: I do not know what you see in him, and I suggest you stay away. It was one thing to frolic about Paris over the summer, but it's another thing to carry on through long distance letters. You do not need a broken heart. At the risk of sounding like "your keeper," you are feeling an onslaught of emotions as you live your dream in Los Angeles, and I don't want to see you conflating your feelings about Los Angeles with the feelings that seem to be contained in the letters you and Billy write back and forth. I know it will happen. I know you. And sadly, I think I know him. He is not too difficult to figure out.

I miss having you here. I look forward to the day that you are rich and famous with your own private plane—so that you can come visit me at my every whim.

Lizzie, don't be stupid.

Love,

Eva

January 18, 1956

Elizabeth,

I will be in Paris until something calls me away. Right now, I'm content with my surroundings, although as the weather continues to cool, I find myself wishing for the days of summer. Tourism slows this time of year. Fewer visitors means less money in hand. The artist stations thin out as the air begins to bite, and those of us who stay also thin down without the extra money for lunch or breakfast. But we stay because we know that all will improve on the other side of May. The tourists will appear, money will feed us, and our Lizzies might, if we are lucky, return.

Billy

February 27, 1956
Elizabeth,
Certainly I did not offend you with the last letter I wrote. I cannot think of a hurtful statement I might have made. Is there another reason I haven't heard from you?

I am hoping that your life in Los Angeles has swept you away into a whirlwind of work and happiness. Yet if you have the chance, I would very much enjoy getting a note from you—to know we are still connected, though more than five thousand miles away.
Billy

April 1, 1956
Oh Dear Billy,
You didn't offend me, and I am so sorry for my delayed response. You might have noticed from my return address that this letter was not sent from lovely Los Angeles. I am back in Northern California—against my will.

My parents discovered my ploy, and through a long and devastating process, they took me home. I do understand their anger, but only to an extent. They have more money than is imaginable, and they've never taken an interest in my sister or me before. Keeping me from Los Angeles is only a way to control me; they have no reason to worry about the money I've spent or the "danger" they say I was in.

But because I have no money of my own and I couldn't find a job on such short notice, I resigned to return with them. I will have to finish school and find my way back to Los Angeles on my own one day. It will be suffocating. They do not trust me to live on campus; I now have to live under their roof and commute to school.

This sudden concern about my life infuriates me. And Eva is so far away. She can't intervene on my behalf the way she did when we were younger, and she can't keep me company in my infuriating, suffocating loneliness. I miss her so much.

They are also making me work to pay back the money I "squandered" over the few months I was living my dream. I secured a job in the library at the University near my parent's home—Stanford. I tried to get a job at my University but could not. My reputation seems to have preceded me. No one thought it wise to put me on payroll, nor did they have a problem telling me so. It has been hard to hear that the fun I had in my prior life has had such a drastically negative effect on the present.

I hope that spring brings you joy and warmth.

Forever yours,

Lizzie

Amy folded the letter and held it to her chest. "She got caught," she breathed. "I don't know if I should feel sorry for her or not."

"I'm rooting for her," Will said. "She's crazy, but I want her to get her way. Most people don't have the guts to pull the stunts she tried." He leaned back in his chair and rested his hands behind his neck. "I wish she were still alive. I bet she had some incredible stories."

Amy nodded and placed the folded letter in the stack of already-read letters. She stared off toward the kitchen window. "I wish Nana would talk. She's the only one who can fill in the blanks."

Will lifted the next letter. "We'll figure out how to tackle that once we're done here. Let's see what Billy had to say in response."

May 6, 1956

Elizabeth,

Perhaps because of your determination, your strength, and your slight, endearing insanity, I thought you would become a wildly successful actress before your parents found you out. How could I have been so wrong? How could they have found out?

I hope working at the library does not bore you. I'm sure it doesn't; how could it? Being surrounded by books—great books—must make your punishment a little more bearable. I am impressed that you chose such a place to work. It reminds me of all the reasons I enjoyed spending time with you. Your intelligence, your sharpness, your beauty—they are all qualities I found in books and knew I wanted to see in real life. That you appeared, embodying them all, was quite a delight to me. I hope knowing this helps you see how lucky you are to work in such a place. If I were not working in Montmartre, I would be jealous.

Tell me stories about your new life.

Yours,

Billy

May 10, 1956

Lizzie,

Is it as awful as it seems? Our parents' house must be like a prison. Between college and the boarding schools, it's been years since we've lived there consistently, yet I still remember the heavy chill that always filled that house. It was so dark, so expansively dark. There's no need for me to describe this to you—you're living it and need no reminder. My heart goes with you. I wish that I could kidnap you and bring you back to Paris with me. I'm not sure that our parents would really miss you.

Enclosed are some pages that I wrote about your last summer here. If you'd like to change anything in them, they are yours to change. I just thought I would send them—perhaps to cheer you up. I hope the memories do not make your heart ache any harder.

Love,

Eva

June 16, 1956

Oh Eva,

Your words are perfect, and I love you so very much for sending the manuscript. (Is that what you'd call it?) I had no idea you were documenting. It's fascinating to see your interpretation of the summer. You are both insightful and imaginative in ways I was unaware. I will certainly cherish this. As much as I hate living at home, I love the escape you've provided me through these words.

Love,

Lizzie

"She's got to be referring to what we read last night." Amy leaned back in her chair. "Insightful and imaginative," she continued. "So, what does that mean? Are we not supposed to believe everything that Eva wrote? Insightful and imaginative. Was *Eva's Words* exaggerated? What do you think?"

Will shrugged. "I think we can only believe what is there on the paper. Maybe you can ask Billy about it—what's true and what's not."

Amy studied the kitchen window. "Insightful and imaginative," she murmured. "It was beautiful, wasn't it? *Eva's Words*—it was beautiful." She drummed her fingers on the table. "I wish I could write that way."

"You can—"

Amy shook her head, cutting him off with the gesture. "No, not like that."

"Just because you don't doesn't mean you can't. You just have to have a reason to."

Amy nodded and turned to the next letter.

June 16, 1956

Dearest Billy,

I miss you. Will you ever come for me? Will you ever take me out of this hellish world otherwise known as my parents' house? Their sudden interest in my life is stifling. Eva and nannies raised me because our parents were so distant—their new-founded desire to know everything has born a resentment in me I never knew I could harbor. I could have used parents for the first fifteen years of my life. Now is not the time. It's too late.

I do, however, understand their distrust. I have given them reason to doubt my character. Still, I feel imprisoned. I work at the library more than necessary—only to evade their constant watch. Just yesterday I found my mother going through the shoebox of letters you've written to me. I fear I will need to keep them under lock and key—or burn them. I have to keep my parents away, somehow.

When will you come for me?

Forever yours,

Lizzie

Twenty-one

Amy flipped through the letters they had just read. "That's it—no more letters from the *Huck Finn* book." She reached for *The Odyssey* and fanned through the letters it had held. "It looks like these are all from Lizzie to Billy. There aren't any that he wrote back to her." Amy pursed her lips together. "That's strange. I wonder if we've misplaced them—or if they're somewhere else."

"Or maybe they don't exist." Will looked over Amy's shoulder as she flipped through the letters for a second time. "They all look really short. What do they say?"

Amy scanned them, shuffling through them yet again. "*Billy, I miss you…Billy, when are you coming to California…Billy I miss you…I don't think my parents will let me visit Eva this summer…Billy, why haven't I heard from you…Eva says you are still around…Billy, I hate working…Billy, I always thought you might just magically show up one day, but it appears you won't…I've been so foolish to think about you so much…Billy, how could you abandon me…Billy, I hate my job, the books, the people who read the books…Eva was right about you...I think I'm going to stop writing to you…Billy, do you want me to stop writing to you…Billy, if you would just answer me once—to tell me I must move on or I must continue writing…Why haven't you come for me…*" Amy shuffled them one final time. "That seems to be the gist of them."

"Desperate."

"Yeah." Amy put the letters back in the *Odyssey* book. "Hey, I've been thinking about what you said earlier. What did you mean when you said that I'm not this generation's Eva? What's wrong with being like Eva?"

"There's nothing wrong with being like Eva. I just think April is more like her."

"Well, I'm not like Lizzie."

Will grabbed *The Divine Comedy* and handed it to Amy. "Maybe you could just be *you* and not worry about being like any of your older relatives."

Amy bit her lip. "Yeah, okay." She took the book from Will and pulled out the stack of letters. Flipping through them, she said, "The letters in here are from both Lizzie and Billy. Good."

December 15, 1956
Billy,
Your surprise visit was the highlight of, well, my year. I know that it took a lot of money and a lot of time for you to come to California and find me at this little library where I work. Thank you, again. Being near you felt like an escape to this morbid reality, even if it were only for a few days. I imagine the look on my face when you walked in was that of complete shock; I'm sure it was funny to you—seeing me so ruffled with disbelief. After all the letters I sent with no response from you…I now realize you were probably planning your trip during that time and wanted to surprise me. Billy, how I adore you.

I only wish that you could have stayed longer. It saddens me that you needed to return to Paris so quickly. Why is it that you needed to return to Paris at all? I know we've already discussed this, but why? Your answers never satisfied me. Why can you not stay here? Then I could truly escape from my parents forever. We could run away. We could go anywhere you want. It doesn't matter if I go back to Los Angeles right now. I could go anywhere. As long as I am with you, and as long as we can find a place for you to practice your trade, we will be fine. In my spare time here, I've learned where my parents keep a secret stash of money. We could take it and never look back.

I miss you, yet again. Please come back.
Forever yours,
Lizzie

January 20, 1957
Elizabeth,
I'm glad that you are still reveling in the surprise of my visit. I am glad that I was able to come and see what you are doing and how you are living. Stanford University certainly is very different from the Sorbonne, is it not? The students are so very different. I recall your sister recently telling me that she spent a great deal of time choosing between those two Universities after both acceptance letters came. I believe she made the right choice.

Perhaps I will make another trip out there one day. Perhaps you will make a trip out here. We both must follow whatever paths lay before us. If they converge, then they converge—and we will be richer in life experiences, won't we? Perhaps we will both steal away from our responsibilities for a time and meet in Los Angeles. You could then show me your life there.

I do hope that you are concocting more plans to escape your current situation. You do not need to live under such an oppressive rule.

Yours,
Billy

February 26, 1957
Dearest Billy,

Your last letter leaves me tentative. I realize that it could be interpreted in various ways, and I am sure that was intentional. My uncertainty does not come from being unable to interpret your true feelings, but instead it comes from being unsure as to why you'd write in such a way. Do you not want to be with me? Do you not know if you want to be with me? Do you not know if it's possible to be with me? I would like a straight answer. I am confused.

Do you want me to escape my current situation with thoughts of you leading my way? Or do you think any escape would suffice? If you could not tell by my letters, you certainly could tell from your visit that my life has shrunk considerably since being forced to live with my parents. My freedoms are minimal, and this current state is killing my spirit. Aside from Eva, you are my only outlet. My only joy. My only hope for something better. I feel helpless and small as I write this; I am not the girl you met in Montmartre, yet I am still me. And I must be truthful with myself and with you. To ever be the girl I was in Montmartre again, I must break free. I am unsure, however, how to do that without you.

Forever yours,
Lizzie

March 30, 1957
Dearest Elizabeth,
Your desperation will not give you the strength to overcome your unhappiness. You are a strong and passionate girl. You must draw on that to come through this unhappiness. I am not the only answer. Relying on me would be a mistake. You are right; you are not the girl I met in Montmartre. She did not need me. And should our paths ever cross again, it cannot be because you need me. A relationship of any kind based on need would not work for either of us. You know that—somewhere in your soul, you know that.
I do hope that our paths will cross again.
The sun is beginning to shine a little more in Paris these days. It is beautiful to know that spring is edging near. The new life, new growth, new colors remind me of you. Of your eyes, your hair, your skin, your smile. You are springtime in so many ways.
Billy

May 3, 1957
Dear Billy,
Would it surprise you to know that I was somewhat insulted by your last letter? It shouldn't surprise you; you've always had a knack for insulting me.
More importantly, would it surprise you to know that I'm engaged? It should—you rarely ask about my life outside the misery associated with living under my parents' rule.
Well, I thought it was quite time I told you. I am to marry a man who attends law school at Stanford. He will be graduating in late June, and soon thereafter we will have our wedding. Shall I send you an invitation?
Lizzie

"What? Engaged?" Will asked, slamming his hands down on the table. "What is she doing?" He looked at Amy, waiting, as though she had an answer. "What's wrong with your grandmother? Is she insane?"

"I think it's been established that she is insane." Amy threw the last letter across the table and slumped down on her chair. "She couldn't have married someone else. How could she do that? Who could she possibly marry?" She pushed her hair behind her ears and shook her head. "Did she go out and grab the first guy she saw at the Stanford library and demand he marry her? She seemed like she was so devoted to Billy. How could this happen?"

Will didn't answer right away.

"Maybe it's a game, just like how she moved to Los Angeles and told her parents she was going back to school."

"For some reason," Amy said slowly, "I don't think so. Faking it wouldn't be hurtful enough." She pushed herself up in her chair and eyed the only letter that came from final book. "And this," she nodded toward the letter, "is all we have from *Canterbury Tales.*" She picked it up, scanning it. "More than two years separate the letter we just read and this one. How can that be? There must be so much more to say." She looked at Will. "We must be missing something."

Will shrugged. "I don't know."

August 15, 1959

Elizabeth,

Eva tells me that your second child is on the way. I believe congratulations are in order. I do hope that you've found some semblance of happiness with the first child, if not with your husband. How is he these days, by the way? Has he managed to get any sun, or do you find paleness to be part of his charm?

I am in New York now. I am no longer making money from artistic ventures. My work is currently far more tedious, but now is not the time to go into that.

As you can see, enclosed are the letters you've written to me over the years. Certainly they are better left in your possession than in mine.

Should you feel the desire to contact me, you know where I am. I may be on my way to the west coast soon—for business dealings, of course.

Billy

Twenty-two

Will watched Amy return the letter to the *Canterbury Tales* book. She rubbed her eyes, and he wondered if she was physically tired or mentally tired. Or both.

He looked clock across the kitchen. It was getting late.

Without thinking, the first words that came to mind left his mouth.

"*What hath night to do with sleep?*"

"Hmm?" Amy yawned. She looked at the clock as well. "Ah, yes. *What hath night to do with sleep*. One of the few lines by John Milton I actually like. Begrudgingly. What made you think of that?"

Will thought of the notebook that he had found in her room. "It just popped into my head."

"I used to understand what Milton meant when he wrote that." She rested her head on a pile of books. "What hath night to do with sleep? *Nothing*, I once thought. I could stay up forever. But now, night has everything to do with sleep." She closed her eyes.

"That sounds like something you'd write about," Will said.

Her eyebrows rose over still-closed eyes. "Really? Maybe." She looked at him and forced a smile. "A long time ago, maybe. So what do we do now?"

Will looked toward the patio door, which had remained open from the time that the sun warmed the sky. Cool air wafted through the screen. "Let's go to Monterey tomorrow and ask Billy about Lizzie. You should come with me to take the books back."

"Tomorrow is Friday. I work."

"Take a sick day. Don't go to work tomorrow."

Amy closed her eyes again. "I can't take a sick day."

Will got up and closed the patio door. "Why not?"

"*Why not?* I *work.*"

He locked the door and returned to the kitchen table. "So? Amy, seriously. *So* what?"

Amy rubbed her eyes again. "I hate my job," she muttered.

"Good. Then you'll come."

Will nodded toward the books strewn about on the table. “Let’s get these boxed up.” He grabbed two books and put them in the closest box.

“Don’t worry about it,” Amy said. “I’ll do it tonight. You’ve helped me so much already—I can do this.”

“You sure?”

“Positive.”

Amy stood, and they walked to the front door.

“Why don’t I come and get you around nine o’clock tomorrow?” Will opened the door and waited for a response.

She nodded.

He reached out and patted the side of her shoulder. “Tomorrow is going to be a good day. And going to see Billy Strath is definitely a good reason to skip work. See you later.” With that, he turned and headed toward his truck.

Amy smiled. “Thanks,” she called after him. She closed the door. Just as she turned toward the kitchen, a knock stopped her. She turned back around and opened the door, finding Will on the front porch.

“Hey,” he said. “Don’t forget to lock this.” He tapped on the doorframe.

Before she could respond, he was on his way back down the walkway.

She smiled, surprised. “Okay, thanks.”

He waved over his shoulder; she closed and locked the door, still smiling.

After putting all the books away and stashing the boxes in the hall closet, she went to the family room where she turned on the television and lay down on the couch. She closed her eyes.

The darkness behind her eyes gave way to an image of the Eiffel Tower. She stood in front of it, looking at the top, knowing that she somehow had to get up there. How? She walked around it, over and over, looking for an entrance and finding none. Desperation quickened her heartbeat as she realized that she *had* to get up there somehow. Something was at the top—something she needed…

A noise came from the front door. Amy lifted her head toward the sound, but once she remembered that Miles was supposed to come over, she dropped it back to the couch.

"Hey," she said as he entered the room. She pinched the inside corners of her eyes toward her nose, trying to wake up.

"Hey there," he replied, sitting down by her feet. "Were you asleep?"

She looked at the clock on the television cable box. "Yeah, I think so. When I laid down here, some silly sitcom was on, but now it's some late night talk show."

"You look tired." Miles reached for the remote and pointed it toward the television. "Any good guests on the show tonight?"

"I don't know. You can change it."

Miles flipped through the channels, finally settling on an old Saturday Night Live skit. Amy felt herself drifting off, but every time the audience on television laughed, she found herself surfacing to consciousness. She wondered if Miles was watching the show or dozing as she was. From where she was lying, she could only see his profile, and it appeared he was chuckling along with the audience—not nearly as tired as she.

"Miles?" she yawned, after being roused from sleep yet again, "are you happy?"

"Sure," he said, his eyes remaining on the television. "Are you?"

"I don't like my job." She yawned again. "I really, really don't like my job."

"You have a great job."

"I don't like it. It's not what I want to do."

"Find something else then."

Amy closed her eyes again, wondering if it was just that simple. "But you're happy? With life in general?"

"Yeah. Things are good. Easy. Right?"

Amy nodded, her eyes still closed. "Right."

***

As soon as Will left Amy's house, he pulled out his cell phone and made a call. It rang only once before being answered.

"Now, why in the world would you call me this late when we aren't even in school?" Kim asked, skipping the usual hello. "It must mean good news."

Will laughed. "There's really no other reason to call—

except for bad news, I guess."

Kim also laughed. "True. So, do you have an update for me about the girl with the book? Have you chased your way across the Grecian Urn to find her?"

"Good memory, Kim," he said, surprised that she remembered the Grecian Urn reference from Amy's book. "It's been something like that. Actually, it's taken a turn you'd never expect."

As he drove home, he told her about everything that had happened since leaving Los Angeles—about meeting Amy at the coffee shop, about her discovery of a long-long grandmother, and about the family history they were uncovering together. When he finished, she didn't say anything right away.

"Kim, are you there? Did I bore you to death?"

"No, not at all. It's just that you're right—I never expected this. Wow. So," she continued, slower now, "what do you think of Amy?"

"Well, she has a boyfriend. It doesn't matter what I think of her."

Again Kim didn't answer right away.

"Tell me more about her," she finally said.

"She's got blond hair and green eyes, and she's probably as tall as—"

"No, that's not what I mean. Tell me why you volunteered to help find Lizzie. What was it about Amy that made you do it?"

Will had been thinking about this very question for awhile. He wasn't often apt to engage inself-reflection, but maybe it was time. Maybe talking about it would help him understand it better himself.

"Honestly?" he asked.

"Of course."

"Okay." He took a deep breath. "Well, when I first met her, if you could call it that, she was just words on a page. And I think what got to me was that she explained how Jocelyn felt when we broke up. She said what Jocelyn never could say. It reminded me of why I wanted to get my act together this year. I didn't want to be that impetuous, thoughtless guy anymore. All it got me was mediocre grades and a bad break up. And all I ever did was hurt myself and hurt others. I know I'm not entirely there yet, but I've been working on it."

He paused, thinking. Kim said *uh-huh* to fill the silence and let him know she was listening.

"Then when I met her, she was so embarrassed by everything she had written in the margins of the book—she was so embarrassed that I had read it. And that made me realize why Jocelyn couldn't have told me what she was really feeling. Who wants to be that vulnerable in front of someone so thoughtless and reckless?" He paused again, letting his own question sink in. "Anyway, there's just something really honest about Amy and the way she expresses herself—"

"Which is ironic since she's lying to her boyfriend about this whole thing."

"No kidding."

"Hmmm."

"And when Chris showed up saying that it was time to go, I just didn't want to leave. I didn't know enough about her yet. I mean, I knew enough to know that I wanted to find out more. I probably would have made up any excuse to stay. Then an excuse presented itself through her grandmother, so I took it."

"Do you know enough about her now?"

He couldn't keep himself from grinning. "Can you ever really know enough about someone?"

"Probably not. Too bad she has a boyfriend."

April's words from earlier that evening rung in Will's head. *Don't shatter her.*

"Yeah," he said, "but I'm not worried about that. I like being around her, and I like trying to figure out what happened in her family, but I'm not going to get between her and her boyfriend. Like I said, I don't want to be that guy anymore."

Will turned into his parents' neighborhood and slowed down.

"Hey Kim, I'm almost home, so I better get going."

"Sure. Thanks for updating me. So far your summer has been much more interesting than mine. Let me know what happens after you go to Monterey."

"I will."

Twenty-three

The doorbell rang exactly at nine o'clock. When Amy answered it, Will was not standing on the porch as she expected. He was down a couple yards on the walkway, his arms extended outward, his lips curved into a great smile.

"It's a beautiful day," he said. "I'd suggest a picnic, but we've got better things to do." He dropped his arms and walked toward the doorway. "Are you ready to go get the rest of the story from Billy?" As he neared Amy, the gleam in his eyes brightened. "Aren't you excited?" He reached out and squeezed her shoulders for a second before walking past her and into the house.

"I think I'm more nervous than excited," she said, following Will.

"Don't be. There's no point in that. This is nothing but exciting. Where are the boxes?"

"In the hall closet. Miles came over last night, so I had to hide them."

As Will opened the closet door and grabbed the first box, he smirked and rolled his eyes—not even realizing he had done so. "Sounds like a pain in the ass. It's too bad that he doesn't understand what you're doing."

Amy didn't answer.

They loaded the boxes into the back of Will's truck and pulled out of the driveway. Amy's stomach flipped and flopped as they passed rows of houses, which melted into rows of shops, which melted into the road leading to the freeway. She couldn't find her voice—although even if she had, no words seemed worth speaking.

"Why are you so quiet?" Will asked once they were on the freeway. He glanced at her. "Oh, you printed directions. Great." He reached over and pulled the paper from Amy's hands. "And where are we going anyway?" His eyes alternated between the road and the directions for a few seconds before he handed the paper back to Amy. "Can you tell me where we're going?"

"You're going the right way," Amy said, keeping her eyes on the road. We've got about twenty miles before you need to worry about getting on Highway 1. I'll let you know." She dropped the directions to her lap and looked out the window.

"What's wrong?" Will asked. "Are you really that nervous?"

"I don't know. Maybe? It seems silly, but I guess I am."

"That's okay. It's not every day that you take your estranged grandmother's possessions to her long-lost boyfriend and interrogate him about events from over fifty years ago. Let's talk about something else then." He merged into the far left lane to maneuver around a line of cars going sixty-five miles an hour. "So, Professor Hollings told me that you were going into journalism—not marketing. What happened with that?"

Amy put her elbow on the window ledge and rested her head against her fist. She stared out the window. "Oh. Nothing. That didn't work out."

"What do you mean it didn't work out? You're, what, twenty-three? You have to give a career like ten years before you can determine whether it's working out. Not a couple of months."

Amy looked at Will and frowned. "What?"

"You can't give up on something so quickly. You know what that comes from? Giving up, I mean? It comes from being too hard on yourself."

Amy looked back out the window. "I'm not sure what to say about that."

"I didn't mean to sound rude. I'm sorry. That came out wrong. But like when you went to New York—"

"I never told Professor Hollings that I was going to New York." Amy turned back toward Will. "How did you know that I went to New York?"

Will cringed. "Oops."

"What?"

"Okay, your sister told me. Yesterday—when you were late getting home."

Amy turned forward again. A moment of silence lapsed before she spoke. "What did she tell you?"

"Nothing." When Amy didn't respond, he continued, "Okay, not nothing. She didn't say anything bad though. She just said that you and your ex-boyfriend planned to go to New York, but then you broke up and didn't know if you should go, but then you decided to go anyway. But then you decided you didn't like it—so then you came back."

All the blood seemed to drain from Amy's head. She grabbed her purse from where it rested at her feet and pulled out her cell phone. She texted April: *Why did you tell Will about Jason?*

"I don't want to talk about it," she said, dropping her phone back into her purse.

"Okay. I'm sorry. I didn't mean to upset you."

"I'm not upset." Before Will could reply she continued, "It's just that she shouldn't have told you about Jason or New York or whatever else she told you. It's not her story to tell."

"She's your sister. We were just talking." He glanced at her before changing lanes to move around another slow driver. "And she wasn't telling me to be gossipy. She was telling me because she loves you. She just wants you—"

"Did she tell you that I can't take care of myself?" Amy pressed two fingers into each of her temples and closed her eyes. "I can't believe her. I'm not—"

"Amy, stop. It's okay. That's not what she said." Will wasn't sure how to dig himself out of the hole he was in, so he just kept talking. "She didn't say anything that made you look bad or weak. She was just making conversation. You even said that she doesn't always think before she speaks, and clearly I don't either. It's not a big deal, and plus, we're on our way to do something pretty exciting. Let's just think about that. Let's just forget the last sixty seconds, okay?"

They sat in silence as Will continued driving. Amy tried to push the heat off her face by taking deep breaths inconspicuously. And she tried to figure out why she was so angry—yet she couldn't.

"Are you going to ignore me the whole way there?" Will said after a few minutes. "C'mon, don't be like that. I can't stand silence." He reached over and pushed her shoulder. "This is supposed to be fun, remember?"

Amy forced a half smile, keeping her eyes on the road. "You need to start getting over to the right."

***

Will slowed as he pulled onto a thin, winding road leading to Billy's house. Amy stared out the window, seeing more and more ocean as the road grew steeper and steeper. Soon she realized the house they approached sat atop a cliff—almost entirely surrounded by water crashing against rocks below. Upon arriving at the circular driveway, complete with a fountain in its center, she wondered if they had mistakenly gone to a hotel rather than Billy's house. She halfway expected a valet to appear from between the great white columns on either side of the front door and whisk their vehicle away.

"You ready?" Will asked, throwing the truck into park and reaching for his door handle.

Amy nodded. Taking a deep breath, she opened her door and stepped out.

The front door was elaborately engraved and sounded heavy as Amy knocked on it. When it opened, a small, wrinkled woman stood behind it. "Yes?" she asked without smiling.

"Hello. I have a delivery for Mr. Strath," Amy said. "Some boxes of books." She searched the woman's face for a sign of recognition.

"Is he expecting you?"

"Well, he knows there were some books left to him," she said. "May I have a word with him?"

The woman opened the door wider, inviting them in. Amy stepped inside.

"I'll go get the boxes," Will said.

Amy nodded, walking behind the woman. Dread settled in her stomach. She turned back to Will and suddenly heard herself saying, "I think I should talk to him by myself."

He turned and saluted her as though saying *anything you want.*

The hallway was wide and long. On either side of it were rows of closed doors, and between doors, leather chairs lined the walls, looking starkly black against the white paint and the sunshine flowing through skylights. It ended with a winding staircase.

The woman led Amy upstairs and into a small room with a hardwood floor and velvet furniture. There, the woman told her to wait. Amy sat down in a chair and examined the paintings on the walls. They reminded her of Monet, but she knew they weren't Monet. She wondered if Billy had painted them—or if his artist friends from Montmartre had painted them. She tried to remember the name of the artist who had told Billy about Lizzie the first day they met, but before the name struck her, the woman was back and asking Amy to follow her into another room.

It was a library—a library bigger than the bookstore in Los Gatos. Books lined the walls from floor to ceiling, and toward the back of the room was a desk. Behind it sat a gray, unsmiling man—and behind him stood a wall of windows.

"Hello," Amy said walking into the room. She stopped a few paces in and looked around herself. She stifled the urge to say *wow.* Then she continued into the room and stopped by the empty chair at the edge of the desk. Through the wall of windows she could see the ocean waving at her, and she told herself not to let the beauty sweep her off task.

"My name is Amy Winthrow. I'm Elizabeth Hathaway's granddaughter." She sat down, knowing she hadn't been invited but needing to—the icy look on the man's face made her legs shaky. "I know that you said you didn't care about the books that Lizzie left you—"

"Why are you here?"

The man's hollow, scratchy voice made her wince. He stared at her through dark eyes surrounded by leathery skin. His thin lips pursed into a short frown. His wrinkly fingers tapped a pen on the edge of the desk.

"I'm here because I was coming out this way, and I thought I would save you the trouble of—"

"And is that why you needed a moment to talk to me? To tell me you brought me something I care nothing about?"

Downstairs, Will finished unloading the books into the hallway. He sat down in a black leather chair to wait for Amy. He looked around, wondering why everything looked so bare.

Amy winced again at Mr. Strath's voice. "Well sir, I wanted to tell you that the books were here—"

"And what else? My housekeeper could have dealt with that. Can't you tell I'm too old—and too busy—to have conversations with someone like you?"

Amy fell silent, afraid to ask anything of Billy yet also

afraid to leave without trying. Softly, more meekly than she would have liked, she said, "I was hoping that you could tell me a little about my grandmother."

His eyes narrowed. "Who is your mother?"

"My mother? Deborah Winthrow."

He huffed. "I'm not telling you anything."

Amy's heart dropped. She took a deep breath and folded her hands in her lap. "Why not?"

"You don't have any right to know."

Amy pushed a couple of curls behind her ear and leaned forward in her chair, politely, earnestly. "Lizzie was my grandmother. Doesn't that give me a right to know?"

"No."

The answer stunned her. She leaned back. Her eyes wandered over the walls, waiting for the sting to subside. "Okay," she said.

"Miss Winthrow, you might as well stop wasting my time with these questions. Please show yourself out."

Amy rose from her chair. She left the room without a word and remained silent all the way down the stairs and out of the house. Will stood when he saw her coming and watched her walk past him. He followed her outside, trotting to catch up, and unlocked the truck's passenger door for her. He jumped into the driver's seat and drove away from the house, waiting for her to say something.

As they cruised down the winding road, Will fought the urge to ask what happened. It couldn't have been good, he figured, or he would have heard about it already.

She didn't speak until they were back on the freeway.

"That man!" she began, putting down the window to cool her burning skin. "He wouldn't tell me anything. He wouldn't even tell me why he wouldn't tell me anything. All he said was that it was none of my business. And he was so mean about it. Why does everybody think this is none of my business?" She rubbed an eye. "I'm telling you, as soon as I get home I'm going over to Nana's house. Again. And I'm going to tell her that she can't do this to me. That she has to tell me something. Because she has to. She does, doesn't she? I mean, she can't just leave me in the dark like this. It's already gotten too deep into my head.

She has to tell me something."

Will looked into the rearview mirror and merged into the fast lane. He glanced at Amy and nodded. "Right."

She shook her head, looking out the window. "I can't believe this."

Will glanced at Amy. "Hey, we'll figure something out. This is only a minor setback. It's not over."

She nodded.

"I'm sorry he was so mean. There was no need for that."

She closed her eyes. "I should have expected it. We already knew he wasn't a nice person. I just—I don't know—I just was hoping it would have gone differently. Maybe you should have gone in there with me."

"That probably wouldn't have changed anything. Let's just think about what our next step should be."

Amy opened her eyes and nodded out the window.

***

Back in the library at the Strath residence, Billy opened his top desk draw and drew out a single sheet of paper. He unfolded it and read it slowly, as though he hadn't already read it one hundred times before.

Dearest Billy,
In so many ways my life began when I met you. And in so many other ways, my life ended. I don't know if I should thank you or curse you. I do, however, know this: I love you. Cancer has eaten away at me, and I couldn't let it finish me off without telling you. My daughters have refused to acknowledge me, and it has been decided that my granddaughters should never know who I was. But my life has not been a waste because I have loved you.
Ever yours,
Lizzie

He swung around in his chair and looked out the windows behind his desk. The sight of water calmed him. *It has been decided that my granddaughters should never know who I was.*

The words rolled through his mind again.

"Oh, Liz," he muttered to the water beyond the windows. "She's got your determination. She knows something whether or not she's supposed to."

He turned back around in his chair and returned the note to his desk drawer, wondering whose wishes he was heeding when he refused to tell Amy about her grandmother.

Twenty-four

"So what are you going to do now?" Will asked. "Are you going to Eva's?"

He and Amy were back in Los Gatos. He didn't plan on staying long at Amy's house—he went in only to grab a bottle of water before heading home.

Amy shook her head, reaching for the refrigerator door. "No. I'll probably just go into work."

"Why? You have the day off. You might as well take advantage of it. Go shopping or surprise your boyfriend for lunch or something. Do something fun."

Amy placed a bottle of water on the kitchen counter. "Lunch with Miles would be a good idea. I haven't done that in a long time."

Will nodded, reaching for the water. He twisted off the cap and gulped half the bottle. As he set it back on the counter, he said, "Hey, I was thinking—you know that note I put in your Renaissance poetry book? Can I see it? I was trying remember something that Kim wrote in it."

"Sure." She stood up and moved toward the family room. "I think I left it in here last night." Will followed her. "It should be on that end table," she said, pointing to the table at the far end of the couch, "but I don't see it." She placed her hands on her hips and walked around the coffee table. "Where is it?"

"Could it have fallen behind the couch?" Will asked.

"Maybe," Amy muttered. She was on her hands and knees looking beneath the coffee table. "It's not here. Is it on the floor over by you?"

He tilted his head to look underneath the end table closest to him. "No, I don't see it."

She sat up on her heels and pushed her hair behind both ears. "Where'd it go?"

"Did you pack it up with the rest of the books yesterday?"

She shook her head at the wall and then walked on her knees to the fireplace opposite the couch. She looked behind the plant sitting on the hearth and then behind the nearby television set. "I don't know where it went."

"I bet you sent it to Monterey with the other books."

Amy scanned the room again, her face getting loose and long. "I couldn't have. I'm sure I brought it in here with me last night." Her shoulders dropped. "I couldn't have possibly given up that book twice."

Will walked around the room, looking in all the corners, behind all the furniture. "Well, it's not here anymore."

Her shoulders dropped further. She bit her upper lip, her eyes on the couch across the room. "I'm sorry. Now I can't give you that note."

Will sat down on the couch. "That's okay. Not a big deal. At least no one else will see it—except Billy, of course." He grinned at her. After a moment he noticed that her eyes were still focused on the couch. "Amy?"

"Yeah." Her eyes didn't move.

He waited, watching her, wondering if silence would bring her eyes upward. When it did not, he said, "You want me to go back and get that book for you?"

She shook her head. "No. That's all right."

"I could go get it for you tomorrow. This afternoon, even."

She shook her head again.

"Why not?"

Her eyes finally rose to his, and she managed a weak smile in return. "It's not important."

"Of course it is. It's yours." He winked at her. "I'll go get it this afternoon. I don't feel like going home right now anyway. And you had enough of Billy Strath today. Now it's my turn."

She nodded at the couch. "Okay."

Will walked back into the kitchen and grabbed his water bottle. "Okay, I'm leaving now—I will call you after I get the book." He stood in the hallway and saw that Amy hadn't moved. "You go surprise Miles for lunch. I'll talk to you later." He turned to walk toward the front door.

"Will?"

He stopped, his hand on the doorknob. "Yeah?" He looked down the entryway toward her voice.

"Thank you."

"No problem."

When Will jumped into his truck, he grabbed his cell phone

and pulled up his voicemail. The first was his mother, asking if he was going to be home for dinner. The second was Chris.

Will, buddy, I haven't heard from you in a couple days. What's going on? Give me a call when you get a chance. It looks like I got a job. I start next week. It's going to be a pain in the ass, but I think it'll look good on my resume. Anyway, talk to you later.

He dialed Chris' number and waited to see if his roommate would pick up.

"Hey Will," Chris said after a few rings. "What are you doing?"

"Nothing. Just leaving Amy's. So you got a job?"

"Yeah. I'm going to be working at my dad's company. Not that interesting. You're still hanging out with that girl?"

"Yeah." Will merged onto the freeway, embarking on the same path he and Amy had taken to Billy Strath's house just a couple hours before. "What kind of job is it?"

"I'll be in the sales department. They tried to make it sound cool, but I'm basically just some guy's assistant. So why are you still hanging out with that girl?"

"I don't know. Because it's more fun than getting a job where I'll be some salesman's lackey. Hey, since you aren't going to be around much once you start working, do you want to come with me on a little field trip this afternoon? I'm heading out to Monterey to do a favor for Amy. Want to come?"

Chris hesitated. "What did you get yourself into now?"

"Nothing. She left something at this super-old, super-crazy-rich guy's house, and I'm going to get it for her."

"Sounds interesting. Who's this guy?"

"Billy Strath." Will checked his mirrors to see if he could move to the right lane.

"That's not what I meant," Chris said, exasperated. "Who's this guy? I mean, if he's so rich, how'd he—never mind. I'm sitting at my computer. I'll Google him. It could take years to get a useful explanation from you."

"Are you coming with me or not?" Will said, equally exasperated and speeding up to pass a car on his right. "I have to get off the freeway if I'm coming to pick you up."

Chris' only answer was the sound of fingers pecking on a keyboard. "William Strath? Born 1933 in Florida—"

"Yeah, yeah—that's him. Good idea to Google him. I didn't think of that."

"Then let me finish." Chris scanned the information in front of him, muttering under his breath along the way. "Did art design work on television shows in late fifties," he scanned further. "Moved to New York and spent the early sixties doing art design on movies. Won some awards. Oh, this is random. He opened his own publishing house in 1965. It was called Strath Publishing—unique, huh? He sold it to Harper Collins in 1980 and started investing in real estate. In the early nineties he moved to Northern California and finally settled in Monterey in 1996. Wow—interesting guy. Yeah, I'll come. Maybe I can ask him how to work my way up the corporate ladder. Hey, why are we going to see him again?"

Will tried to visualize a timeline of Lizzie and Billy's interactions using both Chris' information and the letters he and Amy had read the night before. "I have some questions I want to ask him about Amy's grandma."

Twenty-five

Amy wandered around the house after Will left, wondering if she should really go into work. Will was right—she had taken the day off. She should take full advantage of it.

She made herself a cup of tea and lay down on her bed, listening to the quiet, never having noticed it in the house before. Slowly, the events of the morning replayed in her mind. She thought about Billy and his crotchety attitude. She thought about his beautiful house and wondered how he ended up there—and whether it could have been due to the tedious work in New York he referenced in his letter to Lizzie. She thought about Will going back for the book and wondered how he ended up in her life.

And she thought about April telling him about Jason. Anger heated her cheeks and quickening her heart, and yet she didn't know why. She and April had never really spoken of her time in New York; she figured April already knew why she needed to come home. What had April said to Will? Staring at the ceiling, she wished she could decipher answers to her questions in its textured patterns.

She placed the tea on her nightstand and walked to her closet. The top shelf was lined with boxes. She pulled the middle one down and lifted its lid. The spiral notebook at the far end was what she wanted, and she pinched its corner to draw it out. She returned the box to the closet and settled herself against the pillows of her bed.

She flipped through the notebook until coming to the journal entry she wanted to reread.

October 4, 2008
How do I love thee? Let me count the ways.

I opened my eyes, and there it began. The pen I had been holding was no longer in sight, and the rough draft of my history paper remained unmarked. I stared at the white wall behind my desk, listening to the music coming from outside my room. It had begun slowly, softly, until it finally roused me from my unexpected nap. I breathed the music in, feeling calmer and happier than I had since beginning the history paper hours ago.

I found the pen that had rolled to the corner of my desk and scrawled across the top of the paper, I fell in love with you on a Wednesday.

The hall was empty. Strangely empty. Door after door was closed, as though to say midterms had taken everyone captive, silencing the laughter and yelling that normally reigned. The only rebel—the only one unburdened by schoolwork—was the one playing the guitar around the corner.

I sat down next to my door, listening, playing with the carpet surrounding me. How do I love thee? Let me count the ways.

His rough voice whispered beneath the sound of the guitar, murmuring the words that he no doubt had composed only moments before. And she left me in shades of gray, *he murmured.* Shades of gray, shades of gray.

I could have stayed there, listening, until the sun rose. But I knew the moment was going to pass, and I didn't want to miss it. I crawled around the corner toward the sound of the guitar.

And there he was, strumming softly, sitting outside his doorway.

"Hi," I mouthed.

Jason smiled as I continued to crawl in his direction, watching until I stopped and sat down across from him.

He turned the song he was playing into chords. "Am I bothering you? My roommate kicked me out so that he could study in silence."

I shook my head. "I need to take a break. It seems like everyone is studying tonight." I felt myself getting sleepy—as though the music had drained away the urgency of the history paper.

He continued strumming, looking down the hall. "You know, I think that there are nearly eighty people living on this floor, and only you and I aren't busy fulfilling other people's expectations."

"Seems like it, huh?"

"It's nice."

I closed my eyes again, listening to Jason's music. Yes, the history paper vanished. The rough draft, my pen, my desk, tomorrow's deadline—all gone. Suddenly the night seemed bearable. "It's a good thing that you don't stay at home every night and play out in the hall. I'd never get any work done."

He smiled, continuing to strum.

"What were you playing before I interrupted you? Something new?" I asked.

He nodded. "Something I've been working on today."

"I liked it."

"Thank you." The chords turned back into the song he played earlier. "This one?"

I nodded. He continued playing, leaving out the vocals. In my mind, I could still hear his voice beneath the guitar. Shades of gray and a pale goodbye, it's thinning into lie after lie. *After a while I said, "It's so sad."*

His eyebrows rose. "Paul—my roommate—his girlfriend just broke up with him." He grinned a sideways grin. "Poor guy. His heartbreak inspired me."

I listened awhile longer—until the history paper reemerged from a place of obligation I had tried to bury. I rose to my feet, slowly, smiling. "I have to go," I said. "I've bothered you long enough, and history calls."

He shook his head, strumming away. "You never bother me. If I'm playing in the hall and you don't come out, I think that I'd be disappointed."

"Thank you. Good night." I turned to walk around the corner.

"Hey," he said, stopping me. "You know how bands play down in Westwood Village on Friday nights? I'm going to do that with a couple buddies tomorrow—playing down there. If you and some of your friends want to come, it might be fun."

"You mean, like, you and your band?"

He smiled. "Yeah, I'm cool. I have a band. And yeah, we're playing tomorrow. About eight-thirty."

"Maybe my roommate will want to head down there with me."

"I'll see you down there then."

I smiled at him as I turned the corner, thinking How do I love thee? Let me count the ways.

Twenty-six

Will knocked on Billy's door. The wood thudded under his knuckles, reminding him that the door probably weighed more—and was worth more—than he. Turning to Chris, Will said, "Don't talk when we go inside. Just follow me." Chris continued to stare up at the ornate engravings around the doorframe, but he managed to nod while craning his neck upward.

Will recognized the woman who answered the door. Just a couple hours ago she had stood in the same place with the same unfriendly expression on her face.

"Can I help you?" she asked.

"I would like to have a word with Mr. Strath."

The woman narrowed her eyes at Will. Her sight was getting bad, but her ears were still good. His voice sounded familiar.

"Do you have an appointment?"

"No. I was here this morning to drop off some books, and there was a mistake. One of the books wasn't supposed to be sent. May I come in?"

The woman's lips formed a straight, knowing line. Her ears were correct; he had been there before. She opened the door a little wider. "I'll see if Mr. Strath has time for you."

Will stepped into the house, feeling more comfortable in its opulence than he had that morning. The woman walked down the entryway to an intercom at the foot of the stairs, and Will motioned for Chris to join him inside. "Hey, close your mouth and get in here."

Chris' mouth never quite closed, but he managed to step into the house. "I need to get into real estate."

"You need to go sit down on that black chair over there and be quiet."

Before Chris could follow Will's command, the unsmiling woman began walking back down the entryway toward the boys. "Mr. Strath will see you now. It's the third door from the top of the stairs."

"Can I come?" Chris asked, his eyes wide.

"Fine."

They followed the woman's instructions and went straight to the third door at the top of the stairs. Will knocked.

"Come in." The words were garbled, like the speaker hadn't used his voice in years.

Will opened the door. Slowly, he and Chris walked into the library, looking around the way Amy had. The hard wood floor looked even darker next to the brightness let in by the wall of windows. They hadn't expected to see the ocean decorating the far end of the room; it drew their focus away from their purpose.

The man sitting behind the desk tapped his pen against a book. "What do you want?" he grumbled in that same garbled voice.

The demand drew Will's eyes toward Billy. Chris continued to take in the room—the walls of books, the overhead lights, the statue of *Nike* in the corner.

Will stepped toward the desk. "Sir, my name is Will." He extended his hand toward Billy. "It's very nice to meet you."

Billy ignored Will's hand. "I'll ask you one more time. What do you want?"

Will dropped his arm. "I was here this morning with a friend who came to drop off some books—"

"Get out," Billy growled. "Can't any one of you people leave me alone?" Every word grew louder than the last.

"Sir, I promise to leave you alone in just a minute. I'm only here to grab a book that was accidentally mixed in with the ones we brought to you. That's all."

Billy upper lip twitched. He looked at Chris. "And why are you here?"

Chris' head snapped to attention. "Me? Um—"

"If you can't answer a simple question in a reasonable amount of time, get out."

Chris looked at Will. He began walking backwards to the door. "Okay. Sorry to have bothered you. Have a nice day."

As Chris disappeared through the doorway, Billy's lip twitched again. A snarl seemed imminent, but he kept it from surfacing.

"Sir," Will said, "If you can just direct me to the boxes of books that came this morning, I'll pull the book I'm looking for and be on my way."

Billy narrowed his eyes. After a moment, he nodded toward the back corner of the room. "Over there," he said. "I want to see the book you are talking about before you take it."

"Absolutely," Will said was he walked toward the back corner.

The boxes were hidden behind the replica of *Nike*. Will maneuvered around the headless statue, avoiding the outstretched wings and kneeling next to the closest box. He took off its top and began unpacking books. As he scanned the cover of each one, he thought about Lizzie's library. He wondered if all old, rich people had rooms filled with books. It seemed so cliché somehow, and yet, he wouldn't mind having a library like that himself one day.

Two boxes later, Will found the volume of Renaissance poetry. He packed the boxes again and returned them to their original positions behind *Nike*. "Here it is," he said, holding up the book and walking toward Billy. He sat down and placed it on the desk.

Billy took the book in his wrinkled, knuckly hands, turning it over and over. He fanned through the pages, looking at specific ones intermittently. "This isn't Lizzie's book."

"That is why I made another trip out here. To take back—"

Billy waved a hand at Will as if to silence him, all the while keeping his eyes on the book. "You say this belongs to Lizzie's granddaughter?"

"Yes." Will smiled sheepishly. "There's actually a really funny story about how many hands that book has gone through in the last—"

"I don't want to hear it." Billy continued to flip through pages. "And this is all her handwriting in the margins?"

"Yep."

"So she is a writer."

"She was. I'm not sure she is anymore."

"Why not?"

Will shrugged, stretching back and slouching in his chair. He laced his fingers behind his neck and sighed. "I'm trying to figure that out. I get the feeling that she's weighed down by responsibility. Her life is sort of boring now. I have a theory—"

"I don't care about theories." Billy placed the book on the desk and leaned back in his chair, chewing on a pen. "Following the path of her grandmother?"

Will thought about the letters detailing Lizzie's imprisonment in her parents' house and wondered if that's what Billy meant. "Sir, I hope not."

Billy narrowed his eyes at Will again. He took the pen from his mouth and pointed it at Will. "Don't you let her. You keep her from making those mistakes Lizzie made."

Will nodded. He sat up straight. "Is there any chance you'd be willing to tell me more about those mistakes?"

Billy didn't answer right away. He studied his guest and thought about the note Lizzie had sent him from her deathbed. *It has been decided that my granddaughters should never know who I was.*

"Tell me," he finally said, "what do you and your friend Amy know about Lizzie?"

"We know that you two met in Paris. We know that you wrote letters to each other when she was in California. We also know that she told her parents she was going back to college, but then she went to Los Angeles instead. And when they found out what she had done, they basically put her under house arrest. After that, you visited her one time, and then she got mad at you, and then she got married. We think she did that to get back at you somehow. We don't know what happened after that."

"No one in Amy's family will tell you?"

Will shook his head.

"Why do you think that is?"

"We don't know. Something bad obviously happened. Something that had to do with her mom."

Billy nodded. Then he nodded again as though filling the extra time it took to formulate his thoughts. When he spoke, his voice was still gruff, but it had lost its snapping edge.

"Will, Lizzie and I knew each other for a very long time. Over the course of those years—those decades, actually—Eva and I did not often see eye-to-eye about Lizzie. Eva tried to temper her. She tried to protect her. I, on the other hand, indulged her. I am not proud of all that happened between Lizzie and me. I regret some of the decisions I made. But this I will say: I am not at fault for the hardships faced by Lizzie's family. When she came to me for help, I did my best to help her."

Will nodded.

"Someone doesn't think your friend Amy needs to know what happened to Lizzie," Billy continued, "and I won't dishonor those wishes." Billy pointed his pen at Will again. "But you keep your friend Amy writing. You know enough about the mistakes that Lizzie made early on—don't you let Amy make the same mistakes that Lizzie made."

"Sir, that's the plan."

Will rose and walked out of the room.

Downstairs, he found Chris sitting in a black leather chair.

"Come on, let's go," Will said, pointing toward the front door. "Hey, can you forward me that website you found about Billy? I want to send it to Amy."

Chris stood. "I didn't even get to ask him questions about his business experience."

Will shrugged. "Life is funny that way." He pushed the front door open, and they headed toward Will's truck. "If you had just cracked open your English 151 book while taking Hollings' class, you could have been the one to find Amy and help her with all this stuff. Then Billy would have told me to leave just now instead of you, and you could have asked him all about his business experience."

Chris shook his head at his feet. "No, that's not true. This would never have been my thing. It's playing out just as it should. I just wish I had gotten to find out how he had become a millionaire."

Will gave Chris a sideways glance but didn't comment.

Upstairs, back in Billy's office, the sound of waves crashing against the rocky shoreline filled the air. Billy listened for a long time, musing over the conversation he had with Will.

Sir, that's the plan, Will had said.

Billy had never much liked plans. He knew, though, they were a necessary evil.

He picked up the phone and dialed a number he hadn't thought he would ever dial again.

"Eva," he said when the line was answered. "Tell me about your granddaughter, Amy."

Twenty-seven

Amy jumped at the sound of knocking on her door. Instinctively, she threw the notebook that had been resting on her stomach to the floor, caught off guard by the fact that she had fallen asleep, and caught even further off guard by the sound of April at her door.

"Hey," Amy said, pushing herself up to a sitting position. She blinked and rubbed her eyes. "I think I fell asleep." She looked at the clock on her nightstand. Four hours had passed since Will left.

"You think? I could hear you snoring from the driveway outside." April entered the room and sat at the foot of Amy's bed. "I have something for you." She leaned toward Amy to hand her a stack of papers.

Amy looked at her sister for a moment before taking the stack. When her eyes fell to the paper, she saw April's handwriting.

Amy,

There is more to Nana's story. Will only brought you half of it. This is the second section—one that Lizzie apparently never saw. It's been in Nana's closet behind her shoe rack since we were little girls.

I'm sorry I told Will about Jason. It wasn't my place. I hope this makes up for it.

When you're done reading this, we need to talk.

Love you,
April

Amy looked up at her sister. She was glad that April had written her thoughts in a note rather than spoken them; it was easier that way. She said, "It shouldn't be a secret." As the words left her mouth, she realized that she was talking about both Lizzie's story and her own.

April smiled and stood. "I'm hungry. What do you want for dinner?"

Amy glanced at her alarm clock to check the time. "Miles

is supposed to be bringing Thai food over in about fifteen minutes. He always gets way too much, so there will be plenty if you are in the mood."

April nodded, her eyes following Amy's to the alarm. "I think I will be." She turned toward the door. "I'm going to water our pathetic little patio garden before he gets here. And I know you're going to call Will—you better do that before Miles gets here. Then hide those papers."

Amy nodded. "Before you go, just one question."

April turned around in the doorway.

"How did you get this?"

April shrugged. "I found it a long time ago, but I never read it. I didn't know what it was, and I didn't care. When I saw that Will found something similar in Lizzie's house and you were reading it together, I realized what I had found in Nana's closet. I still don't care, but I know you do, so I brought it to you."

Amy smiled, and her sister disappeared down the hallway. She leaned toward her nightstand and grabbed her cell phone. She found Will's number and called him.

"Hey," she said when he answered. "April just brought me another section of Eva's story about Lizzie. It's been in Eva's closet since we were little girls."

Will laughed. "Are you serious?"

"Yeah."

"Why didn't she tell you about it before?"

Amy paused before answering. "As with much of what April does, I don't know."

"So what's the plan?"

"Miles is coming over in a couple minutes for dinner. Should I call you after we eat? Maybe—" Amy stopped, feeling something different in the air. She twisted around, craning to see the doorway behind her. Miles stood with his arms crossed and his lips pursed, and Amy surmised that he had been there a while—at least long enough to figure out what she was doing.

"I'll call you back," she said into the phone. As she pressed the off button, she could hear Will's voice trailing away. "Is everything okay? Amy? What's—"

"How long have you been standing there?" she asked.

Miles continued his silence in the doorway, unmoving, his

jaw clenched.

"What?" Amy said. Upon first seeing him, she was worried—caught off-guard and feeling like a child accused of wrong-doings. But as he continued to stare, annoyance itched up the back of her neck. "So you're going to let yourself into my house, eavesdrop on a conversation, and then get mad at *me*?"

"Amy, I don't think you'd be saying that unless you knew that you were doing something wrong." He shook his head.

She crossed her arms. "I said it because we have different ideas of 'wrong,' and I'm irritated that you think you have a say in the way I deal with family issues."

Miles remained motionless for a few more seconds and then nodded his head slowly, his eyes averted to the window across the room. "Maybe I should just go. I don't want any part of this."

As he turned from the doorway, Amy called after him, "You never had any part in this, so yeah, you should go." She fell backward on the bed, feeling the cushion reverberate against her force and waiting to hear the front door slam. It never did. She heard Miles's car start outside, and she felt silly thinking that a door might have slammed. She was a door-slammer. Not him.

Her cell phone buzzed as a text message came in. She looked at her phone and read Will's words: *Hope everything's okay. Talk later?* She tossed the phone on the bed and blew a deep breath toward the ceiling.

After a long moment, she sat up and looked at the stack of papers on the bed. There it was. The next section of *Eva's Words.* She shook her argument with Miles from her mind and felt her fingers itch to pick up the papers. Instead of reaching for the stack, however, she reached for her phone.

Can you come over? she texted Will.

Within seconds, he responded, *I'll be there in twenty minutes.* Another text followed a few more seconds later. *Check out this website.*

Amy opened the link embedded in Will's text and saw an article about Billy Strath. Her eyes grew. She scrambled toward her desk for a piece of paper and a pen.

***

Will wasn't too far off—in just under twenty minutes, he walked up the driveway to Amy's house.

Renaissance poetry book in hand, he knocked on the door, somehow feeling as though he had lived this moment before. And actually, he realized that he had. The last time it happened at the coffee shop, though, and he hadn't known what to expect. This time, he did.

When Amy opened the door, he held up the book and said, "I wanted to give this to you before we lost it again." He handed it to her, and she smiled.

"Thank you so much." She opened the door further and continued, "Come in."

Will stepped into the house and closed the door behind him. He followed Amy toward the family room. "Is everything okay?"

She shrugged. "I'm sure it will be. When I called you earlier, Miles had just gotten here, and I didn't know it. He heard us talking on the phone about Lizzie, and he's not happy with me." She sighed. "So we had one of our thirty-second arguments. I'll call him later when we're both not mad, and it will be fine." She sat down on the couch.

Will sat down on the other side of the couch. "A thirty-second argument?"

"We don't see eye to eye on this, and we never will. We are both too hardheaded to give in, so why argue? We'll just drop it and move on once we've both calmed down."

Will squinted at her. "Is that how you always argue? Do you ever get anything resolved?"

Amy bit her lip and looked at the ceiling, thinking. "I don't know. It's just easier this way." She looked back at Will. "So, was Billy awful when you saw him?"

Will shook his head. "It wasn't so bad. I knew what to expect."

"Thanks again for getting the book. It's probably the nicest thing anyone's done for me—" she interrupted herself with a laugh, and then continued, "twice."

He wasn't sure how to respond, so he nodded toward a piece of paper on the coffee table. "What's that?"

"I'm making a timeline to keep track of everything that's

happened."

Will picked it up.

Summer 1955: Billy and Lizzie meet in Paris
Fall 1955 – Spring 1957: They exchange letters
Spring 1956: Lizzie moves home
Spring 1957: Lizzie gets engaged
1957 – 1960: Billy moves to Los Angeles and does art design work
Summer 1959: Lizzie is married, has one child, and is pregnant
1960: Billy moves to New York
?
?
1965: Billy opens publishing house
?
?
1985: Billy sells publishing house
?
?
1996: Billy moves to Monterey

"Good idea," Will said. He put the timeline down. Now we just need to figure out what goes in the blank spots." He pointed to a stack of papers on the table. "Is that what April brought you?"

Amy's eye grew as she reached for it. "Yes. And I'm so glad that you got here when you did. It didn't seem right to read them without you, but I didn't know how much longer I could wait."

"Well, let's get started."

Twenty-eight

June 5, 1970

Liz,

When I first wrote about you meeting Billy, I did so because I was intrigued—and bored. You were both interesting.

I'm writing this now, so many years later, for catharsis. Much has happened since I first wrote about you meeting Billy in Montmartre. Too much has happened. And now much healing needs to take place. It's long overdue, and perhaps these pages will prove to quiet and calm the pain that has filled our lives for so long. Will I ever send this to you? Will I ever find you? I don't know.

Now, the events seem like dreams—snapshots of a former life—and here they are, taking the form of disjointed, dreamlike snapshots. It is all I can manage.

I do love you.

Eva

***

Lizzie sat behind the desk, her head resting on its surface, her eyes glued to the clock. Her shift at the library ended at midnight, and she was beginning the final hour's countdown. She wondered why she had to be there at that ungodly hour; all the books had been shelved long ago, and now only four library patrons remained. Yet again she wondered why her supervisor despised her and forced her to work those miserable hours.

She lifted her head from the desk and propped it up with her arms. Her eyes wandered from the clock to the center of the room where the four students sat at different tables, buried by books. She wished they were not there. She wished they were the normal kind of students who took their library books home and only intended to read them—not the kind of students who stayed at the library and actually read them.

Go home, go home, go home, *she thought as frustration and fatigue crept across her mind, ventured down her neck to her shoulders, and threatened to fill her body.* Go home so I can go home. I'm suffocating. I need to get out of here.

Yet none of the students could read her thoughts. Especially not the sandy-haired gentleman sitting furthest away with his head bowed low to his book.

"How late do they make you work here?" a voice said from behind. "Shouldn't you be at home getting your beauty sleep in preparation for your wedding?"

Lizzie whirled around, the voice tearing her away from her bored self-pity. She saw the man standing behind her desk and nearly said his name but caught herself before the word took flight. Her eyes narrowed. In the dim library light, his skin looked darker, tighter, older. His eyes looked sharper. Smarter.

"Are you expecting me to think this is a pleasant surprise?" she said.

"I'm not expecting you to think anything, my dear Elizabeth. I simply wanted to congratulate you in person on your upcoming nuptials." Billy bowed his head at an angle. "So, congratulations."

"Well, thank you. Now, if you're done here, you can go back to Paris. Good night."

Lizzie turned her back—but a moment later found herself facing him again.

"How dare you?" she began in a hushed voice. "How dare you show up at my library and begin with your games? I am an engaged woman. It is eleven o'clock at night. Why are you here? What are you trying to do to me?"

Billy leaned against a bookcase, his hands in his pockets. "I've already told you. I'm here to congratulate you. After all, you and I are friends, are we not? Did we not share a nice time in Paris and a pleasant exchange of letters over the last few years? Why wouldn't I wish to congratulate you?"

"A nice *time in Paris?" Lizzie hissed. "A* pleasant *exchange of letters?" She glanced toward the four remaining people in the library and then continued, "You ruined me with that* nice *time in Paris and that* pleasant *exchange of letters. You made me believe that you felt something for me. When my world was crumbing, you were all I had. And you knew that. You let me believe that...that—"*

"Not quite sure what I let you believe?" Billy said, one

eyebrow high. "Could that be because I didn't let you do anything? Lizzie, let's be honest. No one makes you do anything. No one lets you do anything. No matter what anyone does around you, you create your own reality and do with it what you like."

Lizzie winced. She felt like her breath had been taken away, and she knew the look on her face portrayed this. "What does that mean?"

Billy's eyebrow remained high. "It doesn't matter what I wrote in those letters to you. You would have construed the meaning in any way you wished."

Lizzie pursed her lips. "That's not true. You're playing another game with me."

Billy shrugged. "You and I have two separate realities then. Two irreconcilable realities." He walked around the desk and Lizzie turned to watch him. He pulled up a chair and leaned back in it, his fingers interlaced behind his neck. "So tell me about your groom. Is he here?" He nodded to the students scattered amongst the desks.

"Yes, he is."

Billy scanned the room. "The man in the back? The one with glasses and the stack of books?"

She didn't answer right away. Finally, she said, "So?"

"So nothing. Picking him out of a group of four wasn't magic. But here's a question for you: shouldn't it bother him that you are talking to a strange man?"

Lizzie looked toward her fiancé, John. "He is clearly busy. His exams are approaching quickly, and he has better things to do than feel jealousy over an insignificant man having an insignificant conversation with me."

"Insignificant. Ah, yes. That would be the appropriate way to look at things. Well then, I should be on my way. I wish you a happy marriage and a happy life. I assume I will not be receiving a wedding invitation?"

The anger brewing in Lizzie bubbled over. "Why are you here? Why would you travel this far—just to torment me?"

Billy smiled. "Lizzie, I didn't have to travel far to see you. And I am simply here, as I have said, to congratulate you. Good night." He stood, and without a second's hesitation, walked toward the library's exit.

***

Lizzie stood before a full-length mirror, alone, frozen, looking at her reflection. She wore a wedding gown custom made by her mother's favorite designer—someone whose name she didn't care to remember. It was nothing like the wedding dress she imagined wearing as a young girl. It flowed to the tips of her fingers and the tips of her toes in extravagant lace, camouflaging both her body and her soul.

Behind her a door opened. In the mirror she could see Eva entering the room.

Continuing to stare at her reflection, Lizzie said, "I don't feel like myself. Is that how it's supposed to be? A new chapter is beginning, so I should feel like a new Lizzie?"

Eva approached and smiled. "That sounds about right."

Neither sister spoke for a moment. Eva sat on the chair next to the mirror.

"John is a good man, you know," Lizzie muttered, her eyes staying away from Eva's.

"I know."

Lizzie nodded. Her stomach tensed. "Do you think you will ever like him, Eva?"

"I don't dislike him."

"But you don't like him. You think he's boring."

"So do you. And you are marrying him despite this. Maybe you just can't put into words what you see in him, and that's okay. You don't have to justify your feelings to me."

Lizzie turned her eyes toward her sister. "Eva, it would be better if you stopped trying to protect me. Just tell me what you really think. Tell me I shouldn't marry him. Tell me that I'm making a big mistake because there is nothing about him worthy of me. Just tell me. Tell me."

Eva locked eyes with her sister and stood. She reached for Lizzie's shoulders and squeezed them. In a low voice, she answered, "Liz, I won't do that—not now that you have promised to marry him." She tried to smile. "Everything will be okay. Okay?"

Lizzie paled.

She squeezed her sister's shoulders again. "It's time to go. Dad sent me in here for you." She reached behind Lizzie's head and pulled the veil down over her face. She took Lizzie's hand and led her from the dressing room to the church's narthex.

Lizzie said nothing.

Eva said nothing.

Their father said nothing. He didn't look at his daughters.

Eva stepped toward the heavy doors separating them from the church and pushed one forward an inch—just enough to see who was there. The Hathaway's family lawyer, their father's business partner, their mother's hair stylist. Their father's country club friends, their mother's bridge club friends. Stranger, stranger, stranger. Grandmother and grandfather Hathaway. Grandmother and Grandfather Task. Stranger, stranger, stranger.

"Are you ready?" Eva asked, turning toward her sister. She smiled, hoping to bring warmth to her words.

Lizzie nodded. She took a step toward her father and took his arm.

Eva nodded as well and then looked back down the aisle toward the front of the church. She gave the organist the cue to begin. Turning a final time to Lizzie, she said, "Here we go." She tried to ignore Lizzie's glassy eyes, and then, as the only bridesmaid, she walked down the aisle.

Eva tried to focus on the alter at the end of her long walk, but she found her eyes scanning the guests, looking for familiar faces. Her first childhood nanny. Her father's best friend from college. Her second childhood nanny. Her mother's decorator. Her father's—

And then she saw him. He sat half way back on the far side of the pew. Eva's eyes caught his swarthy smile for only a moment before he fell from her range of vision, but she was sure it was him. She continued down the aisle, her heart quickening. Oh dear God, *she thought.* Please—it can't be him. *Her feet carried her faster, and although she tried to stop herself from picking up speed, her body no longer seemed capable of communicating with her mind.*

Once she reached the priest's side, Eva turned and smiled at her sister and father who were only a quarter of the way down the aisle. Her heart now pounded in her temples. Still smiling, she looked across the congregation, her eyes only resting on him for a moment before continuing.

Eva turned her gaze to Lizzie. She and their father neared the midway point, Eva held her breath. Just a little further and Lizzie would miss seeing him. Just a couple more steps, and Lizzie would never know.

But then Lizzie's head snapped to the left and stayed there. As she continued walking, her eye remained fixed in one place behind her. Soon, her father seemed to be pulling her forward, away from the point on which she focused.

Eva's heart thundered.

And then looked forward again and caught Eva's eye. With questioning eyebrows, she mouthed Billy? *Eva furrowed her own brows, playing dumb. She scanned the crowed and saw him with that same swarthy smirk on his face. Her eyes returned to Lizzie and she shook her head, almost imperceptibly. Lizzie mouthed* Billy! *and tried to point in his direction with her eyes. Eva followed her eyes, saw him again, then looked back at Lizzie. Again she shook her head, adding a slight shrug.* No, *she mouthed.* Not here.

Once Lizzie and her father arrived at the end of the aisle, they went through the formalities of giving her away—a short ceremony that seemed ridiculous as Lizzie barely looked at either her father or John. When her father turned to sit down, Lizzie stepped toward Eva to hand off her bouquet. "He's here," she whispered. "Billy's here."

Eva shook her head, barely. "Liz, no. It was someone else—just someone who looked like him."

The sisters looked toward the congregation as Lizzie stepped back toward John, both again looking for the uninvited guest. He was gone. Eva felt a surge of relief. Lizzie paled.

The ceremony passed in a blur. As John kissed his bride and prepared to journey down the aisle with his new wife, Eva prayed that Billy would not appear. Lizzie was visibly shaking; she couldn't handle seeing him again.

Eva and John's best man followed the newly-married couple down the aisle. Eva kept an eye on the attendees, hoping that she would spot Billy before Lizzie—should he reappear—so that she could keep her sister from him. She could not find him.

Outside the church, Lizzie pulled away from John's arm and rushed to Eva. Wedding guests began filtering out behind them, ready to congratulate the bride and groom, but Lizzie moved around the corner of the church, Eva in tow, avoiding the well-wishers for at least a couple moments.

"Eva, he was there. I saw him. He was here—why was he here?"

Eva shook her head. "Lizzie, it was your imagination. It was probably the son of some rich investment banker that Dad knows—something like that. You're tired and emotional. It wasn't him."

Lizzie's eyes filled with tears. "It was him," she whispered.

Eva shook her head again. "I was at the altar the entire time you were walking down the aisle. I looked and looked—right where you thought you saw him. It wasn't him." She took hold of her sister's shoulders and locked eyes with her. "Lizzie, do not do this to yourself. It is your wedding day. Do not be any more self-destructive than you already are."

Lizzie nodded, touching the corners of her eyes with her lacy sleeves. "Yes, yes. Okay," she swallowed.

"John is a good man. Billy is not," Eva continued.

Lizzie nodded again.

"That is all that matters."

Lizzie continued to nod. She closed her eyes.

"Can you do this?"

She opened her eyes and took a deep breath. "John is a good man. Billy is not," she repeated.

Eva squeezed her shoulders once again. "That's all that matters."

***

Will leaned back against the couch. "Wow. Billy was an ass."

"He still is an ass."

"I know, but he's sort of scary. I can be a jerk, too, but I don't really mean to. I wouldn't try to ruin someone's wedding day."

Amy turned to face Will. "So intention matters? If you don't mean to be a jerk, then you are a better person than someone who is a jerk on purpose—even if you are both jerks?"

"Yeah, I think intention matters. A lot of guys can be impulsive and stupid. My roommates and I can be that way. Billy was just evil. Who would you rather have around? Someone stupid or someone evil?"

Amy looked toward the papers on the coffee table and shook her head. Her mind began wandering. "Why is Billy doing this to her?"

Will stood up. "Hold on a second. I'll be right back."

Amy watched him walk toward the front door and heard it close behind him. A couple moments later, she heard it open again. Will reappeared in the family room carrying a San Francisco Giants baseball cap.

"I needed my thinking hat," he said, putting it on backward. He sat down on the couch. "Now I'm ready."

Amy smiled. "It's getting intense, isn't it? I'd need my thinking hat, too, if I had one."

Will pulled off his hat and put it sideways on Amy's head. "We can share mine."

Twenty-nine

Lizzie stared out past the Avenue des Champs-Elysees, her eyes fixed in the direction of the Arc de Triomphe. She began counting. One, two, three, four, five, six. *She was counting nothing in particular—just running through the numbers in her head to pass the time. When she hit one hundred, she counted backwards.* Ninety-nine, ninety-eight, ninety-seven. *As she finished, she looked across the table at her husband.*

"How's your book?" she asked.

John lifted his eyes from the thick volume he was reading, a lost look on his face. "My book? It's fascinating. It's a critical analysis of how Eve has been represented in retellings of the Creation story throughout the last five hundred years."

Lizzie leaned back in her chair. "Ugh," she spat. "She's been vilified over and over—you don't need to read a book to know that."

John was already reading again. "Really," he muttered.

"John," Lizzie said, leaning forward in her chair again. "Let's do something. Here we are in beautiful Paris—you've never been here before—let's do more than just read. Let's go for a walk. I'd love to show you Montmartre. It's incredible this time of year, filled with brilliant artists and great coffee. Let's go. What do you say? We've been sitting here for ages."

John continued to read. "Okay," he said into his book. "Let me finish this chapter. Then we can go."

Lizzie leaned back in her chair again. "How many more pages?"

He didn't check. "Probably about twenty."

She sighed softly, impatiently. One, two, three, four…

She watched the sun glide across the sky, itching to tell John that she was going to Montmartre and that she would meet him back at the hotel for dinner. Would he care? Would he protest? What would she do if he did in fact protest?

Just as she worked up the nerve to say that she was leaving to spend the afternoon on her own, he closed his book.

"Fascinating read," he said, smiling at her. "I think you'd enjoy it. Now, where is it that you want to go?"

Calmness washed through Lizzie, and she felt as though she had taken a deep breath, although she hadn't. Finally, finally, *they were going to do something. Finally.*

"Montmartre," she said. "You are going to love it."

***

Lizzie lay awake, listening to John's breathing slow as he drifted off to sleep. She gazed out the window of their hotel room, wondering what time it was, but knowing that it wasn't very late. If she had been in Paris with anyone other than her husband, she would have been at a club, listening to music—perhaps drinking, perhaps dancing. Even so, she wasn't disappointed to reach the day's end. She had been the one who suggested retiring early.

Once his breathing had settled into a familiar pattern, she slid out of bed and wrapped a robe around her shoulders. Carefully, quietly, she slipped out of the hotel room and tiptoed to the lobby.

"May I use your phone?" she asked the receptionist. She didn't bother to speak in French; this hotel had nothing but American patrons, and all employees spoke English. John had insisted that they stay somewhere that English was spoken—so that his wife was not the only one who understood conversations around them.

The receptionist nodded and presented her with a phone; then she stepped away.

When the operator came to the line, Lizzie asked to place a collect call. A few moments later, Lizzie had given the operator the information needed, and she heard the connection going through.

"Lizzie, what's going on?" Eva said through the phone.

"Eva, he's here. Billy is here. I saw him today—twice. First on the Metro as John and I were going to Montmartre and then at a restaurant in the Latin Quarter. He was following me."

"Lizzie, stop. He's not there."

"Yes he is. I already told you. I saw him twice."

Eva sighed. "Did you talk to him?"

"No."

"How long was he in your sight? Did you make eye contact?"

"I only saw him for a second each time. There were big crowds, and he got away before I could make eye contact."

"Liz, you did not see him. It was someone else."

Lizzie's voice was fringed with despair. "Why don't you believe me? I did see him. He's following me."

"Honey, you just thought you saw him. Billy's not in Paris anymore. He's in California. Shortly after you announced your engagement, I found out that he was moving to Los Angeles."

Lizzie didn't answer right away. She covered her forehead with her hand and closed her eyes. "My God. Am I going crazy? Am I hallucinating?"

"All those crazy artists in Paris look the same. It would be an easy mistake."

"But first I thought I saw him at the wedding and now here. I don't know what's going on. I'm losing my mind."

Eva was silent. Softly, she said, "He's just gotten under your skin. He's the kind of person who does that. You have to put him out of your mind."

Lizzie nodded as though her sister could see through the phone. "I don't know why this is so hard."

"Well, first of all, because you took your honeymoon in Paris. What were you thinking to—"

"Wait a second. John's never been—"

"And second of all, because Billy is an awful person."

Lizzie closed her eyes. "Yes."

"Put him out of your mind. Enjoy your vacation. And get some sleep. It's getting late there."

Lizzie hung up the phone and handed it to the receptionist. Then she crept back upstairs to their hotel room. As she slid back into bed, John raised his head from the pillow and squinted toward her.

"Where'd you go?"

"Bathroom," she answered. "It was occupied when I got there. I had to wait."

John dropped his head back to the pillow. "I'll never understand why there are communal bathrooms in European hotels."

"Mmm." Lizzie turned over so that her back was to her husband.

Within seconds, John was snoring. Lizzie began drifting off moments later, the image of Billy on the subway floating through her head. The further she drifted, the stronger the image became—until it finally came to life and she saw Billy walking toward her. He pushed through the crowd of travelers to where Lizzie sat next to John.

"What are you doing here?" she asked, looking up at him. "Eva said you moved to California."

Billy sat down on the other side of her. She glanced at John who didn't seem to notice the visitor. He stared off into the crowd as though the passengers swaying with the movement of the Metro were the most fascinating sight in Paris.

"To find out why you married this man." Billy nodded in John's direction. "I can't understand what you see in him."

John continued to stare into the crowd. Lizzie wondered if he realized Billy was there—he seemed not to notice at all.

"John is not you. That is what I see in him. He is everything you are not."

Billy smirked. "So I am the man against whom you measure all others? I'm flattered."

"Don't be."

"My, Lizzie. He looks like a lot of fun. Is he alive?" Billy stood and stepped in front of John, who continued to stare as though he could see through Billy. "Sir, are you alive? Are you asleep with your eyes open?" John made no movement or sound. He continued to stare. Billy moved away and sat back down next to Lizzie. "He's practically non-existent. Is that what you like about him?"

Lizzie could not bring her eyes to meet Billy's. "Non-existent is a bit dramatic. He is calm, he is smart, he is kind, he is introspective, and he is patient. He does not challenge me. He will not hurt me."

"But is there anything to him?" Billy shook his head.

"I just told you. He is everything you are not."

"He's so empty."

Lizzie glanced at John before turning to Billy. "He's not. He's brilliant—and fascinating. He's a wealth of knowledge—a lawyer, you know."

"Fascinating, yes. Obviously. I'm sure you have long talks into the night about court cases and the Constitution. Am I right?"

"Billy, I'd like you to leave now. Please get off the Metro at the next stop."

He stood and looked down at her. "Why don't you come with me? We both can go—now. John seems like he's content here—he can stay. Let's find parts of Paris that neither of us has before seen."

Lizzie hesitated; she entertained the idea for a split second—until she could see that Billy recognized she was entertaining the idea. "No," she blurted out, shaking her head. "No, I'm married. You must leave me alone."

Billy laughed, and she knew from his look that he had caught her—he had seen her doubt and insecurity; he had yet again gotten under her skin.

Anger crossed her face. "Leave," she seethed. "Leave now."

Billy shook his head and laughed again. "You married a ghost. Enjoy." He tuned and disappeared into the crowd.

Lizzie awoke from the dream, gasping. She had to get out of Paris—right away. "John," she breathed, shaking her husband's shoulder. "Let's go to Nice tomorrow. I'm tired of it here. Can we go? First thing in the morning?"

"Hmm," he responded. "Long train ride? I can finish my book on Eve then. Sounds good. First thing in the morning."

***

Amy looked at Will.

"She's falling apart."

Will nodded. He could think of nothing positive to say.

Thirty

Eva waited for John and Lizzie at the baggage claim. She did not know what to expect upon seeing her sister and brother-in-law. Would they be tired from the long plane ride? Would they be relaxed and satisfied with their honeymoon? Would they be excited to share stories about the places they saw? Eva felt that any one of those scenarios would be good; she prayed that they did not exit the plane with divorce on their lips.

When they came into sight, Lizzie was leading John by the hand, pulling him along the walkway and into the open air of the baggage claim. Her dark hair and tan skin was a stark contrast to the paleness of the man following her, but their matching smiles let loose the floodgates of relief in Eva's mind.

Lizzie dropped John's hand when they were a couple yards from Eva and trotted the rest of the way to her sister. She threw her arms around Eva's neck and squeezed.

"I'm so glad to be back," she breathed into Eva's hair.

"Did you have a good time?" Eva asked, pulling away and searching her sister's eyes.

Lizzie nodded, smiling. "Paris was a disaster, as you know." She turned and looked at John who was approaching but still out of earshot. "But Nice was wonderful. I think John and I will be okay." She nodded again, still smiling.

Eva returned the smile and then looked toward her new brother-in-law. "Hi, John. It's good to see you again. Did you have as much fun as your bride?"

"I did," he said, joining his wife and putting his arm around her shoulders. "It was wonderful having Lizzie show me around France. She knows so much of the country."

Lizzie leaned into her husband for a moment before saying, "Our baggage should be coming soon. I am going to run to the restroom while we wait." She pulled away from John and continued, "Don't you two move. I'll be right back."

John and Eva watched Lizzie move through the crowd. As Lizzie disappeared, she seemed to take with her the little bit of personality that John had displayed moments ago. Without her, a heavy awkwardness settled in the air between them. It grew heavier and heavier, and for one of the first times in her life, Eva didn't feel at ease.

"So it really was a lot of fun?" she asked. "What did you and Lizzie do? What did you see?"

John continued to gaze in Lizzie's direction. "Paris. Nice. And of course the little villages along the way. Although we didn't really see them. We just passed them on the train. Still, they were interesting to see."

Eva nodded. "I am very glad. Planning a wedding can be quite stressful, and I'm sure you could see that Lizzie needed a vacation."

Lizzie had been lost in a mob of people for a couple moments now, but John continued to stare after her as though he knew exactly where she was. Eva wondered if he could in fact see her—perhaps from his vantage point. After a few more awkward seconds passed, John spoke.

"Lizzie clearly felt stress before our wedding, but I don't think it had much to do with the planning of it. That was primarily taken care of by someone else, but I appreciate that you are trying to blame her stress on that. Lizzie has told me that you are someone to be completely honest with, I believe she's right. You pull honesty out of people, so I know that you are already aware that Lizzie and I are not well suited for each other."

Eva's initial impulse was to protest, but he had preempted the protest by pointing out her penchant for honesty. He too, obviously, appreciated honesty.

"I would not have thought that you would be a viable suitor for Lizzie—or that you would ever have proposed marriage to a girl like her. But I was clearly wrong. You must be well suited in ways that I don't see. And did you not have a wonderful honeymoon? Something must have gone right."

"The relationship is mutually beneficial, which is the primary need in all relationships. We both need companionship. I need someone to cook and occasionally pull me away from my work. And she needed someone to save her. I'm not sure what she needed saving from, but I know it was something poisonous. On that level, it works."

Eva stifled a shudder. "I don't understand. You've reduced your marriage to some sort of anthropological study in human needs. And why are you explaining this to your wife's sister?"

John looked toward Eva. "I knew that I would need to have this discussion with you sooner or later, and the opportunity presented itself now. As I said before, you pull honesty out of people. That's one reason. The other is that you have been your sister's keeper for many, many years. Now that job has gone to me, and you should know that she is in good hands. I will keep her well. Beyond the highs and lows of love and romance, there is logic and sturdiness in our relationship. As long as she desires to be with me, I will offer her protection from whatever has plagued her."

Eva tried to swallow a sour taste in her mouth. "I appreciate your perspective on marriage, but you would do well to forget about needs and mutually beneficial relationships. I suggest you have fun with her and take the chore out of it. If you don't, it may not last long. She will not like being saved or protected if you are not also interesting."

John looked back toward the crowd. "She's on her way back," he said upon spotting Lizzie in the crowd again. "I believe we will face that as it comes."

***

Will leaned back against the couch. He stared across the room, squinting. "I don't like him." He shook his head. "I know Billy is awful—crazy, even—but this John guy seems worse to me. He's so, I don't know, cold."

Amy stared at the pages before her. Slowly, she said, "He's my grandfather."

Will turned his eyes toward her. "I'm sorry. I didn't mean to insult your family. I—"

"No, no. Don't apologize. I don't like him either." She kept her eyes on the papers. "He's soulless." She ran her fingers along the bottom edge of the stack. "I mean, Lizzie used to be so soulful. He's the opposite of that. And," she paused, "he's my mom's father."

"I keep forgetting that these people aren't characters in a story."

Amy nodded. "Me too."

***

Lizzie wandered through the house, looking at the walls, the furniture, the carpet. None of it felt familiar. Her parents had been thrilled that she was marrying an attorney—so thrilled that they bought the pair a house and had it decorated while they were on their honeymoon. John enjoyed this surprise, and for once his mild manner was overcome with joy that he overtly expressed. Lizzie, however, felt like she had changed places with him. The house barely interested her. If anything, she was disappointed; this was not her house or her decorations. It was everything that she had wished to escape when running away to Los Angeles, including her parent's grasp.

It was two in the afternoon. John would be gone for at least another three hours, and Lizzie's boredom was edging toward overwhelming heights. Once John was home, it would subside, she knew, but not enough. It never did. With him there, she had someone to talk to. Unfortunately for her, he did not always talk back. He often filled his end of the conversations with hmm *and* oh. *It was not much for Lizzie to feed from.*

She continued to move through the house, one room at a time, looking for something to hold her interest. And one room at a time, she felt her boredom turn more and more into frustration, then more and more into anxiety. I'm going crazy in here *she thought.* This place is like a prison, just like Mom and Dad's house. They've created my very own prison now that I no longer reside in theirs.

Arriving at her room, she fell to her knees and crawled to the space beneath her bed. There, behind three shoeboxes was a fourth box. She pulled it out and poured its contents onto the carpet. Letters fell all around her.

Lizzie stared at the mess now surrounding her. She felt calmer knowing these letters once kept her spirit alive. Perhaps if she read them often enough, they would continue to do so. She picked up one and unfolded it, slowly, gingerly, as though the paper were as frail as her sanity.

January 18, 1956

Elizabeth,

I will be in Paris until something calls me away. Right now, I'm content with my surroundings, although as the weather continues to cool, I find myself wishing for the days of summer. Tourism slows this time of year. Fewer visitors means less money in hand. The artist stations thin out as the air begins to bite, and those of us who stay also thin down without the extra money for lunch or breakfast. But we stay because we know that all will improve on the other side of May. The tourists will appear, money will feed us, and our Lizzies might, if we are lucky, return.

Billy

"Elizabeth?"

Lizzie threw the letter to the floor—as though holding it would implicate her in some crime—and whirled around. She saw John and felt a guilty lightheadedness enveloping her.

"John, hello. I'm surprised that you are home already. Is it past five?" She began pulling the letters toward herself, scooping them up and piling them back into the shoebox. "I didn't realize."

John shook his head and walked into the room. He sat down on the floor a few feet from where his wife feverishly tried to hide the evidence of her crime.

"It's not yet five. I came home early. Work was slow."

"I'm glad that you are here," she lied, her face turning warm.

"What are you doing?" John asked.

"I am—I am just looking through some things. Nothing really. Just," she shook her head at the shoebox as she placed a lid on it, "nothing."

"Lizzie," John said. "Are those the reason you married me?" He nodded toward the shoebox.

She sat with the box in her lap, her eyes glued to it. She shrugged. "I don't know. I'm not sure."

John nodded as though he expected that answer. "I know that you were running from something. I didn't know what, but I still knew you were running. You don't have to tell me what from."

She set the box next to her and brought her eyes to John's. She waited for him to continue.

"We've been married for nearly a month now," he said. "Are you happy? Was getting married the right decision?"

Lizzie pursed her lips, unsure of the right answer. "We have a very nice life, John. We have a beautiful home, and you are very kind to me."

"We have a home that is barely lived in, and kindness can only get us so far."

Lizzie shook her head, her eyes again falling to the floor. "We've never discussed this. You've never spoken so frankly with me."

John nodded. "I do love you, Lizzie. I do want you to be happy. I know that I am often absorbed by books, and they often seem to take priority over you. I don't mean for that to happen, and I'm not entirely unaware that I may have been more convenient for you than whatever alternative was out there. Despite being so absorbed by books, I know this about you." He paused for a moment before continuing, hesitating. "Are you happy with your choice to marry me?"

Lizzie was unsure how to respond. She remained silent.

"It seems that you aren't."

She shook her head. "No. I'm just not sure what I got myself into." She again brought her eyes to meet his. "John, I think I need to find out. I need to find out if I made the right choice. I need to go on a short trip. May I?"

"Will you be traveling alone?"

She nodded. "Yes."

"Where you are going?"

"I'm not yet sure."

John rose to his feet. "Will you come back?"

She again hesitated. "If I don't come back—wouldn't it be better for that to happen now rather than later?"

John nodded.

Lizzie slid the shoebox back under the bed. "I will know soon after I leave whether it was right for me to marry you. John, I am sorry to put you through this. I imagine I was a bit young to think that marriage was appropriate. But I will do the right thing—whatever that may be—and if I come back, I will be a true wife. I will have banished the ghosts that haunt me, and I will be entirely devoted to you."

John turned and walked toward the door. "I'll be here." Before he crossed into the hallway, he turned and said, "When will you leave?"

"Tomorrow, perhaps."

He nodded and then disappeared.

Lizzie took a cab to Eva's house the next morning and asked the driver to keep the car running. As she walked to the front door, she felt her heart's pace quickening. She feared that the meeting wouldn't be as short as she told the cab driver—but she needed to hope that her fears were unfounded.

Lizzie knocked, wondering if she were crazy to think Eva would be the person to speak with. Once Eva answered the door, she knew that coming to see her sister was a mistake.

Eva's eyes went from Lizzie to the cab waiting in the street and then back to Lizzie. Her face darkened.

"What did you do?" she asked.

"I need your help," Lizzie began. "Billy told you he was in Los Angeles. Where in Los Angeles?"

"You must be crazy to think that I would tell you where he is." Eva crossed her arms and leaned against the doorframe. "Are you leaving John?"

"No, I don't think so. But I need to see Billy. I need to see if I made the right decision in marrying John."

"Lizzie, it doesn't matter if it was the right decision or not. It was the decision you made. And you need to make it work. Billy has no part in that."

"I think he does."

Eva shook her head and rolled her eyes. "You aren't a twenty-year-old romping around Paris and breaking hearts anymore. That chapter is over. You must move on. Stop letting Billy torture you. You have to move on."

Lizzie let Eva's words sink in. When she didn't speak, Eva continued.

"And don't think that John is doing you any favors here. Letting you run off to see another man—that's not gallant or smart

or loving. He thinks he saved you from something, but if he really did save you—if he saved you because he loved you—he would be fighting to keep you right now."

Eva's words lashed at Lizzie's plan; their sting disoriented her.

"You know what?" Eva continued. "The three of you deserve each other. Go ahead Lizzie. Go off and find Billy. Realize that he will continue to haunt you as long as you let him. Then run back to John and pretend that you've decided not to let Billy haunt you. That will be a great way to live your life."

Lizzie found her voice, but only a few words came to her. "Eva—what?"

Eva shook her head. "Some things are sacred. Marriage is one of them. I may be flippant about many other things, but not this. I know not to learn the hard way, and you should have learned that as well."

"You won't help me find him," Lizzie said, her voice flat.

"I will not." She looked over Lizzie's shoulder toward the cab. "And you have a decision to make. Either you go home to your husband, or you go on your little journey alone—with no help. You decide."

Eva closed the door without saying goodbye. Lizzie stood, dumbfounded, for a moment. She turned and walked toward the cab.

"Can you take me to the airport?" she asked the driver upon opening the car door.

Thirty-one

Two months passed. John continued to work, and his days grew longer and longer among the books. He missed Lizzie. He missed having contact with another person, although he wondered if any human contact would have been sufficient—or if he craved his wife in particular. That the question even arose troubled him.

But when the phone rang and he heard her voice on the line, his heart swelled. He had truly missed her.

"John, I'm coming home," she said. "If you will still have me."

"There will always be a place for you here." Relief flooded him. "When will you arrive?"

"Tomorrow. Is that fine?"

"I can't wait to see you."

"Tomorrow, then." Lizzie paused, wondering if she should wait until tomorrow to share the news resting on the tip of her tongue. "And John, you're going to be a daddy."

***

"You better put that away," April said, passing by the family room on her way to the front door. "Mom and Nana are walking up the driveway." She stopped abruptly, unplanned, and looked into the family room. "What the hell is on your head, Amy?"

Amy's hands flew to Will's baseball cap. "I forgot I still had this on." She took it off and handed it to Will, somehow feeling as though she had been caught in the act of some wrongdoing. He put the hat on his head.

April narrowed her eyes at them and then continued on to the front door. "Seriously, put that stuff away."

Amy stuffed the stack of papers under the couch. "Why are Mom and Nana here?" she called in April's direction as she stood up and pushed her hair behind her shoulders.

"The three of us are going to get coffee," April called back.

"You couldn't have warned us five minutes ago?"

Amy walked toward the entryway. Will followed.

"What's the fun in that?"

April opened the door for her mother and grandmother. Eva entered first, followed by Debbie who was holding a phone to her ear.

"Hello, my sweet girls," Eva said, hugging both her granddaughters at once. "How are you doing?"

"Good, Nana," Amy said.

Before April could answer, Debbie dropped the phone into her purse and said, "Amy, I was just listening to a message from Miles. He wants me to call him. That's kind of odd." She smiled and hugged her two daughters.

Amy pulled away from her mother and felt her mouth drop. "What? He called you?" She pushed a curl behind her ear and felt her face warm. "Don't call him back. He's being ridiculous."

Debbie's eyebrows furrowed. She laughed. "Is he trying to get you in trouble with me?"

"Sounds like it," April said. "I'd break up with him."

"April, stop now," Debbie said.

"Seriously, Mom, don't call him back," Amy said. "I'll take care of it."

Debbie gave April a look that said *Not another word from you* and then smiled at Amy. "Okay then. He's all yours." Her eyes moved beyond her daughters and landed on Will. She waved at him and said, "Hi, I'm Amy and April's mom, Debbie. And this is the girls' grandmother, Eva."

Will squeezed past Amy and April to shake hands with their mother and grandmother. "Hi, I'm Will. I'm an old friend of Amy's from college."

"Have I met you before?" Debbie asked. "You look familiar."

"Probably," April said. "He spent a lot of time at Jerry's Famous Deli when I worked there." She pushed both Eva and Debbie's shoulders toward the door. "C'mon, let's go. We have lots to talk about, and I'm in the mood for a five dollar drink made almost entirely of caramel and foam."

"Oh, I miss Jerry's," Eva said while April guided her through the door. "It was one of my favorite parts of visiting you in Los Angeles."

"Goodbye kids," Debbie said over her shoulder. "Have a nice evening."

Amy and Will waved, and then Amy closed the door. She turned toward Will. "You spent a lot of time at Jerry's Famous Deli? What does that mean?"

Will readjusted his baseball cap and shifted his weight. "Kind of a weird thing to say, wasn't it? I don't know."

Amy walked toward the family room. "My sister. Geeze." Her voice sounded far away—like the words she spoke weren't the words she was thinking.

Will followed her. He watched her pull *Eva's Words* from underneath the couch. She sat down, her body rigid, her eyes fixed on the paper. The red of anger clung to her face.

"Are you okay?" he asked.

Amy looked up at Will through ever-so-slightly narrowed eyes. "Miles called my mom to tell her what I was doing with Lizzie's stuff. He was going to tattle on me. Like I'm a six-year-old. Who does that?"

Will sat down next to her and nodded. "Yeah, that was a bad move."

"Of all the things he could have done, he decided to call my mom?"

Will continued nodding. "A really bad move."

"I'm not going to call him. I can't even imagine talking to him right now."

"I wouldn't want to call him either. But let's put this in perspective. He didn't try to ruin your wedding day."

A wry smile crossed Amy's face, and she shook her head. "If that's all he has going for him, we're in trouble." She pushed a piece of paper toward Will. "Read."

***

Dearest Eva,

I'm writing this letter to say goodbye. It won't be a long goodbye, but it's a goodbye nonetheless. The last time I said goodbye to you did not go very well, and I'm coward—I don't want to repeat that awful scene. So I am saying goodbye in a letter.

You know I've not been happy. It's been twelve years since my last summer in Paris with you, and my sanity is slowly draining. I have a husband and three children, none of whom bring me joy. I am exhausted by how mundane my world is, and when I look in the mirror I see a stranger. I am plagued by my former life. I am plagued by the mistakes I've made and the reason I made those mistakes.

I look at you and find myself seething with envy. Aidan is everything you've ever wanted; he is your perfect match. You had the patience to wait for him. You followed your heart rather than the demands of our parents. You never questioned your decisions, and the love you two share is worth so much more than the inheritance you lost. I was not patient. I did not follow my heart. And now I am paying the price.

I cannot go on like this.

I will be mailing this letter from the airport. I leave for New York at the end of this hour. John is aware that I am leaving; however, he believes it simply business that needs tending. I did not tell him what that business was. I could not tell you the same. As much as you will hate me for this, I could not tell you the same lie.

I will be back. I do not know when—perhaps a week, perhaps a month.

You love my children more than I; for their sake, please see them and make sure John remembers to care for them in my absence. I fear he will forget to bathe and feed them.

I do hope you will forgive me by the time we next meet. I loathe myself for sinking so low in your eyes, but I know not what else to do.

All my heart,
Lizzie

Eva laid the letter on the table where she sat. She said a silent prayer for her three nieces. Moments later, she rose and crossed the room to get her coat.

***

"Dad, tell Debbie to leave us alone," Mary said while

walking into the kitchen.

John stood over the stove, turning on a gas burner. He looked toward the sound of his daughter's voice.

"Daddy, they won't let me play with them," Debbie complained, following right behind her big sister.

"Dad, Anne and I are working on a drawing. Debbie keeps messing it up." Mary turned to her five-year-old sister. "You can't draw like me and Anne. Why don't you just go and draw your own picture?"

"But I want to help you." The little girl's eyes were huge, disappointed.

John set the teakettle on the burner. "Debbie, leave your sisters alone. Why don't you go play outside?"

"That's no fun if I'm by myself."

Mary turned around and left the room, feeling as though her task had been accomplished.

"Well, then why don't you go up to the attic and play with all those dolls you've got up there?"

Debbie looked after her sister. "Why don't they want to play with me?"

"That's just what happens when you're the youngest. I'm sorry, darling." He wiped up the water spots on the counter and left the dish towel between the stove and the sink. "Come. I'll go with you up to the attic." He led her out of the kitchen and up the stairs.

The attic was full of boxes and trunks, old toys, and baby furniture. John looked around the room, spotting a box marked dolls. He pointed to it. "There—why don't you play with what's over there?" He walked to the box and opened it. Debbie followed him.

"There you go. Okay?"

He looked at his daughter. She nodded at him, and he smiled.

"Alright. I'll be down in my study if you need anything." He patted her on the head and went back to his second story office, forgetting about the teakettle on the stove.

Debbie picked up the top doll in the box. It was a cloth doll with button eyes and a painted-on nose. Mary had drawn whiskers on it long ago. Debbie put it back and grabbed another one. It too had whiskers drawn on it. She put it back, feeling just as unhappy as before. Mary and Anne were too old to play with her, and all the dolls had been ruined.

She went down the stairs, deciding she'd rather be outside than up in a stuffy attic. She walked by her dad's study, looking in a moment. Her father sat at his desk, immersed in a book, holding a pencil poised a few inches above the text. She continued on her way, passing the room where her sisters had been drawing. She looked in, finding that they were gone. As she walked out of the house, she saw them outside, sitting on the curb.

The day was warm and windy. The teakettle, boiling, whistled. Yet, no one was near enough to hear it. It whistled and whistled, the searing sound holding steady until the water evaporated.

Soon the whistling had ceased, and the aluminum bottom of the kettle began melting. The melt was slow at first, but soon the kettle itself caught fire and the melting quickened.

The kettle glowed red as it curled in the flames. A spark jumped from the stove to the dishtowel drying on the counter. A moment later, the dishtowel was drowning in flames with its own sparks jumping in every direction. One caught a hold of the curtains lining the window above the sink.

John lifted his head from his book. Something was burning—he could smell it. He strode across his study, breaking into a run down the hall as he remembered the teapot.

The kitchen was engulfed in flames when he got there. His heart thudded in his chest as he assessed the scene before him. Debbie, he thought. The attic. He sprinted away from the kitchen and toward the stairs.

"Debbie! Anne! Mary! Get out!" he yelled as he ran through the house. "Get out now! Fire!" His heart continued to pound. Upon climbing into the attic, he scanned the room. "Debbie!" he called. "Debbie, where are you?" He turned around in a circle, his eyes unable to find his daughter.

He ran to the window and peered into the front yard. At the curb he could see his three girls staring in horror at the house. Mary held Debbie and Ann in a sideways hug, half hiding their staring eyes. John threw open the window's latch and yelled down to his daughters, "Go across the street and call the fire department from neighbor's house. Now!"

Mary released her arm from Anne's shoulders and nudged her sister toward the neighbor's house. Anne followed the silent orders and ran.

"Dad!" Mary called. "Dad, you have to get out of there! Climb through the window!"

Debbie hid her face in her sister's shirt. She knew her dad had gone up to the attic to look for her.

John turned from the window and looked around the attic. It was full of boxes—boxes of their family treasures. He grabbed the closest box and threw it out the window. It landed with a bounce in the yard, books flying in all directions. Mary peeled Debbie from her shirt and ran into the yard to collect the books. Just as she had gathered them and moved them into the street, two more boxes flew from the window.

"Dad! That's enough!" she said as she pulled the box that had remained in tact to the street. "Get out of there!"

John could feel the floor warming under his feet. He needed to climb out the window and jump. There was one more box labeled books. He would throw that one out the window and then jump.

He lugged the box to the window and hoisted it up. His feet were beginning to burn through his shoes. He shoved the box out the window and—

The roof collapsed beneath his feet.

John disappeared from Mary and Debbie's sight. Both girls screamed.

***

Eva stepped on her car's breaks as she neared her sister's street and saw that it was blocked by fire trucks and police cars. Fear overtook her initial curiosity as she saw Lizzie's charred house, smoking but no longer burning. She threw the car in park and ran down the street, weaving between police cars and fire trucks.

Panic strangled her as she tried to find her nieces and John in the crowd of people that had gathered across the street. They weren't there.

But a moment later she saw the girls sitting on a curb talking to a police officer. She ran faster toward them.

Debbie caught sight of her first. She pushed herself up from the curb and ran to her aunt. Mary and Anne followed. Tears streaked their ash-dusted faces. They clutched at Eva's waist, sobbing, and she tried to hold them all closer and closer.

"Where's your daddy?" Eva asked. "Girls, where is he?"

Debbie sobbed harder as Mary answered.

"He was in the house," she bawled. "He was in the house. It's gone now." Her words slurred beneath the sobs. "It's all gone. He was in there."

Eva closed her eyes, feeling life drain from her.

"My sweet girls," she said, trying to pull them closer. "Oh my sweet girls."

Lizzie, *she thought, her eyes to the sky,* how could you do this?

She squeezed each of the girl's shoulders.

"Let's go home."

***

Amy looked up from the paper—the very last one in the stack that April had brought—and stared straight forward, silently. Will watched her. He waited.

That's it. The end of the story, she thought.

"I want to go get a drink," she said.

Thirty-two

Will and Amy walked from her house to North Santa Cruz Avenue in silence. Will wondered where they were going—and he wondered if they would run into Amy's family on the way there. April hadn't said where they were going to get coffee; Will hoped it wasn't at the coffee shop where he and Amy met. And he hoped that Amy would say something—anything—but when nothing came, he decided to keep quiet himself.

Once on the strip, Amy pointed toward a bar that Will had seen many times before. "There," she said. They walked through a doorway, up a set of stairs, and into a darkened room filled with loud music. Amy pointed to a table close to the bar; they walked to it and sat down.

Amy drummed her fingernails against the wood table. Her eyes focused on something over Will's shoulder as though she was concentrating on gathering her thoughts. "Billy was in New York, wasn't he?" she finally said. "That's why Lizzie was going to New York."

Will nodded. "That is one way to connect the dots."

Amy leaned toward the table and looked at Will. "But we do know that Billy was in New York at one time—he told her where he was in a letter. And that letter was after her first child was born. He could have still been there."

"Yep."

"So Lizzie left her family to see Billy, and while she was away, *my* mother watched *her* father die in a house fire—which she could, possibly, blame on herself because he ran up to the attic to find her."

Will nodded again.

A waitress brought them each a beer. Amy immediately lifted hers to her lips. Will slumped back in his chair and stared at his.

"How does my mom know about Billy?" Amy asked as she set down her glass.

Will shrugged. "She probably went through Eva's stuff when she was a kid just like April did. Don't all kids do that?" He glanced at Amy before refocusing his eyes on the glass before him.

"But I don't think it really matters. She obviously knows about him—that's the bottom line. How she found out is irrelevant."

A chill traveled down Amy's arms. She shuddered. "My mom saw her own father die. In a fire. And she was a little girl." She shook her head. "I can't imagine. How could I have not known this?"

Will kept his eyes on his beer. "I can see why your mom wouldn't want you to dig all this up. It's got to be pretty painful."

Amy pursed her lips and nodded. "I know." She paused and then leaned back in her chair. "Should I feel guilty? Now that I know what happened—now that I know how bad it was and why my mom didn't want to talk about it? Should I feel guilty that I pursued this, despite my mom's wishes?"

"Do you feel guilty?"

Amy took a deep breath and let it out slowly. "I don't think so. I mean, I had no idea that we'd find something so tragic. But that being said, should something be hidden because it's tragic?"

"I don't think your curiosity would have gone away if you didn't find out what happened." With his head still angled downward toward his glass, Will lifted his eyes to Amy. "When I saw Billy today, he said something kind of interesting."

Amy's eyebrows rose.

"He said," Will continued slowly, "that he regrets some of the decisions he made with Lizzie, but when she came to him for help, he did his best to help her. He said that what happened to your family was not his fault."

Amy shook her head. "How could that be? I don't know if I believe that." Her eyes wandered across the wall behind Will. "I have to think about something else now. There's too much—it's too much." She gulped more of her beer.

Neither of them spoke for a moment. Will went back to stating at his drink. He thought about different ways to change the topic of conversation. Anything about UCLA would do the trick. He could ask her where she lived in Westwood, what classes she liked best, or what she did for fun. *Anything* would do. But he didn't feel like small talk.

"So you're really not going to call Miles tonight?" he asked.

Amy shook her head. "No. Not tonight. I'm too mad at him."

"Maybe talking to him while you're mad would be good. You could have a real fight where you yell and say what's on your mind. It's good to get those feelings out sometimes."

Amy shrugged. "You can express those feelings without yelling."

"True. But I think Miles needs to be yelled at. For a mistake like the one he made—he needs to be yelled at. You can clear the air and move on instead of harboring any resentment."

He hadn't planned on bringing up Miles. He hadn't *ever* planned to initiate this conversation. But after reading about Lizzie and John, he couldn't stop himself.

"You know, I don't really understand you and Miles," he said. "You don't seem like a match. You don't seem to connect."

Amy nodded. "I know."

Hesitating—knowing he might step over the line—he continued, "Is that why you still write letters to your ex-boyfriend?"

Amy stared at her half-drunk glass of beer.

"I don't write him letters. He and I used to write letters, a long time ago, but there came a time when I stopped sending them. Now I just write my thoughts. Maybe they're kind of like letters. I don't know who they're really written to though. They're just written."

Will leaned back in his chair, unsure how to phrase the thought in his mind, but deciding not to waste time choosing the perfect words.

"I know you didn't like when April told me about Jason, but she didn't tell me that much. It seemed like it was pretty important though."

Amy smiled at her glass, barely. "I guess everything is important in its own way. I wouldn't be sitting here now if things had gone differently with Jason. Important or not, though, the story really isn't very interesting. He was my boyfriend. We were together for three years. Then he fell out of love with me. And I didn't understand. Nothing had changed—no one had done anything wrong. It simply was over. Suddenly I had a big hole in my life, and nothing I did could repair it."

"You didn't know it was coming?"

Amy shook her head. "I had no idea. And that was just about the time I had Professor Hollings' class and began writing in the margin of my book. Jason had been my outlet for so long, and without him, I felt like I was spinning out of control with my thoughts."

Will found himself nodding even though Amy wasn't looking at him.

"It was hard. I missed not getting to talk to him on the phone some nights, hearing his voice in my ear as I drifted off to sleep. And I missed the way he'd twirl my hair around his finger while listening to me talk about whatever. But then I met Miles. And he really was so nice to me."

"It wasn't the same though, right? Being with Miles wasn't the same as being with Jason, was it?"

Amy forced a smile and shook her head. "Sometimes I wonder if I feel about Miles the way Jason felt about me toward the end of our relationship."

"But you won't break up with him?"

"I don't know if I should. Maybe we have what all good relationships have. Security, ease, contentment. Maybe it's not realistic to want more than that."

"Amy," Will said, trying to bring her eyes toward him. When she looked up, he continued, "Do you really think that? C'mon, we just spent the last hour reading the story of your grandmother's life—and what happens when people settle. Sure, Billy wasn't the right person for Lizzie, but neither was her husband. She had security and ease and contentment with John, but that wasn't enough."

"Lizzie and I aren't the same person though. She was wild and stubborn and passionate. I'm much more mild, and—"

"That's not the point. It doesn't matter if you and Lizzie are the same; we all need someone who understands us, no matter what our traits are." He paused, thinking, staring at his untouched beer. "John didn't twirl Lizzie's hair either."

She shrugged and dropped her eyes back to the table. Will bit the inside of his lip. Perhaps he had said too much.

"So you and Jason remained friendly enough to exchange letters, but then at some point you stopped sending them?"

"Yeah. I knew that Jason had headed to New York, but I didn't tell him that I was still going there myself. I just went. I didn't want him to think that I was following him. And I couldn't send him letters with a New York postmark—so that's when I stopped sending them. About a week after I got there, I saw him. I was walking down the street, and through the window of a pizza place, I saw him. He was eating and talking with a girl. I stopped and watched them for a minute—and they looked so happy together. I guess they could have been just friends, but," she shook her head, "I didn't think so. When I had stared at them long enough, I continued on my way, feeling different. I didn't go to New York thinking that I would find Jason and we could live out the plan that we had created so long before. I mean, after all, Miles was supposed to join me. But I guess after seeing Jason with that girl—I don't know. It all changed." She blew out a deep breath. "I kept going. I kept getting up everyday, doing my stupid job and coming home every night. Then repeating the process over and over. It wasn't turning out to be the way I thought it would be. It wasn't fun. And I realized that I couldn't bring Miles out there—he would be as miserable as I was. So I came home. I figured I could live the same boring cycle with the same stupid job here, but at least I would have my family with me."

The waitress walked by and Amy ordered another beer for each of them. As the waitress left their table, Amy gulped down the rest of her drink and then forced a weak smile. "You know, Miles was the one who sold back my Renaissance poetry book."

"Somehow that doesn't surprise me."

"He had offered to take my books with him when he was selling back his. I took him up on the offer. I still don't know how he could have thought that book needed to be sold back—it wasn't with the books that were being sold—but he took it with him anyway."

"Were you mad?"

Amy shrugged. "I was more sad and embarrassed. He knew I was upset, and he felt bad about it—but there wasn't anything he could do."

Will sat forward in his chair. "Really? He could have gone back down there and told the bookstore people that he didn't mean to sell it back. He could have offered to go through all the books they had gotten that day to find it. He could have offered to pay full price for it when he found it. He could have had it back to you less than two hours after you realized it was gone."

Amy pursed her lips. "I didn't think about that. I guess he didn't either."

Will wanted to say *That's what I would have done*, but he stopped the words from coming.

The waitress brought the next round of beers. When she walked away from the table, Will said, "Amy, you've only been out of school for a year. Maybe things haven't gone the way you dreamed, but you've got plenty of time to work on those dreams. No one should be settling at the age of twenty-three."

She picked up her second beer and sipped it. Then she nodded. "You're right."

Will looked around the bar. It was starting to fill with people and noise. He leaned toward Amy and grinned, knowing it was time to change the subject. "Hey, you want to know why April mentioned Jerry's Famous Deli earlier tonight? It's because she really did know who I was back then."

Amy sat up straighter. "What do you mean?"

"Remember that night we brought Billy's books to your house and April commented about my truck? She recognized it from the UCLA sticker I have on the back. And then it clicked in her head—I was the boyfriend a coworker at Jerry's Famous Deli. I used to race down the streets of Westwood to pick up my girlfriend when her shifts ended. And no one there liked me because I drove too fast." He leaned back and grinned again. "Well, that wasn't the main reason. The main reason was that Jocelyn and I fought all the time. My driving just gave them another reason to hate me."

Amy squeezed her eyes closed and shook her head. "April knew who you were? And she didn't like you?"

"Actually, she didn't seem to care about me either way. Everyone else thought Jos should break up with me, but April figured we just had one of those bad relationships everyone needs to have so that we recognize when a good one comes along."

Amy smiled. She sipped her beer. "That sister of mine. Full of surprises, I tell you. Sarcastic and brash on one hand; insightful and logical on the other hand. I'll never understand her." She took another sip of beer. "Wait. Jos? Is that the girl from Kim's napkin? Didn't she write something on there about a Jos?

Will nodded. "Yep. Same person."

"Are you still dating?"

Will shook his head. "That ended at the beginning of the school year." He turned his beer around in circles on the table. "I never would have said it at the time, but now I see that we did have a pretty immature relationship. We never really trusted each other, and we never really figured out how to talk to each other."

Amy tilted her head to one side. "Really? I wouldn't have guessed that about you. You seem like a pretty nice guy."

"I messed up a lot during my first two years of college. But after Jocelyn finally had it and broke up with me, I knew it was time to make some changes. I knew I needed to take school more seriously, and I needed to stop being such a jerk. I mean, I now know that Jocelyn and I weren't right for each other, but I don't think the old Will would have been right for anyone. I didn't want to continue being that guy."

"So," Amy said slowly, "Maybe you and Jocelyn just crossed paths at the wrong time. Maybe if you met today, you would be right for each other."

Will shook his head. "No. Because I wouldn't have decided to grow up if I hadn't known her. Like April said, I needed that bad relationship to figure out what I wanted out of a good one."

"Sounds like a lesson that Lizzie should have learned with Billy." She sighed. "You and April. You are both something else." She smiled. Then giggled.

The sound of her laugh caught Will off guard. He looked at the two full beers sitting in front of him and the two empty glasses in front of Amy.

"Did you eat dinner?" he asked.

She shook her head. "No. Miles was supposed to bring Thai food over, but I guess he took it with him when he left. Then I was too upset to eat." She thought a moment. "Come to think of it, I didn't eat lunch either. After you left, I fell asleep. Then April woke me up with the rest of Eva's story, and then Miles came over." She rolled her eyes—for no particular reason—and then giggled again.

Will pulled out his cell phone and looked at the time. "We should probably get you home. Or get you something to eat."

Amy stood up. "I'm fine," she said. "In fact, I feel better than I have in a long time. Sort of like a weight has been lifted." Her eyebrows furrow. "Which is strange, since I just found out my real grandfather died in a fire because my real grandmother was so selfish." She shook her head as though trying to rid herself of those thoughts and then smiled. "Let's not be so serious the rest of the night. We've had too much seriousness already. Let's go dance." She turned and moved through the crowd toward the small dance floor in the back of the bar.

Will watched her go. How quickly her mood had shifted; he hadn't expected this. He grabbed his two beers and picked his way through the thickening crowd toward Amy. At the edge of the dance floor was a line of tall tables and clusters of bar stools. He set his drinks down on one of the tables and leaned against a stool.

He spotted her among the other dancers, moving with the beat of the music. When she spotted him, she waved him over. He hesitated, but then he squeezed through the mass of flailing arms and bobbing heads.

"Will," she shouted, touching his shoulder when he neared her, "this is my friend Becky from high school." She nodded at the tall brunette girl dancing next to her. "We haven't seen each other in forever. Can you believe that we're both here, right now?"

Will nodded at Becky and smiled at Amy. "How are you feeling?" he asked, leaning toward her and shouting over the music.

"Good. Really good," she answered. "C'mon. Dance with us."

"I think we ought to head out."

"I'm not ready to go. Me and Becky need to catch up."

"Okay. I'll be waiting over there." He pointed to the tables. Amy nodded and turned back to Becky. Will maneuvered through the crowd. Taking a seat on a stool, he sipped his beer and watched as a man approached Amy. She smiled and shook her head, and the guy walked away. Will checked his cell phone for the time again. It wasn't that late, yet the inhibitions of bar patrons were fading fast.

One song ended and the next begun; two guys appeared next to Becky and Amy, trying to get the girls' attention. The one nearest Amy took a hold of her hand and spun her around once. She smiled, shook her head, and turned her back. Will grinned. He set his beer down and made his way onto the dance floor.

"Hey, look who's here," Amy called over the music as he neared her.

He smiled a closed-lip smile, finding the rhythm of the music and moving with it. "Look at you, breaking hearts all over the place."

Amy laughed. "Oh, they'll find some other attention-starved girl in a couple minutes. I may be mad at Miles, but I'm not going to be stupid."

Amy forgot about Becky and turned toward Will. She had wondered if he was one of those guys who didn't dance or couldn't dance. What was it that Lizzie had said? She hated when boys danced as though they didn't hear the music? Amy had always felt the same way.

Thirty-three

"I don't want to go home right now," Amy said as Will guided her through the bar's exit. "April is going to yell at me for drinking."

"If you go home any later, she's going to yell at you for being out so late," Will answered. "And she's going to yell at me for keeping you out so late."

"You're not keeping me out. I want to be out. If anything, I'm keeping you out."

Will's eyebrows rose in agreement. He looked around. Some people milled around outside the bar. Further down the street, more people were milling around, probably in front of another bar. "If you don't want to go home, what do you want to do? I think you really need some food."

"I'm not hungry. Let's go that way," she said, pointing down the street toward the park. She began walking, and Will followed. "When I want to get away from whatever is gnawing at me but I don't feel like sitting at a coffee shop, I go down here. There is a park bench that I've taken over as my own. Sitting there," she sighed, "it feels like you can see the whole city."

Will put his hand on Amy's shoulder to slow her momentum. She stopped walking.

"What? You don't like parks?" she asked.

His eyes were toward the sky. "I want to show you something."

Amy's looked in the direction of his gaze.

"Up there," he pointed to a bright star in the eastern sky. "See that? The bright one? It's Jupiter."

Amy looked at the shining planet and then at Will. She smiled, almost skeptically. "How did you know that?"

Will shoved his hands in his pockets and began walking. This time Amy followed.

"I took an Astronomy class my first year of college. I hadn't thought too much about it lately, but I just ran across an Astronomy book in a bookshop, and it all came back to me."

With her eyes still to the sky, Amy continued to follow Will.

"Ah. What other planets are visible this time of year? Are they aligning for anything special?"

Will looked back at Amy. Her hair hung about her face, tangled from dancing. Mascara was smudged under her eyes, and her skirt had twisted itself a couple inches out of place. She turned around, still moving forward, her mouth hanging open a bit.

He smiled. "Saturn's out there, but it's not as visible as it was earlier a couple months ago. Venus is visible right after sunset." He waited for her to catch up. "They might be aligning for something. Professor Hollings said they were."

Amy drew her eyes from the sky. "He said what?"

They continued walking, now side by side.

"He said the planets were aligning. He said it was fate that I would find you."

"Really? That sounds like Professor Hollings. That's why I loved his classes." As they neared the park, Amy pointed to a park bench in the middle of the lawn. "There's my bench."

They cut across the grass toward it.

She continued, "I grew up believing in all the wonderful stories that I read, and the entire time I was in college, people teased me about it. They said that those stories were just stories—they weren't going to get me a job or help me buy a house. I'd be better off as an Econ major. They said that it was silly to care about those stories. But Professor Hollings believed in those stories like me. He was like my dad. He kept me going."

They came to the bench and sat down.

"Oh yeah?" Will said.

Amy nodded, looking out to the street. She used both hands to comb her hair way from her face. Half of it fell right back where it began. "My dad is a Professor of Classics—so he's the one who got me into those old stories in the first place. April and I grew up hearing Greek and Roman myths as bedtime stories. When other kids were reading *Goodnight Moon*, we were listening to *Echo and Narcissus.* By the time we were in grade school, my dad had us reading children's versions of Shakespeare plays instead of *Ramona Quimby* books. I loved *A Midsummer Night's Dream* before I knew what love was." Amy looked up at the sky. "Where is Jupiter again?"

Will took her hand and pointed her finger toward the white speck far to the east. "Right there." He held her hand toward the sky for a moment.

She smiled. When their hands dropped back to the bench, she said, "April couldn't stand all the stories—all those stories my dad shared with us. She couldn't wait to get away from them. But I loved them. I wanted to be them. I wanted to grow into them."

A breeze whistled through the trees scattered around them.

"Have you? Grown into any?" Will asked.

Amy thought for a moment. "I don't know. Not yet."

The breeze blew again, harder. Amy shivered.

"What was your favorite? Which story did you love the most?"

Amy looked back up to the stars. "A story by an old Roman poet, Ovid. It's called *Baucis and Philemon*, but I always call it *The Linden and the Oak.*"

Will smiled. He hadn't thought of that story in years.

Amy pushed her hair away again and said, "There is an old married couple who loves each other so much that they can't bare to live a second without each other. One day the Gods Jupiter and Mercury decide they want to see how things are going with the humans down below them. So they disguise themselves as weary travelers, and they pay a visit to a little town. No one is nice them—they knock on door after door looking for shelter and a little food, only to have each door slammed in their faces. Finally they come to Baucis and Philemon's house. These two people have been married for ages, and now they are very old and very poor living in a little cottage without much of anything. I know it's cliché, but all they have is love. They invite the travelers in and throw a meal together. And as they bustle around the kitchen, adding a little extra water to the soup and searching for another crust of bread, they chat away with their guests. Even though Baucis and Philemon don't have much, no one notices because their kindness outweighs everything else."

Amy shifted toward Will and smiled at him, her eyes growing wide. "Here's the good part. When everyone sits down to eat, Baucis and Philemon notice the wine jug they've been drinking from never seems to get empty. They suddenly realize their visitors aren't weary travelers—they are Gods—and they are horrified that they've just served these Gods watery soup." Amy laughed. "The Gods stop them and explain that no one else in the town was kind to them, so they plan to punish everyone with a great flood. Only Baucis and Philemon will survive. On top of that, the Gods promise to grant the old couple a wish." She stopped herself, thinking. "Wouldn't it be incredible if the Gods offered you a wish? What would you wish for if you could wish for anything?"

Will reached toward Amy and pushed a stray curl behind her ear. "Probably what Baucis and Philemon wished for."

Amy sighed a drunken sigh. "They did have good ideas for wishes. And they couldn't pick just one, so they asked for two. First, they ask to be guardians of the temple built to worship the Gods. And second, they ask that neither of them live longer than the other. They had spent almost their entire lives together, and they don't want to live even one moment without each other. The Gods grant them both wishes. They spend the rest of their days as guardians of the temple. And one day—the final day—Baucis sees Philemon slowly transforming into a tree, and Philemon sees the same thing happening to Baucis. They look at each other, knowing what is happening and saying goodbye to each other. One turns into a linden tree and the other turns into an oak. And as legend has it, the trees still stand before the temple, entwined for all eternity."

Amy cocked her head to one side and smiled a sideways smile. "And that's it. My favorite story."

Will listened to the breeze for a moment before speaking. "When you took Professor Salt's class on John Milton and you had to read all that Ovid poetry, you weren't assigned *Baucis and Philemon*, were you?"

Amy shook her head. "I grew up hearing that story because of my dad. Did you read it with Professor Salt?"

"No. But I remember it from my sixth grade reading book. Well, I remember the sixth-grader version of it. I always liked it too."

Amy chuckled. "You could have stopped me—you didn't have to let me tell you the whole story if you already knew it."

"It was good to hear again. It had been lost in the back of my head for years."

Amy smiled toward the stars. "Lost stories. Lost stories are good to remember. They—" She straightened up and fixed her eyes on the bench.

"Amy?" Will asked after a moment of silence passed. "What's wrong?"

"You know," she said slowly, "I just figured it out. I lost a book before I met you." She paused, mentally retracing her steps. "You know, the book that I thought I lost at the coffee shop? The one I thought you were bringing back to me? I wasn't at the coffee shop when I lost it." She shook her head. "I was sitting right here. I put the book beside me when I was looking for my notebook—and then I got distracted by Miles. And then I left it here." She scratched her head. "Huh."

"What book was it?"

"Oh, it was called *East of Eden*. By John Steinbeck. I've read it a thousand times." She bit her lip, still staring at the bench. "I guess it's gone now though. Time to go get another copy."

Will smiled. "Did you write in its margins?"

Amy tried to stop a smile from crossing her face but couldn't. "You know it."

Will nodded. "Good." His smile morphed into a sideways grin. "It's a pretty damn good book."

Amy smiled. Silence filled the space between them.

"I know. So you've always liked stories, haven't you? *Baucis and Philemon* in sixth grade, *East of Eden* later on—is that why you became an English major? Because you like stories?"

He shrugged. "I became an English major for the girls. There's probably five girls for every guy in an English class."

Amy's eyes grew. She pushed Will's shoulder. "That's why you became an English major, really?"

"Yeah. Remember the old Will I told you about earlier? Girls were his motivation for everything. But a guy has to be far more charming than I am to get those girls to help write English papers. I stuck around, despite having to do my own homework, and professors like Hollings and Salt won me over. In the end, the professors—and the stories—kept me there. And I'm glad they did."

Looking toward the street, Amy somehow felt warm in the cool morning air. After a moment she turned to Will and said, "What a beautiful night. Thank you."

Will winked at her and then pulled out his phone to check the time. "We need to get you home." He stood and held out his hand to help her up from the bench.

As they headed across the park, Amy looked over her shoulder at the bench. "We came with nothing, and we leave nothing behind."

***

"It's almost three o'clock in the morning."

Amy looked up from the sink where she was washing her face and found her sister standing in the bathroom's doorway. Sleep clung to April's eyes, and she kept them half-closed to keep out the bathroom's bright light.

"Oh," Amy said, grabbing a towel to dry her face. She watched April disappear from the doorway and down the hall.

"Miles came by," April muttered, only loud enough for Amy to hear. "He said he wants you to call him. Now. He doesn't care what time it is." April stopped in the middle of the dark hallway, sensing her sister's eyes peeking around the bathroom door. "I don't care where you were, but, where were you? When we got back from having coffee, you were gone."

Amy didn't answer. She hung up the towel, and by the time she went to turn off the bathroom light, April had disappeared.

She walked down the dark hallway and opened her sister's bedroom door. Faintly she could see April's lumpy outline against the queen-sized bed. Amy kicked off her shoes and lay down next to her sister.

"What happened?" April whispered, her eyes still closed.

Amy remembered something Lizzie had said to Eva over fifty years ago. Channeling her grandmother, she whispered back, "I met a guy tonight."

"Have you been drinking?"

"Yeah."

"Go brush your teeth."

"Don't you want to hear about the guy?"

April moaned. "Not particularly."

"Don't you even care that I met a guy?"

April felt herself reeling in a state of semi-consciousness. "What happened?" she asked, fighting off wakefulness.

"I went to a bar with Will."

"And you met a guy there?"

"Yeah."

"Who was he?"

"Will."

"Will? The one you went to the bar with?"

"Yeah."

"What happened?"

"Nothing. We danced."

"Did you do anything that you're going to regret tomorrow?"

"No. I have a boyfriend." Amy giggled. "He was a perfect gentleman."

"If you're going to wake my ass up in the middle of the night with some story, have the decency to brush your teeth beforehand." April took the pillow from beneath her head and slammed it over Amy's head.

"We were dancing, April," Amy said, her voice muffled underneath the pillow. "And I realized he is the missing puzzle piece."

April waited for more. When nothing else came, she found herself climbing toward clearer consciousness. "What do you mean?"

"When we were dancing and I wanted to tell him something, it was so easy to lean into him."

"Oh, Amy." The tone of April's voice dropped in warning.

"I mean, he's the perfect height."

April pulled the pillow off Amy's face and tucked it under her head. "Oh, Amy," she repeated.

"But what I mean really," Amy said, her words slowing dramatically, "is that he knows what I mean before I even say what I'm thinking. And he knows all the great stories I know. He knows *Baucis and Philemon*. No one else knows that story. No one. Miles doesn't know that story."

April agreed silently, not realizing in her sleepiness that was what she was doing. "*Baucis and Philemon.* Right."

Amy yawned. "He has really nice arms. And he even knows *East of Eden.*"

"Are you going to call Miles?"

"In a minute." She felt so tired. Her limbs had turned to lead. "I'll call him in a minute. Just give me a minute."

April gave herself over to the sleepiness, and soon dreams swallowed the words Amy had left hanging in the air. In the morning, however, when she awoke to find Amy asleep, crumpled into a ball on the corner of her bed, she began to understand what her sister had said.

***

After Will walked Amy home, he jumped into his truck and headed toward the freeway. He thought about Lizzie's story. He thought about Amy's story. He thought about his story. And he thought about the point at which all three stories converged.

He reached for his cell phone and dialed Jocelyn's phone number. When she picked up, her voice was low but her words were fast.

"Will?" she said. "What's wrong?"

He almost chuckled. Even now, months after they had broken up, she still answered the phone with the same greeting when he called at the middle of the night. "Hey Jos. Everything's fine."

"Then why are you calling me?"

Will took a deep breath—almost a sigh. "Because," he said, "I didn't really treat you well when we were together. I sort of knew it then, but I didn't know how to change. Now I'm starting to get it. And I wanted to apologize."

"Have you been drinking? Are you okay?"

He smiled. "I'm fine. More fine than you'd expect."

Jocelyn was silent for a moment. "Well, thanks for calling."

"Don't say that. Don't hang up and blow me off. I really want you to know that I'm sorry."

"Will, that's great," she yawned. "But you couldn't have waited until morning?"

"My epiphany didn't come with magical intelligence. Sorry."

She laughed softly, tired.

"Jos, we'll never get back together, will we? And we'll never really be friends, right?"

He could almost hear her shaking her head through the phone. "No, we won't."

"I guess that's why I want you to know that I am really, truly sorry. I'll never have the chance to make it up to you—so you'll just have to accept my apology."

"Will," she said, "Don't be sorry. Just be nice to the next girl who comes around."

An image of Billy surfaced in his mind. *Don't you let her make the same mistakes that Lizzie made,* he had said.

"That's the plan," he said to Jocelyn. "That's the plan."

Thirty-four

A voice echoed somewhere in the back of Amy's mind. It was female, and it was familiar. But there was something else about it that drew Amy from her slumber. Something urgent in its tone—

The bedroom door swung inward, and Amy's eyes shot open. She saw her sister in the doorway with a phone to her ear. She looked around. Why was she curled in a ball at the edge of April's bed? Why was her head pounding?

"Amy, Miles is on the phone for the fourth time this morning. I told him you were asleep, but he said if you don't talk to him right now, he's coming over."

Amy sat up and rubbed the inner edges of her eyes. "Miles?"

April leaned against the doorframe and nodded. "Yep," she said, half into the phone, half to Amy. "Your boyfriend, remember? The one who tried to tell Mom yesterday that you were going through Lizzie's stuff."

Amy closed her eyes and tried to shake the fog out of her head. "Tell him I'll call him later."

April nodded. "Amy says you're a loser." She turned toward the kitchen and disappeared from Amy's sight. "She'll call you later. Goodbye."

Amy slid out of April's bed and pulled her hair away from her face, stretching her arms along the way. "Thank you," she called down the hallway.

Her body ached as she walked toward the bathroom. She was still wearing the same clothes she wore to Billy's the day before, and in the bathroom mirror she saw the wrinkles and beer stains they had acquired since the trip to Monterey. She splashed water on her face. Monterey felt like it had happened a year ago, but the wrinkles and beer stains proved otherwise.

As she reached for her toothbrush, she saw her cell phone on the counter, left there the night before. She picked it up and saw an alert for seven voicemails. Six were from the night before and one was from this morning—and they were all from Miles. Each asked her to call him as soon as she got the message. *I'm getting worried*, he said somewhere in the fifth or sixth message. By the last message, she stopped listening. She finished brushing her teeth and deleted all seven messages.

After a quick shower, she threw on some clothes and grabbed her purse.

"I'm going to Nana's," she told April while passing through the kitchen. "I didn't call Miles, so I halfway expect him to show up here. Please don't tell him where I am."

April looked up from her cup of tea. "With pleasure."

As Amy reached for the doorknob, she heard her sister's voice again.

"When you get back, I want to talk to you."

"Okay." She waited to see if April was going to elaborate. When no explanation came, a thin layer of guilt settled across Amy's mind, dampening her memories of the last day. She waited a moment longer and then left.

Driving to Nana's house, she tried to ignore that guilt. She tried to figure out why it was there and why it wouldn't evaporate. Was it because she knew what April wanted to talk about? Was it because of the family history she had discovered yesterday? Was it because she hadn't called Miles?

When Amy knocked on Eva's front door, the guilt disappeared and was replaced by worry. Maybe she should have called first. It probably wasn't a good idea to show up unexpected. Normally she would have called—but this morning she just wanted to get out of her house before Miles showed up.

Aidan answered the door.

"Hey kid!" he said. "What are you doing here? This is a nice surprise."

He beckoned her to step into the house. "Here to see your grandma? She's at the grocery store. Should be back any minute now. Can I get you something to drink while you wait?"

Aidan turned and headed into the house with Amy following him.

"Grandpa, why is my mom so angry when it comes to Lizzie?" Amy blurted out. "I mean, I know why she's angry, but why is it such a big deal for me to want to know what happened?"

"You still talking about that wack-a-doodle Lizzie?" Aidan said, poking his head into the refrigerator. He pulled out two sodas and walked to the kitchen table where Amy was sitting. He shook his head at the drinks. "I don't know for sure, Amy, but I believe it's because Lizzie was so darn crazy. Who wants a crazy mom?" He sat down and placed one soda in front of Amy. As she picked it up and cracked the top, he leaned toward her and said in a softer voice, "So what do you know about her so far?"

Amy's eyes grew as the answer rolled out of her mouth. "I think I know a lot. I know that she married John even though she wasn't over Billy. I know that she disappeared just in time for John to burn his house down. I know you and Nana ended up adopting mom and her sisters because John died in the fire." Her shoulders slumped involuntarily. "I just don't know what happened after the fire."

Aidan sat back in his chair and nodded. "I'm impressed."

The center of Amy's eyebrows turned inward, pleadingly. "Are you impressed enough to tell me what happened?"

Aidan laughed. "I think you know as much as I do. And I think you answered your first question about why your mom is so upset." His expression turned serious. "Wouldn't you be mad if your mom walked out on you—and then you saw your dad die in a fire? If it were me, I'd want to pretend it never happened."

Amy nodded at her drink.

"I think your mom is coming around. Just remember, she's buried her feelings about Lizzie for years and years. It's all resurfaced since Lizzie's death. She needs time to work through those feelings, just like you've needed some time to figure out what happened."

Amy glanced at Aidan before fixing her eyes back on the soda can. "Did you know I was digging for answers?"

Aidan smiled. "I figured. And I think this project is good for you. Your job has bored you to tears." He chuckled. "I've been bored to tears watching you do that job. I'm glad to see you interested in something."

"Thanks, Grandpa."

"You know, there's a shoebox under our bed filled with photos of Lizzie and such. I think you probably have a couple minutes before Nana gets home if you want to check it out."

Amy leapt to her feet. "You're the best," she said, patting Aidan on the shoulder before heading toward the stairs and taking them two at a time.

Upstairs, she dove underneath her grandparents' bed and pulled out a couple shoeboxes. The first one had shoes in it, but the second was filled with pictures. She grabbed a stack from one end of the box.

The top picture showed two young women sitting at a café, sipping coffee, looking at each other instead of the camera. Amy flipped it over and read the handwriting on the back.

Eva and Lizzie, Paris, 1955

In the next, one of the young women from the first picture walked down a cobblestone road toward the camera, a soft smile painted across her face.

Lizzie, Paris, 1995, read the back.

Amy studied the first two pictures. They—Eva and Lizzie—were so young. And they looked just as she imaged they would. Defiantly long hair. Glowing, amused eyes.

She looked at another picture of Lizzie talking to a shorter woman outside a market, a bag of groceries sitting on each hip. She went through each one, slowly, checking the captions on the back. Then she flipped through all the pictures a second time, faster now. Lizzie staring at the sky, her hair hanging to her waist and swaying in the wind; Lizzie and Eva looking directly at the camera at close range, their eyes and smiles hinting at mockery; Lizzie sitting on a stool next to a painter, handing him a cup of coffee.

Amy was about to grab another stack of pictures when she heard footsteps in the hallway. Her heart jumped. She knew they weren't Aidan's; his weren't so rhythmic—his weren't so fast. She shoved the pictures into the shoebox and pushed it under the bed. Then she slouched down, her back against the box spring.

The footsteps stopped at the doorway. Amy held her breath.

"Honey, do you really think you need to hide from me?" Eva said. "I've never been much for those kinds of games. I didn't think you were either."

Amy got to her feet and looked toward her smiling grandmother. "Sorry, Nana."

Eva walked into the room and sat on the edge of the bed. "The second I came in—do you know what Grandpa said to me? He looked up from his drink and said, 'Amy's upstairs going through the shoeboxes under your bed.'" She laughed. "How do you like that? He's the one who told you about those pictures—it seems like he'd be the first to cover for you."

Amy crawled onto the bed next to Nana. "Grandpa just can't hide anything from you."

Eva continued to smile, though it faded slightly as she picked out her words. "That's true." She nodded. "And Grandpa has never quite known how to handle the topic of my sister. It's always been a little touchy. You know how it is with sisters—even when you're mad at April, you'd go to the end of the earth for her. Right?" Eva nodded again at Amy as though answering her own question. "Grandpa always understood that relationship, although he hasn't always known what to say or do about it. And he probably wants you to know about Lizzie but doesn't want to say the wrong thing."

"I'm sorry Nana," Amy interrupted. "I should have waited until you came home—I shouldn't have come up here. My curiosity just got the best of me."

"I am glad you are curious. Your curiosity has always been something that I've admired. And I know this has been a tough—"

"Nana, I know everything," Amy said before Eva could finish. "I know about the fire, I know that Lizzie abandoned her children for Billy, and I know that you were stuck raising them when she left. I know that my mom never got over it."

Eva absorbed Amy's words. She nodded. Then she smiled. She reached over and patted Amy's leg. "I always knew that you were an excellent investigator. That's part of why you became an English major—you always knew how to analyze what was in front of you. It sounds like you've done a good deal of exploration on this matter."

"I just wanted to know what happened. And I still just want to know what happened. Where was Lizzie during the fire? Had she gone to see Billy in New York? Did their relationship ever end?"

Eva thought a moment and then sighed. Her eyes searched the walls of the room before finally settling back on Amy.

"Honey, your mom has spent most of her life plagued by that last question of yours. She's been swallowed by it—so much so that Billy and Lizzie have become a single monster in her mind. They're a monster that stole her father and her childhood." Eva shook her head. "I never told her that Lizzie went to New York right before the fire, but she is an investigator like you. She found out on her own. And when she found out, she declared that no one in the family was ever to speak of Lizzie in her presence—or your presence." Eva's eyes searched the walls again. "I think that's starting to change. Last night April brought Lizzie into conversation when we were at coffee. She—"

"April did what?" Amy had heard Eva just fine, but she couldn't stop the words from coming.

Eva tilted her head toward her granddaughter and smiled. "She wants to protect you. She knows both you and your mom have a lot of emotions invested in Lizzie—different emotions of course, but emotions nonetheless. And she knows that if you two had the conversation, those emotions could clash and cause an ugly scene. She wants you both to make peace with this."

Amy raised an eyebrow at Eva. "Mom has a lot to make peace with, but I don't. This didn't happen to me. And I understand why Mom would be so upset, but," she thought about something she had said the night before to Will, "should something be hidden just because it's tragic?"

Eva pursed her lips and shrugged. "I don't know, honey."

A moment passed. Then Amy asked, "What about Lizzie and Billy? *Did* their relationship ever end?"

"Ah, yes, back to that." Again Eva's eyes floated away from Amy as she thought through her words. "No, it didn't. I know that she loved him until the very end. But any relationship that lasts over fifty years is going to be complex—and to classify their relationship as romantic, platonic, spiritual, emotional," she shook her head, "I'll never know what they had. Even when she was dying of cancer, we never spoke about what happened. I lost a piece of my sister when she went to New York. For years I thought I had lost that piece to Billy, and even at the end, I never got that piece back. We could never talk about that fateful trip—it was out of my reach."

Amy absorbed Eva's words. "And despite everything that happened—despite having to raise your sister's children and never getting an explanation, you forgave her."

Eva nodded. "Raising your mother and her sisters was one of the most wonderful experiences of my life. Of course I wish that they could have been raised by their own mother—for their sake—but I loved every minute of it." She looked at Amy. "After the fire, we tried very hard to find Lizzie in New York. So did three private investigators. I needed to get her back home to her girls. But we couldn't find her anywhere. We all knew that Billy had an enormous amount of money by that time and perhaps could have hidden her behind that money." Eva's face darkened. "And I was so mad at him for refusing to talk to us." She paused, the darkness in her expression disappearing as quickly as it came. "But our inability to reach her has always given me pause. Even though investigations in the 1960s were nothing like they are today, it seemed like finding Lizzie in New York shouldn't have been so difficult. After awhile I began to wonder if I didn't lose a piece of my sister to Billy. I began to think that I lost her to something else. Something bigger. I just never knew what."

Amy collapsed backward on the bed and looked at the ceiling. "I wonder what happened."

Eva looked at her granddaughter. "She did come back years later. She came back, and she was devastated to hear what had happened. She had no idea—and I do believe she really had no any idea. She never quite overcame her guilt. And she certainly didn't know how to build a relationship with her children at that point. Soon she left again—and again, we didn't know where she went."

"Nana," Amy said through a deep breath. "It's amazing that you forgave her even without knowing the whole story. I think I would have needed an explanation. I would have needed a reason to forgive her."

"She was my sister, Amy. That was reason enough. I didn't know how she ended up a sad, emaciated woman dying in a gigantic house not even thirty minutes from here—and I didn't care. She was my sister. My tragic, self-destructive sister. The only one I'll ever have. When we were little girls, she and I practically shared the same heart—we were so close. When I was still fairly new to adulthood, her daughters filled my heart. And I'm sitting here with you, now, because of her—she continues to share my heart through you." Eva shook her head. "My tragic, self-destructive sister. Her tragedies became the greatest blessings in my life. Not forgiving her would have resulted in my fall from grace."

Amy nodded at the ceiling. After a moment, she said, "Do you really think my mom is coming around? Do you think she might be okay with me poking around Lizzie's past?"

"April's pretty good at getting people to listen to her. I always thought she would have been a great lawyer." Eva chuckled. "Maybe that's why she's such a good kindergarten teacher—she knows how to break everything down in such a simple, logical way. As for your mom—I think at this point you could talk to her about Lizzie. Cautiously." Eva patted Amy's leg again, this time as though to alter the course of the conversation. "Now you know as much as I do about Lizzie. And it's time to stop looking backward and begin working on your own story."

Thirty-five

"I'm sorry about last night," Amy said into the phone.

Will laughed on the other end. "Don't be. You were a lot of fun. You should get out more. I think it was good for you."

Amy smiled, "I just hope I didn't do or say anything too stupid."

"I wouldn't tell you even if you did. What are you up to?"

"I just left Nana's house," she sighed. Stepping on her car's break, she slowed on approach to a stop sign and continued, "I have a five-minute drive home, and I'm certain Miles will be there waiting for me."

"You don't sound excited about that."

"No," Amy said. Her voice disappeared into thoughts she didn't seem likely to share.

"How was your visit with Eva?" Will asked.

"It was good." Amy looked in both directions before proceeding through the intersection. "She told me a lot—nothing particularly new—but still a lot of important stuff. I'm having a hard time wrapping my brain around it."

"You've got five minutes before you get home. Talk through it."

Amy tried to organize her thoughts. "Nana hired private investigators to find Lizzie after the house burned down, but no one could find her. They knew she had gone to New York, and they all suspected she had gone to find Billy. Even now, though, that's never been confirmed. They tried contacting Billy directly, but he wouldn't help them find her. And Lizzie never told Nana what happened during the years she was gone, but oddly, Nana was okay with that. She said that Lizzie's greatest tragedies became her greatest blessings, meaning my mom and the rest of us. And because of that, she forgave Lizzie—for everything." She paused, again slowing toward another stop sign. "I think I have a hard time understanding that kind of unconditional forgiveness."

Neither spoke for a moment.

"Maybe you do right now," Will said, "but that's because it's never been tested in you. Just because you haven't needed that kind of forgiveness in your life doesn't mean you aren't capable of it."

Amy bit her lower lip, thinking. "Part of me really wants to drive back to Monterey and ask Billy to tell me what happened in New York. That's the missing puzzle piece. Everyone has just assumed they know why she went there and what happened when she went there—but…" she couldn't find the words to finish the sentence.

"You think there's more to it."

"Maybe. Nana said after awhile she started to think that she hadn't lost Lizzie to Billy but instead to something else. Something bigger. And I think she might be right. Lizzie died a very wealthy woman. How did that happen? Nana doesn't have that kind of money. If their parents took away Nana's inheritance because she married Aidan, certainly they would have taken away Lizzie's after she destroyed her family. Did Billy have a hand in that? Did he give it to her?" Amy tapped her fingers on the steering wheel. "Nana said she didn't know how Lizzie ended up a sad, emaciated woman dying in a huge house, and she didn't care—because they were sisters and no explanations were needed. But I need an explanation." Slowly she continued driving toward the corner where she would turn onto her street.

"I think you should go tell Billy that. He might turn you down flat, but he also might surprise you. He's a strange old guy. But you need to try. You don't want to look back and regret not trying." When Will's words were met with silence, he continued, "I'll go with you—if you want."

Amy smiled. "Thank you." At the corner where she should have turned left toward her house, she turned right and headed toward the freeway. She thought about what waited for her at home, and she thought about what stood at the end of a long stretch of freeway before her. Her stomach felt raw with excitement and worry. "I think I want to do this on my own. And I need some time to think about everything."

***

A slow, continuous knock on the door pulled April away from her spot on the couch where she was reading a magazine.

"I'm coming," she called. And when the knocking didn't stop, she repeated, this time louder, "I'm coming, stop knocking."

But the knocking continued.

April checked the peephole and swung the front door open.

"Geeze Miles, what the hell is wrong with you? I said I was coming. No need to break the door down."

"Is Amy here?" he asked, looking past April's shoulder and into the house.

April stepped further into the open space of the doorframe, blocking as much of the house as possible, and put her hand on her hip. "Nope. And I don't expect her any time soon."

"Can I come in please? I need to talk to her."

"She's not here. There's no need for you to come in."

"But she will be back at some point. She won't answer my calls or texts. I just want to come in and wait for her."

"Nope. Not a chance. I don't like the smell of coward." She started closing the door, but it met the resistance of Miles' hand.

"How am I a coward?"

"Oh my gosh—are you kidding? Do you really think it's your place to call our mother to tattle on Amy? You know, you're not part of this family, and what Amy's doing has nothing to do with you—"

"I'm her boyfriend. I want to make sure she doesn't do anything stupid."

"You are not her keeper. She doesn't need one. And if she did, it would be me." April tried to close the door again, but again Miles resisted.

"April, please just let me in."

"No way. If you want to wait for her, you can sit outside." She pushed hard against the door, and Miles relented. It closed, she locked it, and Miles sat down on the porch.

Thirty-six

Amy stared at the heavy, dark door standing between her and Billy's study. She took a deep breath and knocked three times. When no one answered, she turned the handle and pushed the door open a sliver.

Billy looked up from his desk. When he saw her eyes peering around the door, he scowled.

"It's you," he said.

Amy opened the door further and stepped into the room. "Yes, it's me." She concentrated on keeping her eyes toward Billy rather than running up and down the walls of books, and, hands clasped behind her back, she walked slowly toward his desk and sat in the chair opposite him.

"I suppose it's no surprise you came back," he said. "You are a Hathaway girl, after all."

Amy nodded and then swallowed. "Yes sir, I am. But I'm as much Winthrow as I am Hathaway."

Billy raised an eyebrow at her. "What do you want?"

"I want to know what happened," she said. "I want to know why Lizzie left her children—why she left my mother and why she didn't come back after her husband was killed in the fire. I know everything else. I've seen the letters that you two wrote back and forth, and I know about the time that you spent together in Paris. But I need to know why you let Lizzie abandon her children because—"

"Are you blaming me for the difficulties of your mother's life?" Billy's eyes narrowed.

Amy blinked and swallowed again. "Do I have reason to?"

Billy glared at her from the other side of the desk, his eyes still narrow, searching and evaluating. "You have your grandmother's eyes. Not the color—not even the shape, really. But the determination in them is the same. And you carry yourself the same way. Lightly. Did you know that?" He didn't wait for a response before continuing. "Of course you didn't. You couldn't—no one but Eva would know it, and she would never speak of it to you."

Amy nodded.

"Tell me," Billy said as he leaned back in his chair and pressed his fingertips together. "What did Lizzie leave you in her will?"

Amy straightened up. "She gave me and my sister money to continue our educations. And she left us a room full of books."

Billy nodded. "And you already know that she left me a specific list of books. Seems odd, doesn't it, given that I own every great book written?"

Amy thought she detected a fleeting smile on Billy's lips as he waved his hand toward the rows of bookcases around the room. She nodded again.

"Lizzie was foolish," Billy said. "She was brilliant with her talents, but she was foolish. Are you the same way? You have the same determined eyes. Do you have the same foolishness? Or the same brilliance?" Again Billy continued without giving Amy a chance to respond. "Your friend was here yesterday. He picked up a book of yours. I saw the notes that you wrote in the margin. You were a poet. Is that correct?" As he finished his question, he opened a drawer to his desk and pulled out a short, wide book.

Amy's heart quickened. She wasn't sure if he really expected an answer.

Billy picked up a pen from his desk and began writing in his book. "Young lady, I asked you a question. You are a poet, correct?"

She shook her head. "No."

Billy tore out the piece of paper.

"Miss Winthrow, I do believe that you are lying. Perhaps you are lying to me. Perhaps you are lying to yourself. I do not know. But I don't tolerate liars—and neither should you. I have seen your grandmother in your eyes, and I have seen your words in that book. Lizzie lied to herself, and we both know the effects of those lies. Do not lie."

Amy nodded.

"The boxes of books she sent to me were boxes of regrets. She read all those stories in school because she had to and not because she wanted to. To me, those stories were gold—particularly when I was young, poor, and stupid. Do you know why she would send me boxes of regrets and send you back to school?"

Amy shook her head.

Billy looked at the piece of paper he had torn away from the book before turning his eyes to Amy. "Then you better go back to school and find out. Lizzie must believe the answer is there." Billy held the piece of paper up and waved its two short corners at her. "I have been thinking a great deal since you first came to see me yesterday. It seems that you should know the rest of the story—if for no other reason than to keep you from telling these disastrous lies you like to tell. I, however, can't be the one to tell you." He laid the paper on the desk, face up, and pushed it toward her. "You will need this to get the rest of the story."

Amy picked it up. Her head felt light and she looked back and forth from it to Billy. "This is a check. It's made out to me."

"I want you to go to Paris. I want you to get on the next flight. I don't know how much a last minute round trip ticket costs, but that check should cover it. On the memo line is an address. I want you to go there upon arrival." He leaned back in his chair and pressed the tips of his fingers together. "Miss Winthrow, there is nothing for me to tell you. However, you will find all your answers at that address."

"Mr. Strath, I can't take this—"

"You do know that I am made of money, correct? I have no time for protests about this. Take it and leave me to my work."

Amy stood, automatically, ready to obey his wishes, but feeling confused.

"Thank you, sir." Awkwardly, she continued, "Do you want me to tell you what I find when I come back?"

"No," Billy snapped. "I already know what you'll find. I lived the story, did I not? Just go—leave me be. Right now."

Amy turned and walked toward the door, fighting the urge to thank him again. When she reached the door, his voice stopped her.

"Miss Winthrow," he said, scribbling across the paper on his desk and keeping his eyes down. Amy turned toward him. "Remember, you are just as much Hathaway as you are Winthrow."

"Yes sir. Thank you." She stepped through the door and closed it behind her.

Half way down the stairs, Amy felt her cell phone vibrate against her purse. She pulled it out and looked at the text message that had come through.

FYI—Your boyfriend is still here. I wouldn't let him in, so he's been sitting on the porch for nearly two hours.

Amy thought about how to answer April's message as she walked through the house toward the front door. What she wanted to say was too complicated for a text.

She pulled up April's cell phone number and called her.

"Hey," Amy said as her sister answered. She pushed Billy's front door open and squinted in the sunlight. "Earlier you said you wanted to talk to me, and with Miles camped out on our porch, I figured it would be easier to talk now rather than when I get home."

"Can I just break up with him for you? I'm happy to do it."

Amy unlocked her car door and slid into the driver's seat. "No, that's not your responsibility."

April huffed. "Well, can I at least tell him that you've moved to Florida so that he'll go away?"

"You're being silly."

"Where are you?"

Amy started her car and steered it toward the winding road that led to the freeway. "I'm in Monterey. I'm on my way home now, but," she took a deep breath, "I'm only going to be there for a little bit—just long enough to pack. I'm going to Paris. Lizzie's old boyfriend told me that I could get the rest of her story there, and he gave me money for the trip." She cringed, bracing herself for April to freak out.

"You are driving me nuts, little sister." April sighed, exasperated. "Is this whole thing almost over? Will this trip to Paris be the end? I can't take much more of this."

Amy rolled her eyes. "Yes, this will be the end of it. I think."

"Okay. Good. Listen, before you leave, there are two things you need to do."

Amy waited for April to continue.

"First, you need to go talk to Mom."

"I know. Nana told me what you did last night at coffee."

"I'm not promising anything—I'm not saying that Mom will volunteer to take you to the airport when she hears you are going to Paris—but it's still time for you to talk to her."

"I know, you're right. Thank you."

"Second," April's tone dropped, "you need to talk to Miles. This is getting ridiculous."

"You're right."

"I don't care what you say, but you need to say something."

"You're right."

"Do you remember where you woke up this morning? Do you remember why you were there?"

"Yes, I know." It was Amy's turn to sign an exasperated sigh. "You're right, of course, as usual."

"Good. I'm glad that's settled. I'll start packing for you."

***

Amy pulled into her driveway. Her head felt light; her limbs felt tense and weak. She put the car in park, climbed out, and walked toward the porch where Miles sat waiting.

He stood as she neared him. "Amy, where have you been? I've been waiting here forever. You haven't answered any of my—"

She motioned for him to sit back down. He stopped talking but didn't seem to understand what she meant until she sat down herself. He stood for a moment, staring at her sitting on the porch, and then sat next to her.

Wrapping her arms around her knees, she said, "Miles, we need to talk."

Thirty-seven

They sat in Will's truck outside Debbie and Spenser's house. Amy stared out the windshield; Will stared at Amy.

"Hey, I know this isn't easy," he said after a moment. "But there's no way around it."

Amy nodded, still staring out the windshield.

"And I'd come with you, but then your dad would recognize me as the guy who picked up Lizzie's books, and your mom would recognize me as the guy at your house last night. That would probably be pretty confusing."

Amy nodded again. Then she turned toward Will. "Do you really think I need to tell them I'm going to Paris?"

Will pushed his sunglasses to the top of his head. He raised an eyebrow at her.

"I know, I know." She opened the truck's door and hopped out. "I'll be back soon."

Will looked at the dashboard clock. "You've got fifteen minutes before we need to leave for the airport."

Amy pursed her lips and nodded. "Okay." Taking a deep breath, she turned toward the house and began walking up the driveway.

"Hello?" she called while opening the front door. "Mom? Dad?"

She walked through the house and caught sight of her parents in the backyard. They sat at the patio table, each reading and munching on grapes sitting in a bowl between them.

"Hey there," Amy said as she let herself into the backyard.

Debbie and Spenser looked up and greeted their daughter with big smiles.

"Hey, look who's here," Spenser said. He closed his book. "Come have some grapes and remind your mother that great scholars of Classics shouldn't have to do yard work."

"Spenser," Debbie said, also closing her book. "I didn't mean you have to mow the lawn right now. Just after you finish reading that chapter."

Amy sat down at the patio table and felt her stomach flip. It would be easier to watch her parents discuss lawn care than to bring up an impromptu trip to Paris. For a moment she considered taking that route.

Debbie shook her head at Spenser and then smiled at her daughter. “What are you up to this afternoon?”

“Well,” Amy started slowly, looking at the table. “I’m going to Paris this evening. Unexpectedly.” She smiled awkwardly knowing that the statement sounded ridiculous. “Of course it’s unexpectedly. You would have known sooner if it were expected.”

Both parents stared at her.

“You’re going to Paris?” Debbie asked.

“For work?” her dad asked.

For a fleeting moment, Amy considered answering *yes* to her dad’s question. It would have been so much easier.

She shook her head. “Not for work.” She looked back at the table. “Billy Strath is sending me there. To find out what three of Nana’s private investigators couldn’t uncover decades ago about Lizzie.” She squeezed her eyes shut and took a deep breath. Then she opened her eyes, one at a time, hoping she wouldn’t see red across her parents’ faces.

Spenser looked at his surprised wife and nervous daughter. He stood up. “I’m going to mow the lawn. Professors of Classics need their exercise.” He headed toward the house, patting Amy on the shoulder as he passed by.

“Honey,” Debbie said, shaking her head. “What are you doing?”

“Mom, I know you aren’t thrilled about me looking into Lizzie’s past, but Nana said she thought April had sort of convinced you that it’s okay—”

“Yeah, but you’re going to Paris? Billy Strath is sending you to Paris?”

“I know it sounds strange—”

“Do you really think this is a good idea? Do you really think you can trust that man?”

“I don’t think it’s a bad idea. And I’m not going to Paris *with* him—he’s just sending me there. I don’t think the issue of trust even comes into play. He gave me a check and an address. That’s it.”

“And he doesn’t want anything in return?”

Amy wasn't excited to see such deep lines of concern on her mother's face, but she much preferred them over the blush of anger. She shook her head. "I think he'd be happy if he never saw me again. He probably gave the money to me just to get rid of me."

Debbie didn't answer.

"Mom, I know this is bizarre, and we haven't even talked about what happened with Billy and Lizzie all those years ago, but—"

Debbie interrupted with the shake of her head. "When are you leaving?"

Amy tried to look at her mother, but the second their eyes met, Amy veered hers toward the pool. She couldn't do it. "Now. We have to head to the airport in ten minutes."

Debbie didn't answer right away. "I need some time to gather my thoughts," she finally said. "You are an adult and can make your own decisions, so I'm not going to stop you. But when you get to Paris, please call me. We will need to sort through some stuff." As Amy nodded her response, Debbie continued, "Go say goodbye to your father."

Amy hugged her mom before heading toward the house and zigzagging through it to the front door. From the front porch she could see her father standing at the side window of Will's truck, leaning on the handle of his lawnmower and talking to Will. Amy ventured down the driveway.

"You know this guy?" Spenser said to Amy. He grinned and pointed in Will's direction. When Amy nodded, he shook his head and said, "Small world, isn't it?"

Amy nodded again. "It sure is." She hugged her father. "Bye, Dad. Thanks for not being mad about this."

"How's your mom?" Spenser's eyes filled with concern.

"I think she's okay. April must have cast a magical spell on her last night. I expected her to mad, but she's not. She's a little confused, but not mad."

"That sister of yours." Spenser shook his head. "She gets that talent from Eva. They both have a way of orchestrating events so that they get what they want."

Amy glanced in Will's direction knowing that they needed to get going. She hugged Spenser again and said, "I'll call you when I get there."

"Be careful." Spenser turned to Will. "Good to see you again. Drive safely."

"Good to see you, too," Will answered. "Have a great afternoon."

Amy climbed into Will's truck, and the two of them waved at Spenser as they pulled away from the curb.

"How long were you talking to my dad?" Amy asked.

"Just long enough to tell him that Billy asked me to chauffer you to the airport. I figured that was the easiest way to explain why I was lurking outside his house. Hey," he continued, now with a twinge of excitement in his voice, "I have a going away present for you." He lifted the top of the console between them and pulled out a small brown shopping bag. "Sorry I didn't have time to wrap it." He handed the bag to Amy without taking his eyes off the road.

Amy recognized the bag—it was from her favorite bookstore. She looked inside and pulled out three books. "Oh, Will—"

"Let me explain," he interrupted. "I'm giving you each of those for the reason." He glanced at the stack of books in her lap. "The top one is a guidebook to Paris. I figured you wouldn't have time to get one, but you definitely need it. The second one," he paused, waiting for Amy to flip to the second book, "is the book you lost at the park, *East of Eden.* You'll need something to read on the plane. And the last one," he paused again and Amy automatically flipped to the final book, "is the Astronomy book I got awhile ago. I was hoping you could tell me what planets are visible in the Paris sky this time of year."

Amy's throat felt as though it was closing up. She leaned over and hugged Will.

"Thank you," she choked out.

Thirty-eight

Paris

Amy looked at the Paris guidebook for the hundredth time as she rode the Metro toward what the book said was her destination: *Abbesses Station*. She had never been good with maps—or subways—and she was sure that at some point she would be lost on this trip. She just didn't want her first memory of Paris to include being lost. *Abbesses Station*, she said in her head. *Abbesses, Abbesses, Abbesses Station.* Anxiously, she watched each stop come and go, wondering how much longer—and what she'd find when she got there.

But soon her stop was in sight: *Abbesses Station.*

Once she stepped off the Metro and emerged from the station, her fears melted. She was in the heart of Montmartre—she knew it by the crowds, the shops, the music, the laughter. It wasn't what she imagined while reading *Eva's Words*; it was better. It vibrated with an energy she had never felt.

Amy dropped the guidebook to her side and wandered through the crowd. She was there—where Eva and Lizzie and Billy had spent the summer of 1955—where the story began. She found her way to a church set atop a tall staircase, and although she wondered the name of the church, she didn't look it up. She climbed the stairs alongside the other tourists, taking in its grandeur, excited to see it as it stood without knowing its history or its name. She told herself that she would look up its history later—after she had absorbed the city's joyful chaos. For now, all she wanted was to feel that new, vibrating energy and life of the city.

She found her way to the rows of artists, all chatting and drawing and enjoying the warmth of the day. She wondered where Billy's station had been so many years before. She eyed a spot she thought would be perfect for him—off in the shade, toward the end of the row. From there, Lizzie certainly would be able to spot him from afar, bring him coffee from the nearby café, and watch the tourists as they came and went.

She walked up and down the cobblestone back streets and staircases, taking in the buildings, the shops, the cars, and the people whose everyday lives were centered in this very place. She sensed that even if it weren't the high tourist season there would be a distinct spirit in the air that existed nowhere but Montmartre.

Time slipped away. Without realizing it, Amy had spent an hour meandering through this corner of Paris. Looking at her watch, she thought it wise to find the building whose address filled the memo line of Billy's check—before she let the entire day slip away.

She found the street without much trouble. It was an off-shoot of Monmartre's bustling center—a downhill slope punctuated with short staircases and rows of trees. As she moved down the hill, looking for the address that matched Billy's instructions, the buzz and flurry of the place dissipated into a warm, welcoming residential area.

Halfway down the hill, she found herself standing before a building with the correct address. She walked to the front door, checked the address one more time, and then knocked.

Moments later, a short, round, wrinkly woman answered the door.

"Mademoiselle Amy?" the woman said with a wide smile. "Is it you?" When Amy nodded, the smile widened further than Amy thought possible, and the woman ushered her in, wrapping her chubby arms around Amy's neck. "Welcome," she said, pulling away from Amy and taking the traveling backpack off her shoulders. "Please come in and sit. Billy called and explained that you were coming. We—my husband and I—we are so happy that you are here. I am Marie. It is so nice to meet you."

She led Amy into the house and directed her toward the living room where two vintage, velvet couches stood opposite each other with a coffee table separating them.

"Please, sit."

"Thank you." Amy sat on the far side of the closest couch and smiled at her hostess.

"I have been told that you are Lizzie's granddaughter, yes?" Marie sat down on the opposite end of the couch.

Amy nodded.

"And you are here to learn about her time in Paris?"

Amy nodded again, but then she stopped herself as Marie's words sunk in. "Oh, actually I think I know about Lizzie's time in

Paris. Mr. Strath said that I could find out about her time in New York if I came here."

"Ah, I see," Marie said. "I only know of her time in Paris. Perhaps we are talking about the same thing but giving it different names. I can tell you my story, and then we can decide if my memories are what you are truly looking for. Yes?"

Amy smiled and nodded. "Thank you, Marie."

"Okay. And so I begin." Marie turned her body to face Amy and folded her hands in her lap. "My husband was an artist here in Montmartre alongside Billy so many years ago. It was a wonderful time—especially in the spring and the summer when our little section of the city fills with people and art, and especially money." Marie stopped and chuckled. "My husband Jean and Billy were such wonderful friends. We often spent evenings with Billy, sharing dinner and drinks and stories. He was a fascinating man with so much to say. We enjoyed spending time with him very much.

"But as we know, very few things in life are forever, and one day Billy's stay in Monmartre came to an end. We were able to keep in touch with him through letters sporadically, but we were never certain of where he was because he did not stay in one place for very long. He would send us letters from wonderful places such as, what do call the place?" She furrowed her eyebrows at Amy. "Arizona? Or New Jersey?"

Amy nodded at her.

"Well, wherever he was—we would quickly write a letter back and hope that he would still be there by the time it arrived.

"Years after Billy left, he called our home. It was the first time he called. He said that he had a friend who needed a place to stay in Paris for while, and he asked if she could stay with us. The person he spoke of was our Lizzie. We told Billy that we would be happy to take in any friend he sent our way. So we traveled to Charles de Gaulle Airport on the day she arrived, and we waited for that airplane from New York. We knew her the second she stepped through the gate. She was an angel, just as Billy had described.

"So Jean and I took our Lizzie home. Even from the first day, we loved her. She was a good soul, and we knew it just from looking at her." Marie paused, choosing her words, and then shook her head. “She was a good soul, but a lost soul. We did not know why she was lost, but just as we knew she was good, we knew she was lost. Jean and I would exchange glances from time to time, wondering how we would help her find her way.

“Lizzie spent many nights with us, talking about her dreams of acting and becoming famous. Jean and I encouraged her to pursue her acting, and we promised that she could stay with us as long as she desired. She was so very talented, and we wanted her to shine as we knew she could. As it turned out, she very quickly secured a role in a local play. She told us that she never much liked her name, so her stage name became Lyla deTroyes. Jean and I went to the play almost every night.” Marie chuckled, remembering. “We must not have had much else to do,” she sighed, still laughing, softer this time. “We were just so proud of her. And soon after she began acting in that play, someone in the audience asked her to audition for a commercial, which she then was hired to do. From there, she was hired for more and more commercials. Soon we were seeing our Lizzie’s face on television during our favorite television programs.

“And then the day came when she was offered a role on a television series. She took it, of course, and she became quite famous. We were happy for her, but at the same time we were quite sad because it was time for her to move on. She had enough money to buy her own apartment, and she said that she did not want to disturb our lives any longer. We never felt disturbed by her, but we could not convince her.”

The front door of Marie’s apartment opened, and a tall, thin man walked in. As soon as he saw Amy and Marie on the couch, he smiled.

“Ah, Jean, I am so glad you are here,” Marie said, beckoning her husband with a wave. “This is Amy. She is Lizzie’s granddaughter—the girl that Billy sent to us.”

Jean neared the couch and offered Amy his hand. “I am so happy to meet you. I hope Marie is telling our story well.” After shaking Amy’s hand, he leaned down to Marie and kissed her forehead. “I hope you have had a good day,” he said to his wife.

“It has been very good,” she said, taking his hand and squeezing it.

"Good. I am going to wash up," he said, nodding to Amy and backing out of the room. "It was very nice meeting you, Amy. I will see you in a bit."

Marie watched her husband walk toward the back room, and Amy watched Marie. She couldn't help but feel as though Marie and Jean were the characters in a familiar story—a sweet, kind love story.

"Marie," Amy said, inching a bit closer to her host as though the ground she gained would help her hear more clearly. "So Lizzie came to you from New York? And this must have been somewhere around 1967?"

Marie nodded.

"Do you know how long she was in New York before she came to you?"

Marie shrugged. "Perhaps at one time I did know, but now I am unsure. I do not believe it was very long. Days, maybe."

"And she became a famous actress?" Amy asked.

Marie nodded again. "In France, yes. Of course in the United States, no. No one in the United States cares about French television. But to us, Lizzie was a star. Everyone knew Lyla deTroyes, and Jean and I were so proud to be friends of hers." Marie paused before going on. "But in all the time that Jean and I spent with Lizzie, we never found out what had ailed her so. We never found out what brought her to Paris in the first place. As the years passed, we forgot that she came to us out of sadness. She had so much joy; it was hard to imagine that she could harbor any sorrow.

"But then one day it came out. Lizzie had been very secretive about her past, yes, but a reporter—a terrible, meddling, troublesome reporter—he traced her roots back to the United States. And one night as Jean, Lizzie, and I shared dinner and listened to the news on television as we often did, we saw the sadness of Lizzie's life unfolding. The reporter told of a family in California and a fire that had killed her husband.

"I will never forget it. She crumbled in Jean's arms." Marie shook her head, the sorrow of the memory clouding her face. "Lizzie had not known. She did not know of the fire or that her husband's life had been taken by it. And this, she did not know, had happened shortly after she arrived in Paris—years before."

Amy leaned back into the couch, wishing she had her timeline in front of her. Lizzie had sent a letter to Eva about heading to New York just as she was stepping on a plane. Just a couple days later when Eva received the letter, she rushed to the Mills' house to find it burned to the ground. Lizzie could have already been in Paris by that point according to Marie; she had not been in New York with Billy. Private investigators weren't looking in the right place.

"That night," Marie continued, "we drove her to her apartment where she gathered her things, and then we took her back to Charles de Gaulle—the same place we picked her up years earlier. She flew back to California immediately.

"Jean and I did not know when she would return. We did not know if it would be better for her to come back or to stay with her family." Marie shook her head. "We did not know. It was clear that she had great difficulties in her life and that we knew very little of them. We did not wish to pry; we only wanted the best for her. We just did not know what it was.

"But our Lizzie did return. And when she did, she threw herself into her work. For years and years she worked and worked. Her face was all over town, and no one bothered her about the tragedies in the past. I am unsure how she was able to escape the stare of the media, but they left her alone.

"For many, many years, she remained one of our closest friends. But one day, she came to us and asked that we watch her apartment while she was away on a trip. We wondered how long she would be gone. She said she did not know." Marie smiled. "And I must tell you, we've been looking after her apartment ever since." Marie looked around the room, raising her palms as though presenting it to Amy. "We are in her apartment here, now. This lovely place was your grandmother's." The smile on Marie's face faded. "We got word recently that she had passed away. Our hearts were so heavy at the news. In her will, she gave this home to us, and we feel so blessed for it. But we would give it back in an instant if we could see our Lizzie just one more time."

Amy nodded, letting Marie's words sink in.

"I am sure that you have so many questions," Marie said. "I just told you a very long story and there is a lot to take in. Would you like to have some time to yourself to think?"

Amy nodded again. "Marie, I understand so much more now. Thank you. It would probably do me good to think for a bit."

"You have come from very far. Why don't you take a shower or a nap—or both? I will have a meal waiting for you when you are ready. And we can talk more then if you like."

Amy was suddenly aware of how tired she felt. A shower and a nap—and food—sounded wonderful. "Thank you, Marie. You are so kind." She stood, and for a split second wondered if she should hug Marie for her graciousness. Before she could decide, Marie had wrapped her arms around Amy's shoulders and was guiding her toward a room in the back of the house.

Thirty-nine

Three hours later, Amy emerged from Marie and Jean's flat, feeling refreshed after a short nap and her first meal in France. She roamed around Monmartre, thinking about the story Marie had told her. Somehow, it made her feel both anxious and relieved at the same time.

She sat down in a café, ordered a cup of coffee, and computed the time difference between Paris and California. When her coffee came, she picked up her phone and called Will, hoping eight o'clock in the morning wasn't too early to call.

"Hey," he answered. "I didn't expect to hear from you so soon. How was your flight?"

"Good—it was good. Uneventful. But so much has happened since I got here. I've been dying to call you to talk about it, but I didn't want to wake you up."

"You could have called. You can call me anytime. What did you find out?"

"Lizzie wasn't in New York with Billy. She was here in Paris. Well, first she went to New York, but right after that, Billy turned around and sent her to Paris. She barely spent any time with Billy at all. She was here. He sent her here to get away from her life in California."

"No kidding," Will said. "So the private investigators that Eva hired in New York weren't looking in the right place."

"Right. And get this: while she was here, she became a famous French actress. She changed her name, though, practically erasing all traces of Elizabeth Hathaway. Her stage name was Lyla deTroyes."

Amy could hear typing on the other end of the phone line. She imagined him sitting at a computer. "Lyla deTroyes. Let's check her out on the internet. Is deTroyes spelled like the Medieval writer Chretien deTroyes?"

Amy scrunched up her nose, thinking. "I don't know. Probably."

She could hear more typing on Will's end. A moment later, he said, "Aha, there she is. Lyla deTroyes, famous French actress." He laughed. "Wow, who knew? She's beautiful—no surprise though. I figured Billy would have good taste. She has your eyes."

Amy smiled. "Well, she became a famous actress here and didn't find out about the fire until a reporter dug up her past years later and broadcast it all over the evening news. She immediately went to California, but she didn't stay long. She ended up coming back here and threw herself into her work. And that was it. Paris was her home all that time."

Will blew out a deep breath. "I don't know what I expected you to find out in Paris, but I know it wasn't that."

Amy nodded. "I'm sort of relieved. Lizzie didn't trade in her family for Billy. She didn't choose him over her daughters. In the end, it wasn't about him as much as it was about following her dreams. He may have gotten her to Paris so that she could follow those dreams, but that's where it ended with him." She paused. A knot was beginning to form in her stomach. "But that being said, I think what makes me sad is that her family was torn to pieces because she decided to pursue her aspirations to become an actress. Maybe she didn't trade in her daughters for Billy, but she still traded in her daughters—for her dreams."

Will thought a moment before responding. "I think that's sort of backward. Her family wasn't torn apart because she ran off to become an actress. Her family was torn apart because she tried to deny that dream for so long. She didn't follow it in the first place—and she didn't do it the right way. From the beginning she cut corners. She didn't want to finish school, so she ran off to Los Angeles. Then she got angry when her parents caught her, and she lashed out by making bad decisions. She married John because she was impatient and mad that Billy wasn't going to swoop in and save her. She should have just focused on what she wanted, been patient, and put in the hard work. Marrying John didn't solve any problems. It complicated everything because it led to a family that was then affected by her bad decisions."

Amy took in Will's words and stirred her coffee slowly. She watched ripples of cream turn the drink into a light brown. "If she hadn't married John, she wouldn't have had any children."

"Right. And life with John was like—it was like—" Will searched for words. "It was like being haunted by a shadow. She wanted to squash anything that reminded her of Billy, and that included her dreams of becoming an actress. She hastily got married and tried to start over. And I really think she wanted to start over. She was so hurt by Billy that starting over seemed like the only way to heal. But those dreams couldn't be ignored—maybe she squashed most of them, but the shadow remained. You and I both have read enough to know why—nothing that comes from a strong passion can truly die. There are themes of that in just about all great literature. So her dreams just haunted her in shadow form until she couldn't take it anymore."

Amy closed her eyes and nodded, "You're right."

"Don't get me wrong—I'm glad Lizzie married John because if she hadn't had kids, you wouldn't be here distracting me from looking for a job."

She sipped her coffee and found herself rolling her eyes. "You're welcome."

Will chuckled, his voice trailing off as he thought about what he wanted to say next. He didn't want to hurt her feelings, yet he didn't want to miss the moment to speak his mind.

"Hey Amy, don't let this happen to you. Don't find out what happens to shadows of dreams in your own life. When Professor Hollings told me about you, the last thing I expected to find was a girl working in Silicon Valley's private sector with a boyfriend who wouldn't indulge her curiosity. I expected a girl who was writing for a magazine in San Francisco or something." He paused. "I thought you'd be jumping into your dreams head first."

Amy bit her lip. She looked toward the rows of artists down the way and thought about the pictures of Lizzie she saw at Eva's house. "I know. My job isn't right for me. I guess after I got back from New York, I was so defeated that I just took whatever came my way first. And I don't want to keep going that direction." She looked around the café at the patrons at different tables, all in deep conversation. "I'm going to go back to school. It's too late to apply for the fall term, but I'll do some research and figure out when and where I want to go."

"UCLA, maybe?"

Amy smiled. "Maybe." She took another sip of coffee. "And as for the boyfriend who wouldn't indulge my curiosity, I broke up with him. Right before you took me to the airport. I didn't tell you on the way because I couldn't bring myself to talk about it. I knew it was the right thing to do, but it was still sort of confusing. This whole search for Lizzie—you and Billy and everything in between—I didn't know if I was doing it because of that or because deep down I hadn't really been happy in a long time. Everything converged, and I just couldn't bring myself to talk about it."

"That's okay—you didn't have to tell me. Are you happy with your decision?

Amy nodded to herself. "Yes."

"He didn't seem right for you."

Amy answered with another nod. "I know."

"So what are you going to do now? Are you coming back home soon? Are you going to hang around Paris for awhile?"

"I want to stay for a bit. I left a message on the voicemail at work letting them know that I had to take some time off unexpectedly. I figure I have a week or so. I've never been here before—I don't want to turn around and go home so quickly."

"Good. Make the most of the opportunity."

"Right. Who knows when it will come around again?"

"Can you keep me updated about what you're doing over there? Send me emails and let me know when you plan on coming home, okay? I can come and pick you up from the airport."

Amy smiled into the phone. She didn't expect that she'd ever want to leave Paris, yet knowing that Will would be waiting at the baggage claim for her made the return trip seem worth it.

They hung up, and as soon as Amy set her phone down on the table, she picked it up again to call her mom. The knot that had formed in her stomach while talking to Will about Lizzie returned.

When Debbie picked up, she said, "Hey Mom—I'm here. I made it safe and sound."

"Hi, honey. Is it as beautiful as all the pictures look?"

Amy relaxed. Her mother's voice was normal—not at all angry. She had worried that her mother might have spent the last day thinking about Amy's trip to Paris and working herself into a fit over it.

"It is beautiful. I don't think pictures do it justice."

"That's what I've heard."

Neither spoke for a moment, and Amy wasn't sure where to start.

"Mom, I know I've upset you, and I'm sorry. I've just been so bored with—"

"I know."

"And I've just wanted to understand why I—"

"I know."

"And finally I had a chance to go do—"

"Honey, I know."

Amy stopped her line of thoughts. She didn't have to explain herself. In a softer tone, she switched gears and said, "Mom, I found out what happened with Lizzie. After she left you and your family, she wasn't with Billy. He sent her to Paris where she became an actress."

Debbie didn't answer right away. When her response finally came, her voice had dropped an octave.

"Really."

"It doesn't change the fact that she was gone, but she was here in Paris. Not New York. And Billy might be an awful person who helped her get to Paris—and essentially abandon you and your sisters—but I don't think she chose him over you. She chose her dreams. Her ambition. She chose herself."

Again Debbie took a moment to let the information sink in. "That's interesting."

"And since Eva couldn't find her in New York after the fire, Lizzie *really* didn't know what happened until years later. She didn't knowingly stay away. When she did find out about it, she came back immediately. That doesn't justify the fact that she left at all, but at least she didn't stay away knowing what had happened."

Debbie exhaled. Amy envisioned her mother on the other end, eyes closed, head shaking, trying to internalize the conversation and move on.

"Nana thinks you needed to do this—to settle something inside you. She and April think this was more about you than it ever was about Lizzie. Are they right?"

Amy considered her mom's words. "Two days ago I would have said no. But now, I don't know." She ran her finger along the rim of her coffee cup. She thought about the aching pain she felt when reading Eva's description of the fire. She thought about sitting with Will on the park bench in the middle of the night and retelling *Baucis and Philemon.* She thought about Billy handing her a check and about listening to Marie's story. "Actually, yes. I think they are right."

"And did it help settle something inside you?"

"I'm getting there, I think."

"Then I'm glad. Lizzie never put her daughters first, and I promised myself I would never make that mistake. So if this was good for you, it is good for me."

"Thank you, Mom." Amy wished she could find better words—nothing seemed good enough to describe how grateful she felt.

"So now that you are out there in Paris, what are you going to do? Are you going to travel around? Come home soon?"

"I'd like to travel around some. I've never been here, and I don't know when I'll have another chance like this. I guess it depends on how much time I can take off work."

"Just keep us in the loop."

"I will."

"Be safe. And don't talk to any artists named Billy."

Amy smiled. "Not in a million years. I'm steering clear of all the artists."

***

Just as Amy was placing a call to her mom, Will was placing his own call. Like the time before, when Kim picked up she didn't say hello.

"The last time you called me it was late at night," she said. "Now you're calling me first thing in the morning. I'm guessing you have more good news."

Will laughed. "You're the only one who would appreciate this story—and I had to tell someone. I couldn't wait any longer"

"Well, do tell."

He continued where he left off the last time they chatted. And he told her everything. Three trips to Monterey. One trip to Paris. John and Lizzie. Amy and Miles. The fire. Private investigators. Dreams and shadows.

"I have an idea," Kim said once he finished. Her voice was light and quick as though she had been thinking about this idea throughout Will's narrative. "Hear me out before you say no. Promise?"

Will smiled. "Your ideas have worked out for me pretty well so far. What are you thinking?"

"You're going to have to make one more trip out to Monterey."

Forty

Marie said that Amy could stay as long as she liked, and somehow, Amy believed her. She knew why Lizzie had spent so much time with Marie and Jean—their kindness drew Amy in, surrounding her with warmth. It reminded her of spending the night at Nana's house as a child, it reminded her of April's cooking, it reminded her of Will's constant encouragement, and it reminder her of her parents' unconditional love.

So the next morning, when she awoke to birds chirping outside her window and the sun shining down on her face, she jumped out of bed and prepared for the day. She waved to Marie on the way out and made her way to a small souvenir shop she had spotted the day before. There, she bought a notebook and a new pen. And with her supplies in hand, she went back to the outdoors café where she had placed calls to Will and Debbie the day before.

She ordered a cappuccino and pulled an envelope from her messenger bag. From it she took *Eva's Words* in its entirely. She skimmed the first few pages—the ones that recounted Lizzie's first encounters with Billy. Then she looked up. People were sprinkled throughout the tables of the café, some sitting—deep in conversation—others gazing silently at the artists across the way at their easels. Amy followed those gazes and again imagined Billy sitting there, more than fifty years earlier, this time standing next to Jean as they both painted whatever moved them. The café played American music softly in the background; tourists chattered as they passed by, café patrons laughed and clanked forks against plates, and waiters bustled around taking orders. She opened her notebook.

As she touched her pen to the paper, it seemed to move without command, and as page after page filled, Amy felt the shape of the day changing. The sun moved overhead, warming the table on which her notebook sat and brightening the pages to a blinding white. She finished her cappuccino and ordered another, this time with a sandwich. The sun continued to move, and the throng of tourists thickened. The cacophony of their voices and their actions spurred Amy on; the energy they brought moved directly through her senses to her hand as it tore across the pages.

Page after page, page after page. The sun began its descent, and Amy ordered another cappuccino. Page after page, page after page.

When the day's light had faded to shades of pink and orange, Amy closed her notebook. She thanked the waiters for allowing her to sit there all day, and she headed to Marie's apartment.

The following day, she found her way to the same café and did the same. Again, her pen moved without command. Page after page, page after page.

Late in the afternoon, a thud on the table caught her attention, and she looked up toward the noise. Her book of Renaissance poetry had landed with a bounce in the middle of the table.

"You've got to stop leaving this book behind," Will said. He stood on the other side of the table, grinning.

Before he could say anything else, Amy jumped to her feet and threw her arms around his neck.

"Will!" She pulled away slightly to look at him. "What are you doing here?"

Will unwrapped her arms from his neck and held her hands down at their sides. The sun had darkened her skin and lightened her eyes—and the warmth of her smile spurred him on.

"I came to give you that book. I didn't see how you could be all the way over in Europe without it."

She laughed. "How did you find me?"

He squeezed her hands. "Where else would you be? Coffee shops are kind of your thing, so I figured I'd just keep walking along this row of cafes until I spotted you." He winked at her. "And I figured if I couldn't find you, I always could just call your cell phone."

She laughed again. "I can't believe you're here. How—why—?"

He smiled. "I was at home, thinking about why I brought you that Renaissance book in the first place—and I just realized…" his voice trailed off.

She cocked her head to one side as if to ask *you realized what?*

"Remember 'Ode on a Grecian Urn?' That poem by John Keats we had to read in English 10B?" He looked toward the rows of artists before turning back to her. "I'm not the kind of guy who wants to wait in anticipation. I want to get what I'm reaching for."

He pushed a curl behind her ear and twirled its end around his finger. Then he took her hands and placed them back around his neck so that he would be close enough to kiss her.

Without realizing it, Amy found herself rising to the tips of her toes to meet him halfway.

"So," he said slowly, moments after their lips met, "I knew that if I wanted to reach for you, I better get to Paris. And as it so happens, Billy Strath agreed with me."

Amy rose to the tips of her toes and kissed him again. "It's a perfect ending to my story."

Will smiled. He was just about to ask her what story she was talking about when he noticed the notebook on the table next to the Renaissance poetry book. "Hey, what's this?" he asked, picking it up. "Is this your story?" He opened the book to the first page.

Eva stood at the end of a long, sloping driveway lined by linden and oak trees.

He closed the notebook and picked up the pen laying on the table. Across the front, he wrote *Amy's Words*.

She smiled at him.

He picked up her messenger bag and put the notebook and pen in it. "Come on, let's go," he said while holding his hand out to her. She took it and began following him out of the café.

"Where do you want to go? Do you want me to show you around?" Amy asked. "There's this big church at the top of a staircase not far from here called the *Sacre Couer* or something like that. It's sort of a must-see when you are in Monmartre. Or we could go see the Latin Quarter—it wouldn't take too long to get there."

They stepped onto the sidewalk outside the café and Will stopped walking. He turned to Amy and squeezed her hand. "Let's go to Italy. I think Lizzie and Eva and Billy already wore all the stories out of this place. Let's do something entirely new together—something entirely different. I heard pirates liked to ransack the coast in the north. Let's get on a train and check that out."

Amy's eyes grew and her heartbeat quickened. "Italy," she breathed. "I've always wanted to go there."

"Let's go. There's absolutely nothing stopping us."

Amy listened to his words echo across her mind. *There's absolutely nothing stopping us. Absolutely nothing.*

He was right. No work, no family secrets, no shadows of lost dreams.

She smiled, feeling the sun warm her cheeks. With a deep breath, she answered, "Yes, let's do that."

Made in the USA
Lexington, KY
19 September 2012